I0576152

LUKA

Dianne Hartsock

A NineStar Press Publication
www.ninestarpress.com

Luka

© 2021 Dianne Hartsock
Cover Art © 2021 Natasha Snow

This is a work of fiction. Names, characters, places, and incidents are either the product of the author's imagination or are used fictitiously. Any resemblance to actual persons living or dead, business establishments, events, or locales is entirely coincidental.

All rights reserved. No part of this publication may be reproduced in any material form, whether by printing, photocopying, scanning or otherwise without the written permission of the publisher. To request permission and all other inquiries, contact NineStar Press at the physical or web addresses above or at Contact@ninestarpress.com.

Printed in the USA

ISBN: 978-1-64890-191-1

First Edition, January, 2021

Also available in eBook, ISBN: 978-1-64890-190-4

WARNING:
This book contains sexually explicit content, which may only be suitable for mature readers. Depictions of violence; mention of off-page incest, rape, and physical abuse; forced captivity; death of secondary characters.

Luka makes a desperate wish and the earth shifts to his will. Regretting it immediately, he tries to undo the sorcery, but it is too late. He asked for hope, and to his horror, all the hope in the world is given into his keeping. He desires nothing more than to return this gift to the world.

Aethan wants to get his hands on the Well of Hope in Luka's keeping. If he can ransom out hope to others at his whim, the world will be at his feet. Where it belongs.

With the aid of his lover, Rhys, Luka stays one step ahead of Aethan. But Rhys has his own enemy in Aethan, his estranged father.

Rescued by Luka, his sweet, gentle witch, Rhys now stands with him against Aethan. They have vowed to return the Well of Hope to the earth despite all odds, or die trying. For what is life worth, for anyone, without hope?

Chapter One

Luka settled cross-legged on the hearth with a murmured word of gratitude to the fire as its warmth surrounded him. Keeping a veiled eye on the woodpile, he crumbled a crust of bread and honey onto the stones. The animals had grown skittish of late, and he missed their company on his long tramps through the forest. The cabin had grown lonely without Rhys's vibrant presence.

The thoughts of his lover sent his gaze to the small stack of books he kept close at hand to leaf through during the long empty nights. He'd rescued the young man from a brutish existence at the hands of a madman, and the stories were all that would ease his frantic, tortured mind. Rhys would sit close to Luka while Luka read the heroic tales until his head would nod, and he'd slump into Luka's arms, a warm, living presence in his solitary life.

Luka raised his head, attentive. Winter gathered outside the latched door, wind howling through the trees, sending their limbs scratching along the roof. A shiver traveled up his spine. Something darker than the storm was coming.

The fire snapped in a shower of sparks, recalling his attention. He drew a small bundle of twigs from a pocket, cupped it in his worn, nut-brown hands, and breathed in the scent of juniper and sage. Chanting the words his mother had taught him long ago, he tossed the clump into the flames. A tendril of smoke rose, twirled in lazy circles in the air and brushed against his face.

He breathed deeply, holding in his lungs the heady smoke of the sage and grasses he'd gathered by the stream last autumn. His thoughts cleared. He saw everything! Snow whipped through the darkness between the trees, carried on the fierce wind. His beloved animals huddled in the scrub brush for safety and warmth. The village beyond the forest barred its doors, fires lit, safe inside while the storm raged.

His thoughts soared, bursting into the moonlit landscape above the clouds. Laughing aloud, his spirit flew in wonder, heart aching at the beauty of the night. But something tugged at his heart, his name shouted on the wind. He blinked at tears, bringing the fire back into focus, the cabin solid around him. Night pressed on the shuttered windows. Something was in the night...

Luka's heart leaped. He comes! A soft cry of joy escaped him, and he rose in one fluid motion to his feet. He'd sent Rhys away to find love elsewhere than in the arms of a lonely witch, and yet he came, daring the storm.

"Come to me," he urged the solitary figure in his mind's eye, struggling up the path to reach him. A tremor seized him. Long years of bartering his herbs and potions to the villagers had passed while he waited with hope and dread for Rhys's return, darkness at his heels.

He crossed the wooden floor of the cabin, logs he'd hewn and planed himself, lighting the candles with a word as he passed, filling the room with light. Luka paused at the door, hand hesitant on the latch. He had enemies beyond this safe threshold. What if Rhys had gone to them in his bitterness and returned now for revenge? Luka closed his eyes, seeing again the pain on Rhys's youthful face, the confusion in his eyes when Luka told him to go, and closed the door on his anguished pleas.

A rap on the door sent his pulse racing. Love and doubt warred inside him, but he had to know, see the truth of it. He opened the door a crack; icy wind whistled in. A figure stood on his step, the heavy cloak clutched against the cold obscuring his features. Who was this? He swung the door wider. The energy was all wrong. But Luka would welcome him in whatever guise he wore.

He opened his hungry arms, but Rhys shook his head and looked up, candlelight spilling on his pale face, grown older. "You sent me away—brokenhearted." Rhys's voice was deeper than he remembered. "If I cross this threshold, I won't leave again. Be very sure."

Luka trembled, searching the beloved features, and mourned the sweet innocence that was missing. Snow sifted through the trees adding to the weight on Rhys's shoulders, and Luka swallowed his doubts. "Come inside." He tugged on Rhys's sleeve, unable to mask his eagerness. His heart stumbled, then leaped, seeing a flash of elation in Rhys's eyes.

Rhys stepped into the cottage in a flurry of cold air and snow, and Luka hastily closed and latched the door behind him. He turned, and his lips parted in a startled gasp. Rhys had removed his cloak, snow already melting on the warm floor. His golden hair fell loosely to his shoulders, and his body filled out the tunic and trousers he wore in a way it hadn't five years ago. He had grown into a handsome man, the fine wool of his clothing attesting he'd done well in the village.

Suddenly conscious of his frayed sleeves and ink-stained fingers, the silver now threading his dark braid of hair, Luka glanced away. His gaze fell on the books and parchment littering every surface, candle wax spilled on the tabletops. A thick layer of dust covered the bookshelves, except for the volumes he used for reference. He chewed a lip, troubled.

"Come to the fire," he offered, taking Rhys's cloak to hang on a peg. "There's a stew simmering on the hearth."

Rhys touched his shoulder, halting him. "A moment. I've come to warn you. Your old enemy—"

"Is coming. This I know. We'll talk of it later. Please, come to the fire. You must be cold."

"Luka."

Luka swiveled sharply at the command in Rhys's voice, a thrill rushing through him. So much courage from his once timid lover. Was this the same man he'd rescued? The young lad of seventeen years, chained and beaten in a dank cellar? Rhys wouldn't speak of his parents back then, saying only he'd lived on the charity of others—until he'd been snared, captive to a cruel man's dark appetites.

Rhys's soul had cried out in anguish from his prison, finding Luka's heart, drawing him deep into the forest to the monster's isolated hut. Luka had eluded the dark sorcerer, freeing the lad and taking him into his home. And later, into his bed, a moth to Rhys's bright flame, his heart opened for the first time in uncounted years to love and promise.

He tucked a hand under Rhys's elbow. "Come to the fire, dear heart. Let me see you in the light." He dropped his gaze again, unaccountably shy. "I've missed you."

"And I..." Rhys's voice trailed off into a sigh and he let Luka lead him across the room. Luka ignored the hurt he had no right to feel. He knew Rhys had been with others after they'd parted, had felt his moments of ecstasy and sorrow while Luka sat at his lonely hearth, unable to bring himself to severe the connection Rhys had no knowledge of and couldn't remove anyway.

But he'd also suffered Rhys's loneliness in the dark hours of the night, when Rhys missed him with a physical ache, a longing to see him again, hear his voice, touch his hand. Those times had torn at Luka's vulnerable heart with sharp talons. It was Luka himself who had at last severed the tie, unable to bear the pain he'd caused.

Rhys took the low stool on the hearth and Luka knelt at his feet, wishing he could put his head in Rhys's lap, have him loosen his braid and run fingers through his hair, soothe his troubles as he had so often in the past. Instead, he scooped the last of the stew into a wooden bowl and handed it to him along with a spoon.

"Why have you come?" he asked, watching Rhys eat as if ravenous, wishing he had more to offer. He'd make an extra loaf of bread in the morning and perhaps find some winter berries in the snow for him...

Rhys motioned with the wooden spoon to the pile of books against the hearth. "Sir, do you not recognize your white knight, come to rescue you?"

Luka snorted at the old jest between them. "Perhaps I am the ogre under the bridge?"

Rhys shook his head and finished the bowl without answering. He set it purposefully aside and turned a grave face to Luka. Disconcerted, Luka flushed hotly under the scrutiny, and he sat cross-legged on the stones. The fire crackled, and he watched the sparks shoot up the chimney. Luka thanked the flames once again for their warmth, the cold of winter kept outside the snug walls of his cabin.

He heard the moment Rhys grew impatient. The creak of the stool as he shifted, his harshly drawn breath. "Aethan has returned to the forest. Does this not concern you at all? Why do you not flee? With your subtle power you could have a place in the prince's court itself. Why do you tarry within Aethan's reach?" Bewildered and angry, his distress vibrated in the air, and Luka quickly shut his mind to the wave of emotion battering his defenses. He would not look into Rhys's heart. He no longer had the right.

"I have felt his dark presence," he admitted. "My concern is for you. I wished you far from here when he returned."

Rhys clenched a hand. "Did you think I would abandon you to him? I was his slave, Luka! Endured his many cruelties. He would gladly see me dead. But you, my love, he will torment and torture until your mind breaks in exquisite pain—" Rhys bit off his heated words, controlling his fear. "He seeks the Well."

"He will never find it," Luka vowed, and felt the subtle shift in the world, bending to his will. Aethan was strong, frighteningly so, but Luka had far more to lose, something more precious than life to him.

Rhys watched him and a tender smile curled his lips. "I'm tired, Luka. Do you have a cot for me? Though I would prefer the warmth of your bed."

Luka blinked, torn. Rhys gave him no chance to answer, leaning forward to press kisses to his cheeks, the eyelids he closed in surrender. Their lips brushed, but then Rhys pulled back, drawing a moan from him.

"No. I think not. Not tonight." His calculating expression in the flickering firelight smote Luka's heart. "I believe blankets here on the hearth would be best."

Luka inclined his head, accepting that Rhys had yet to forgive him. He dragged his own mat of twigs and sweet grasses to the fire, laying out the thick comforter of goose down he'd made that spring. Rhys murmured a goodnight and settled into bed. Intensely conscious of him, Luka added wood to the fire, then took a blanket and his troubled heart across the hearth. Rhys had returned. That was enough.

Chapter Two

Luka sat on the stone steps of the cottage and breathed his fill of the crisp morning air. The storm had passed in the night and a pale sun glittered off the snow blanketing the forest floor and weighting the pine branches. A mug of tea warmed his hands and he smiled, recalling the touch on his face that had come with it, sweeter than the honey Rhys had added.

"We need to fatten you up," Rhys teased, but there had been concern in his eyes. Luka hadn't taken care of himself, but the years had grown lonely, waiting for Rhys to return.

He missed his lover, though he'd been the one to send him away. Luka had wanted him to find a better life than he could offer, a solitary witch bartering his potions. And he had wanted Rhys safe from his enemies. But he may as well have cut out his own heart when Rhys had left.

Luka sipped his tea, enjoyed its comfort, then heat flushed his skin as he recalled his dream last night, the feel of Rhys in his bed. Rhys had been tender and passionate and welcoming. Luka had cried in his arms, overwhelmed with the joy of it. Had wept again on waking to find himself alone on the hearth, Rhys across the room, reading a book in the morning light spilling through a window, as far away as the years that had separated them.

A bird fluttered past, calling his attention, and Luka's spirit flew with it, soaring into the sky. The rush of air exhilarated him, and he dropped with a smile back into his body. After hastily setting aside his tea, he pulled a crystal from a pocket and held it up to the faint winter sunlight. He marveled at the earth reflected in glass. Focusing his gaze, his essence slipped easily into the encapsulated world and flew along the pathways, flitting between trees and brush. He scampered with a family of squirrels along a branch, leaping with wild glee from limb to limb.

Hearing the waterfall, he rode with a bee to the river's edge, and spotted Rhys perched on a boulder, naked, his ivory skin pebbled from his brief swim. Luka thrilled at the beauty and strength of his body. Rhys stretched, leaned back on his hands, and Luka's caressing gaze traveled over the long length of his form.

He drew a puzzled breath. This was not the body he remembered, the one he'd dreamed of last night. He'd tasted every inch of Rhys's skin, once upon a time. Drew his tongue along every plane and line and curve. The form before him was stockier, more muscular. Luka missed the lithe limbs that had twined around him, pale against his dark skin, and held him close on the small pallet before the hearth during the glorious nights they'd shared.

He laughed, the unhappy sound floating on the warm air. Maybe his memory was growing faulty. It was five years, after all, and they'd been together for far too short a time. Less than a year. Rhys was bound to have changed.

Rhys stretched again, but Luka wouldn't allow his gaze to drop lower than his waist. He knew the length and taste of that delight as well, but there was little use in awakening a longing for the pleasures he'd pushed away with both hands.

He moved off, but Rhys looked up, and a gentle smile touched his wide mouth. He raised his hand and Luka landed in his palm. Rhys stroked his thumb over his back and pleasure rippled through Luka. "I'll be home soon, my sweet," Rhys said with a fond laugh.

Luka brushed Rhys's cheek as he left, letting the breeze carry him. Reluctant to leave the sunlight, he nevertheless flew toward the dark shadow spreading in the forest. Feeling a rapid heartbeat, his spirit fell into the rabbit hiding in the brush and snow. Terrified, scattered images flashed into his mind. Danger! The trap snapped; searing pain as it smashed the bones of his foot. In agony, he looked through blurred eyes at the forest crowding in around him. The thick ferns hiding him wilted as if with blight. Dead limbs twined with the green of the towering pines.

He flinched back when a figure approached, cloaked, the leering face looking into his with a gleam in its eyes. "Always the fool, Luka."

Luka fought the waves of pain, struggled to leave the rabbit and fly home. But his spirit beat against an invisible wall, escape barred to him. "What do you want?" he asked, his mind touching on the man bent over him.

He shuddered at the cold, calculating thought in return. "I want the Well of Hope. You know this." Aethan drew a hard breath, then Luka felt a hand caress his face. The sorcerer's voice changed, becoming seductive, wheedling. "We can be allies, Luka. Share the energy pulled from the Well. Join me. We can master all others." His thumb brushed Luka's lips, his voice thrumming with passion. "Every desire fulfilled."

The tendrils of Aethan's potency wound through Luka's head, so alluring. They would be lovers and leaders, nature itself bowing to their whim. But Luka had no use for power. He wished only for his quiet life, and Rhys's love.

"This will never be," he murmured, and braced. Aethan's fury crashed into him, bruising his mind. The sorcerer tore at his thoughts, seeking entrance. He pushed on his wounded foot, and Luka screamed in anguish. But then a wish touched him, bound in love, and his consciousness soared on the wind, reaching for Rhys.

"Come to me," Rhys begged, a whisper of longing on the wind. Luka clung to the tendril of thought, let it wind around him, pull him to his beloved. But it stretched taut as if from a great distance, broke before he reached him, and he fell into his body with a cry. Rhys held his splayed form against his chest. There were tears in his eyes, and

Luka swore under his breath. He never wanted to hurt him, but it seemed all he accomplished.

"I am well," he said, pushing up into a sitting position.

Rhys clung to him a moment, then let him go, brushing a kiss against his cheek. "What happened?" he asked, his concern easing Luka's distress.

"Aethan caught me." Luka hurried to add at his sharp breath, "Do not worry. I told him nothing of your presence."

"Luka," Rhys chided. There was a note of censor in his voice. "I worried for your safety. I returned to find you here, lying so still. It took all my will to call you back. I'm thankful you found your way to me."

Luka ignored a sharp prick of jealousy. Who had been Rhys's teacher these past five years, that he had such power? The witch in the village hadn't this talent. "You've grown strong, my heart. But please, Rhys, listen to me. Aethan is coming. He will be here before nightfall. You must go."

Rhys's lips tightened with his anger. "I won't desert you."

Luka's heart pounded in a rush of adrenaline. "You don't understand! Aethan means to use you against me."

"Then you must be strong and not let him." Rhys rose to his feet and held out his hand. "Come, my dear witch. It's time we faced our monsters."

Despite the circumstances, warmth flooded Luka's chest, hope and apprehension trembling in balance. Rhys would stand with him! He had found Rhys broken and bleeding in Aethan's cellar, his spirit a mere flicker in the darkness. But now Rhys burned, his life-force a flame of passion and resolve.

Rhys helped him stand, and power sparked between them where their hands touched. Luka gasped at the bite, clasping Rhys's fingers tighter, keeping him at his side when he would have moved away. He swallowed his absurd pride, the answer important.

"You've grown strong, Rhys. Who was your teacher?" *Did you find him handsome?* He knew he flushed, heat in his cheeks, but held Rhys's blue-eyed gaze. Something flickered in the pretty depths, a secret, and Luka's heart stumbled with dismay. But then Rhys smiled, his eyes once again guileless, clear.

"Widow Ravan took me in. Said she felt the power in me."

Luka nodded, disheartened by the false answer. "I know the witch. Wise and knowledgeable. Rhys, I'm glad you found a safe haven when you left here."

Rhys lifted a shoulder, his gaze shifting to the side. Luka stifled a sigh. He'd known Ravan since she was a fair-haired child growing wild in the woods. Later, when her woodsman husband died of fever, she turned her capable hands to herbs and potions, learning the ways of healing. She prospered, but that didn't account for the fineness of Rhys's clothing nor his strength in magic.

His lover kept secrets.

Chapter Three

Luka held his hands to the fire blazing on the hearth, every candle in the room lit behind him. Aethan came to them with shadow and death. Luka would meet him with light and his fierce heart. Rhys sat at his feet and Luka had trouble not running his fingers over the tousled head bent in meditation. They'd spent the afternoon warding the windows and doorway and chimney flue. Not to keep Aethan out, but to trap him inside. If they were to battle, Luka would protect his forest brethren as best he could.

Rhys caught his breath and stirred, and Luka's heart jumped to his throat. Not fear. He'd locked fear away. But Aethan arrived, cloaked in terror, his hatred battering at the door moments before his heavy hand struck the wooden barrier. He struck again, splintering it asunder. His dark form filled the doorway and Rhys rose to his feet, standing at Luka's side to face him.

Aethan's laugh chilled Luka's heart. "Why, Luka, I'm surprised to find you home. Did you think I wouldn't come for you?"

Tension vibrated from Rhys, and Luka willed him calm, peace. They mustn't let on—Aethan stepped across the threshold and the wards sealed silently closed behind him, trapping them inside with the monster. Rhys flinched, and Aethan turned his attention on him. He was a handsome man with dark hair and eyes as black and deep as Luka's own, but a cruel smile curled his full lips.

"Here you are, Rhys, fled back to *him*." His voice dripped disdain. "But tell me, my sweet lover, does your tender flesh miss the bite of my hand? Are the nights long and dark without my mouth on your skin?"

Rhys whimpered, a lost child, and Luka stepped between them.

"Leave him be, Aethan. This concerns only us."

Aethan arched a brow. "Indeed?" He lifted a hand and Rhys swiftly pressed against Luka's back, grabbing his arms to hold him in place. Alarmed, Luka looked over his shoulder, but Rhys's eyes were hooded, for the first time his thoughts concealed from him. Aethan's laughter shivered down his spine.

"My dear Luka, you should see your face! So shocked." Aethan stepped up to him and touched Luka's hot cheek with a fingernail. "But you have always worn your emotions on your sleeve, honest and true, expecting others to do likewise. How easy it must have been for Rhys to deceive you, playing at love, when all the while it was my bed he longed for."

Rhys muttered something at that, but Luka forced his thoughts away from him, all his senses focused on Aethan. It would come soon...

Aethan flexed his shoulders, his cloak falling back to reveal a fine woolen shirt and britches of the same cloth Rhys wore. Luka couldn't hold back a sound of dismay, and Aethan's gaze turned triumphant. "Yes, Luka, Rhys came from your arms to mine. And when he explained he wanted his revenge on you... Well, how could I resist?"

Aethan scraped his nail down Luka's cheek, and he winced as it burned like fire, with Rhys's body against his back adding heat to the already stifling room. Sweat trickled into Luka's eyes, but he ignored the sting as Aethan's hand covered his heart. He braced.

"Tell me, my dear fool, where have you hidden the Well of Hope?"

He didn't give Luka time to answer. Power slammed into Luka's chest, pouring from the fingertips pressed over his heart. His chest seized, pain boiling through him, liquid fire in his veins. He bit his tongue on a scream and tasted blood. Rhys folded his arms around him, and for an instant his pulse leaped. But he merely held Luka upright.

The agony lessened and Luka straightened his slumped body, drawing in a lungful of air, and cried out at pain sharp as a knife in his chest. He blinked Aethan into focus through his tears. "Hope, Aethan?" he asked. His voice sounded ragged to his own ears. "What need have you for such a thing?"

Aethan looked at him with contempt. "I have no use for it, simpleton. I will withhold it from others. What wouldn't people do for just a taste of hope in a world bereft? I could control kings with a single sip of its possibility. For a people without hope, I would be a god, merciful or cruel, depending on my whim. I want the Well, Luka." His voice rose to a shout that shook the walls. "Give it up to me!"

Luka screamed as the shriek pierced his ears, and he felt the trickle of blood on his neck, eardrums burst. Pain spiked through his head and he could hardly understand Rhys's urgent words, "Come, sweet wizard, give us the Well and be free. You have no hope, alone as you are."

Luka trembled. *Was* he alone? He had to gamble all...

"Please." He wasn't sure what he begged for. Peace, of course. And courage. He pushed the pain away, needing to concentrate. Aethan mustn't get the Well. The nails of Aethan's hand over his heart rent his tunic, and he choked back a cry of anguish as they pierced his flesh.

Aethan crowded close, trapping Luka between him and Rhys. Heat stifled Luka, the air thick with candle smoke and the scent of the grave from the sorcerer's body, rot and decay and endings. Luka leaned back into Rhys, solid and too hot, and breathed in the clean tang of his sweat and the spices of Luka's soap he'd used that morning. Aethan put his free hand on Luka's head, and Luka shuddered as nails scraped his scalp.

"Please" he said for the second time, louder. Aethan's mocking laughter rang in the room.

"Who are you calling to, Luka? There is no one here but us. Now, my dear witch, show me where you've hidden the Well."

Nails bit into Luka's head, the other hand digging for his heart. Agony lanced through Luka, and he would have fallen to his knees if Rhys hadn't kept hold of his arms. Aethan put his lips close to Luka's ear and murmured words Luka couldn't hear, but that wound in his skull, asking questions Luka suddenly wanted to answer, needed to answer. What could be the harm in giving the sorcerer what he sought? He would do no harm with it. And the Well of Hope was a gift to mankind and shouldn't be hidden.

What right did he have to hide it?

The words trembled on his tongue, wanting to spill out. Aethan's voice confused him. Luka drew a ragged breath, the hot air burning his lungs. *Focus.* He needed to find his center. *Breathe in.* The pain receded to a corner of his mind. *Breathe out.* Aethan's crooning became a whisper on the edge of thought, ignored.

Blood pounded through Luka's veins. *Be calm.* His heart slowed. *Breathe in.* The air tasted of smoke and candle wax and the sweat from his upper lip. He cried out as his heart clenched, Aethan's fingers gouging his chest. But he shoved that off. *Breathe out. Are you here?*

Thoughts brushed against his, one after another. The fox on the ridge. Birds on the wing. Deer raised their heads from the snowy fields. Wind pushed against the cottage with the buzz of insects. The earth breathed, waiting. He had only to wish...

No. Time itself would warp to his bidding; he need only ask. Draw on the life force thrumming in the ground and vibrating through the air, washing through him in powerful waves. But he had no right to it. No right to use a life not his own. His mother had drummed that into him along with herb lore, among other things. Better he should die...

"No," he said aloud and felt Rhys flinch against him, his surprise a sharp note in the air. Aethan's hatred was a bitterness on his tongue.

"But you will, my dear," Aethan promised. "I have your heart."

Luka screamed as agony once again tore through his chest, dropping him into darkness.

Chapter Four

Luka startled awake and winced at the pain pounding in his head.

"Easy, dear one," someone murmured, and Luka was drawn back against a warm chest. Arms cradled him, muscular, secure, and he kept his eyes closed, breathed in Rhys's familiar scent and sweet aura. He must be dreaming. This was how he remembered Rhys, strong and vibrant, his love open and beautiful, wrapping around them both.

"Where are we?" he asked. Sometimes his dreams held a kernel of truth.

Rhys's soft laughter was tinged with sorrow. "You have come to me again, my sweet witch, when I called. Though better if I had wished for you to stay away."

"Do you hate me so much?" Luka whispered, his heart torn in two.

The familiar arms convulsed around him, pulling him closer. "No. You are my heart, dearest master."

Luka opened his eyes and drowned in the blue depths peering down at him, so full of love and pain his chest tightened.

"As you are mine," he confessed, and curled an arm around Rhys's neck and pulled him lower until their lips met. Rhys kissed him, tentatively at first, achingly tender; then harder, until Luka surrendered with a groan, sliding his tongue between Rhys's parted lips into heat and home.

"Are you real?" he asked after a delirious moment. His dreams had often started this way, only to leave him broken and alone on waking.

Rhys murmured an incoherent word and slipped his hands under Luka's tunic. Luka no longer cared. He'd die if Rhys stopped touching him. Rhys pushed against him and Luka eased onto his back on the hard floor, Rhys beside him. They kissed, Rhys's hunger matching his own, his hands tracing the scars on Luka's chest he'd gotten over the years. Luka jumped when nimble fingers found a nipple and he greedily swallowed Rhys's chuckle of delight.

His chest swelled with emotion. He'd missed this. Missed Rhys's playfulness and passion. They twined together, needing to be closer, desperate touches and kisses. Luka slid a hand between them and undid the knot on his pants. Rhys frantically did the same, his cock slipping out. Luka grabbed his ass with his free hand and yanked him closer, then gripped their cocks together, Rhys's pale and his darker. If he had oil...

But he didn't and pumped their members, drinking in Rhys's moans against his lips, the joy on his face. This was everything. This moment, when Rhys yielded to him, surrendered to the pleasure Luka gave them both. He watched Rhys's expressive face, his own pleasure rippling through him, mounting with each stroke of his hand, every uncontrolled moan and panted sigh from Rhys.

Rhys's breath hitched, and sudden, glorious color flooded his skin. His body shuddered against Luka, and he tilted his head back in a silent cry as he swept across the edge into ecstasy. Luka's heart burst open, his love gushing out in elation and agony. He clutched Rhys to him as he trembled, hot tears wetting his face. He thought he'd never hold Rhys like this again, never bring pleasure to this sweet man who was life to him.

Rhys's ragged breathing slowed, and Luka loosened his hold, ignoring his own need. But it seemed Rhys would have none of that. Making a low growl sound in his throat, he brushed Luka's hand aside and gripped his cock, still hard, slick with Rhys's spunk, and pulled, drawing moan after moan from Luka until his pleasure spilled into Rhys's hand.

He pushed his face against Rhys's shoulder and fought the sobs rising in his throat, overcome, and only gradually became aware of Rhys's hand caressing his head, the murmured words of love in his ear.

Luka sniffed, drew a deep breath. "Are you real?" he whispered once again, terrified of the answer.

Rhys stilled, pulled away, and Luka scrambled to his knees facing him, reaching for his hands to keep him there. They stared at each other in the early morning sunlight finding its way through the windows, Luka's hungry gaze raking the face before him. It was kinder than the one he'd sat opposite from yesterday. Thinner. More beautiful than words.

"I don't understand," he said, utterly bewildered. Was this some dark machination of his enemy? A shapeshifter to torment him? No. The other had been. His heart knew this man.

Rhys's face softened, and he picked up Luka's hands, kissing each scarred knuckle. "It was not me in your home these last few days. Believe me, if it had been, you'd have no doubts left."

Luka felt the heat rise in his face. He must look a fool, knowing the love he couldn't hide shown in his eyes, curled his lips in an awkward smile. Rhys stood abruptly, pulling Luka up with him. "Come, we can at least be comfortable."

They crossed the flagstones to a pallet against the wall of the circular room of what must be part of the tower, the stone walls thick and tightly sealed. Windows high in the walls let in daylight and Luka heard the wind outside, the screech of a bird of prey in the distance. But the room was warm despite its bareness and the quilts soft as they sat on the pallet, backs to the wall.

"We're above the kitchens," Rhys explained, guessing his thoughts as they shared a scrap of linen to clean themselves, exchanging a grin. "The quilts came from one of the servants. Aethan wouldn't want to see me in such comfort."

Luka reached over and twined his fingers with Rhys's, placing their clasped hands on his thigh. He needed to dispel the bitterness that didn't belong in Rhys's voice. "Tell me," he urged. "Who was it that came to my house and betrayed me?"

Rhys's breath was a desperate sigh in the bright room, and he wouldn't meet Luka's gaze, though his hand in Luka's tightened. "It was my cousin, Lorin. We were born two days apart, though our upbringing was— disparate."

Luka felt the tension in him and squeezed his hand. "What is it? Let me help you, my heart."

Rhys's voice sounded strained as he spoke with great reluctance, "We share the same father."

A coldness settled around Luka's heart. "Aethan."

"Yes."

They sat in silence. Luka watched the play of sunlight across the walls, hurting for Rhys. He would spare Rhys further revelations if he could, though perhaps the telling would be cathartic for him. His next words filled Luka with sorrow.

"He raped my mother, his wife's sister, and she fled to Moss Hollow before he found out about me. He would have destroyed us, had he known." Rhys breathed deeply and continued, unknowingly wounding Luka with each word, "I don't know how he found out about me. Mother had died in the winter of my twelfth year, and I did small chores, ran errands, whatever I could in the village to survive and stay out from under the Watchman's eye. Aethan came the day I turned seventeen, knew me, and took me to that cabin in the forest."

His voice had grown dull, empty of emotion, and Luka gathered him in his arms, kissing his face until he stopped shaking.

"Did you think I would judge you for what *he* did?" he whispered against Rhys's golden hair. Rhys drew a ragged breath as if to speak but Luka silenced him with a kiss on his mouth. "I know the horrors you endured, chained in that dark cellar. That it was at the hands of you own father... Dear heart, it tears at my soul. But there is no blame here for you to bear."

"I didn't tell you who he was," Rhys said, in tears, though hope danced on the face he turned to Luka.

Luka smiled slightly. "I don't remember asking." For just an instant the fury he fought to contain for the monster who'd hurt Rhys spilled out. "I would gladly watch him die for what he did to you, both back then and now."

"Luka, no." Rhys shifted on the quilts and took Luka's face in his hands, stared into his eyes. "Put that thought from your mind. You are all that is beautiful and good in the world. I won't see that tainted by any ugliness. Especially on *his* behalf."

Luka blinked in surprise at his vehemence then rested their foreheads together, breathing in Rhys's scent as he sought his center. What peace he could find filled him, and he raised his face for a kiss, but the rattle of the door sent Rhys springing to his feet. Luka rose more slowly as the door opened inwards.

A familiar face peered around the door then Lorin strolled into the room, the arrogance he'd kept hidden now on display in his walk, the sneer on his face. Rhys's stance changed as well. He held himself ramrod straight, chin raised, as if daring Lorin to do his worse. There was no love lost between these two, longtime enemies. Luka's heart ached for them, both victims of a cruel, selfish man.

Lorin stopped a short distance inside the room, his cool gaze looking them over, and his eyes narrowed. "Aethan wants to see you. Both of you," he amended when Luka hesitated. He followed on Rhys's heels, but when they passed Lorin, he grabbed hold of Luka's braid, pulling him to a stop. He jerked his head back and Luka swallowed a grunt of pain.

Lorin's lusting gaze raked his face, took in his disheveled tunic. He bent close, his breath brushing Luka's cheek. "I should have fucked you when I had the chance, Witch. I still might, and make my dear brother watch," he murmured, and licked along Luka's jawline.

"Let me go."

Luka didn't push, kept his voice even, but uncertainty touched Lorin's face and he released his braid. "Come with me," he said shakily, and stalked from the room.

Rhys stared at Luka a moment, then suddenly bowed to him. "My lord and dearest master," he said with pride and love in his eyes. Luka frowned to be so addressed, but Rhys gave him no time to object, linking his arm with Luka's, and they followed Lorin along the winding staircase downward.

The door at the bottom of the tower opened onto a large room, the flagstone echoing under their feet as they crossed the vast space. The stronghold was newly built, stone walls and oak beams, richly appointed with tapestry and bright rugs. But the servants laying the long table kept their eyes downcast, shoulders hunched as they approached.

Luka grieved, wounded by the thought of the blood mixed with the mortar in the walls. Whispers reached him, faint cries of pain and grief.

"Peace," he murmured on a wave of compassion. If he had his herbs, sage, and sweetgrasses, he could possibly free them. Perhaps...

He closed his eyes, opening himself to the aura of the room. Waves of anguish struck him, days of misery, hunger, the whip. The cries of a child for the loss of a father, an older brother...

"Hush," he whispered brokenly. "You don't have to stay—"

A heavy blow against his back staggered him and he fell and cried out as his knees struck the stone floor, sending pain splintering through him.

"None of that," Lorin hissed. Rhys put an arm across his shoulders to help him stand, but Lorin shoved him aside with a snarl. "No. On his knees is where he belongs." He drew a glittering knife from his belt, held it ready. "Try anything, Witch, and I'll slit Rhys's throat." He looked at Rhys, his malice plain. "Gladly."

Luka raised a hand as Rhys took a step toward him. "Let it be," he begged. He could see Lorin's jealousy as a flame around him, fierce, dangerous. It would take little to push him into violence. Rhys's life was in danger every moment they remained in the castle.

"Yes, brother, do stop. In fact, get on your knees as well. The proper position to great our lord."

Rhys's lips thinned as he contained his fury, and he purposely moved closer to Luka, kneeling beside him. A wild gleam entered Lorin's eyes, but he remained silent, glancing across the room at the sound of boots on the stone floor. Three soldiers in dark livery entered, followed by Aethan, and Luka shivered in the cold, tainted air that proceeded him, affected, but an accurate warning of the deadly nature of the man.

The guards moved to one side and Aethan swept up to them, a false smile on his full mouth, his dark eyes calculating.

"What's this?" he asked with a simper and stopped before Rhys. "Is this any way to greet your father?" He looked up and exchanged a lewd glance with Lorin. "Maybe it is." He crowded closer, the buttons of his pants a hairsbreadth from Rhys's mouth. He licked his lips, face flushing, hand going to the back of Rhys's head.

A growl rose in Luka's throat as he gathered himself, anger a hot knot in his chest. Aethan flicked him a dismissive glance, but then the dark eyes widened, and he took a hasty step back before he recovered himself, standing stiffly, eyes flashing.

"As you wish, *Witch*," he snarled. "I won't touch your whore." His tone turned menacing. "On your feet, both of you."

Luka made to comply, but Rhys lurched up with a shout of hatred and torment and shoved against Aethan, sending him staggering backward. Lorin's sharp cry rang in the room, as did the hiss of a blade leaving scabbard. No! Luka sprang in a burst of energy that radiated outward to crash against the walls. Light flashed, blinding. He threw an arm around Rhys and raced with him to the doorway.

"I can't see!" Rhys called out, his panic resounding in Luka's breast.

"It will return," Luka promised, power thrumming through him he fought to contain. Guards blinked, dazed, as they passed, and Luka prayed his strength lasted. He guided Rhys's steps through sheer will as they crossed yet another long room. The doors came in sight. Once outside, he found men blinking at the sky, rubbing their eyes. His steps faltered on the wide stairs as exhaustion slammed into him.

"I need you," he whispered fiercely. A loud neigh answered from the stables and a horse raced across the wide yard, kicking up dirt. Luka took a perilous moment to help Rhys mount on its bare back, then swung up behind him.

"Hold on to his mane," he urged, and slumped against Rhys as the horse surged forward, the powerful muscles bunching beneath his thighs. They cleared the gates and ran for what seemed like leagues, Luka clinging to consciousness.

Rhys gasped, "My sight returns," and Luka tightened his hold, leaning to his ear. "Find us a safe place," he murmured, and closed his eyes, letting the warmth of Rhys's body drive the cold from his bones.

Chapter Five

Rhys slowed the sweating mare to a walk. He'd run her, then settled to a fast trot, but now her sides were heaving and spittle flecked her lips. Time to find somewhere to stop. Forest had closed around them an hour ago, and he followed the sound of water to a small glen on the frozen banks of the stream. Thick trees and brush surrounded them, hiding them from casual view, shielding them somewhat from the bitter wind. This would have to do.

The horse dropped its head in exhaustion, nibbled half-heartedly at the sparse grass at her feet. Snow hadn't sifted through the canopy of limbs overhead, but the banks of the river were white with frost. Luka was a heavy weight against his back, sound asleep, and despite the circumstances, a smile quirked Rhys's lips as warmth and joy spread through him. Luka had come for him, made love to him, and all the terrible doubts he bore since Luka sent him away were quiet for the moment. Luka loved him. It shown in his eyes, his tender touch.

Drawing a deep breath, Rhys slid carefully from the animal, easing Luka down with him. He staggered a little on the slick grass and then his heart clenched. Luka was so thin, close to being gaunt. A feather in Rhys's arms. He carried him gently and laid him on the grass in a patch of sunlight filtering through the overhanging trees. The place smelled of damp earth and pine and life. Luka would approve.

Rhys studied his continence, peaceful in sleep. But there were lines of worry etched on the nut-brown skin that hadn't been there before, and others speaking of sorrow—and loneliness.

"I know about that as well, dear heart," he murmured, and tenderly cupped Luka's handsome face, feeling the spark and tingle that always accompanied any contact with him. Luka sighed in his sleep, and leaned into Rhys's hand, a small smile playing on his lips. Rhys's chest tightened, his love spilling from his heart, and he bent to place a soft kiss on Luka's lips.

"I'm all yours, whether you want me or not," he murmured, then hesitated, a crease between his brows. He stripped off his tunic and placed it under Luka's head on the frozen ground, then rose to his feet. The horse stood nearby, sweat drying on its russet coat. Rhys sighed, hoping it wouldn't become chilled. They'd come away without blankets or supplies and there was nothing he could do for him. He went to the river and knelt, splashing water on his face and chest. He'd need to see to food and a fire if Luka didn't wake soon.

As if roused by his thoughts of him, Luka made sounds of stirring and called his name. "Rhys?"

"I'm here," he answered but didn't turn. What did Luka see when he looked at him? He'd lost weight these last trying years as well, stomach flat, ribs showing. Did Luka compare him to his more muscular cousin? Did he find him lacking? His thoughts came back around to the question that tormented him. Why had Luka sent him away?

Silence stretched between them, then Luka knelt behind him, pulling Rhys back against his chest. His hands feathered around his waist, caressing, and Rhys twined their fingers together, light and dark, beautiful. An ache started in his chest.

Luka moaned as if in pain. "I love you, Rhys. I always have, from the moment your spirit touched mine, bright as a flame. Don't," he begged, pushing his face into Rhys's neck as he tried to turn. Rhys felt his tears. "Let me say this. You walked into my heart when our eyes met in that terrible cellar room. You are my heart. It tore me to shreds to send you away, my heart torn out. But I didn't make you leave because I didn't love you. Never think that. I sent you away to keep you safe from my enemies." He drew a sorrowful breath, his anguish clear. "In that I failed, dear one, and I grieve."

"Hush," Rhys admonished, emotion a hurtful lump in his throat. He leaned back in Luka's arms and Luka shifted, bending his head to kiss him. Rhys had only meant to comfort him, but Luka's arms tightened desperately, his face etched with pain and a longing that touched on his own. He deepened their kiss, hungry for Luka's sweetness, sucking on Luka's tongue, and felt the hard shudder that passed through him.

Luka gasped against his lips, pulling away with a breathy laugh. "You make me forget everything, where we are, the enemies searching for us, all but my fierce need for you."

"Then take me," Rhys offered in a whisper. The ground was too icy, but there were plenty of trees he could brace against. The thought of Luka sliding into him sent his pulse pounding in his ears. Luka's groan was all the answer he needed, and Rhys twisted in his arms and pushed him down, pinning him. He kissed him again and again, drawing moan after moan from him.

He needed more and shoved a hand between them, slipped fingers through Luka's loose pants and found the hot, thick member he craved. Luka bit off a cry of pleasure and turned his head to the side. "Rhys, no. We need a warm room, soft bed—"

"No," Rhys hissed, made desperate, achy and yearning. "I need you inside me, scouring the memory of—" He broke off, dropping his head to Luka's shoulder. He hadn't meant to say that.

"What?" Luka seemed bewildered, but then a wounded sound rose from his throat and he shoved against Rhys, struggling to stand.

"Stop," Rhys begged, putting his weight on him. "It doesn't matter. You're here—"

"It was Aethan," Luka said in despair. It was not a question, and all the fight seemed to leave him. "I sent you from my protection, right back to him. How long?"

Rhys shook his head. "It doesn't matter—"

"How *long*?" Luka said through gritted teeth.

Rhys rolled to his side, cupped Luka's stern face and met his stormy eyes. "It makes little difference now." He gently rubbed his thumb over Luka's full bottom lip until the tension eased from his body. He couldn't help it and leaned down and kissed him. "What happened means nothing. Make love to me, Luka! I've known nothing but pain and shame at his hand, while your touch is fire, all passion and love, exquisitely sweet, infinitely pleasurable."

Luka blinked at him, then a blush flooded his cheeks, a small grin erasing his grim expression. "You flatter me," he said, embarrassed.

"I love you," Rhys countered.

"Come here." Luka snaked an arm around his neck and drew him down. They kissed long, deeply, their passion mounting, until Luka begged him to stand. Rhys jumped up, heart racing, and leaned with his arms braced against the trunk of a nearby tree. Luka was slightly shorter and placed a hand between his shoulder blades and pushed until Rhys bent, legs spread to hold his balance.

Luka leaned over him, moved his hair aside, and kissed the nape of his neck, causing a pleasant shiver down his back. He kissed along Rhys's spine, sending warmth through his chilled skin, while his fingers stroked heat over his chest. Luka undid Rhys's pants with nimble fingers, and they fell about his boots. Naked, exposed, sudden panic swept through him. Aethan often had him like this, to rape and wound while others watched. He wasn't sure he could—

Luka gathered him in his arms, placed kisses on his neck and shoulders. "You're so beautiful," he murmured brokenly, breath warm on his skin. He turned Rhys and captured his lips, then kissed his face, jaw, along his neck, whispering words of love with each caress, his mouth warm on Rhys's skin. He slid lower despite his protest, nibbling each nipple until Rhys grew hard again. Luka went to his knees and took Rhys into his hot mouth, making him gasp. Tears stung his eyes at the beauty of the moment. Aethan would hurt him, see how far he could push the pain until Rhys broke. This was different. That Luka enjoyed himself was obvious in the happy sounds he made, the soft groans around Rhys's cock, his touch tender, caressing, healing.

If they were somewhere else, he'd undo Luka's braid and twine his fingers in the dark silk. Luka liked it when he tugged a little. At that instant Luka glanced up at him, and the joy in his eyes sent pleasure surging through Rhys. Luka took one last hard suck, and love spilled from Rhys's heart as he came in his mouth. Weakened, he leaned back against the tree before he fell.

Luka chuckled, kissed his thigh, and pushed to his feet, mischief dancing on his face. "As delicious as ever," he murmured in Rhys's ear and Rhys delighted in the teasing. He nudged him back, cupped his face in his hands. Luka was always comely, but the happiness in his expression made him beautiful. Rhys kissed him, tasting himself, and his desire stirred once again.

"Your turn," he whispered and walked his fingers down Luka's chest. It surprised him when Luka grabbed his hands, raised them to his lips to kiss his palms.

"No, my heart," Luka murmured, shaking his head. "I want a warm room and a soft bed when we make love again. For hours," he added with a flash in his eyes, his face kindled with passion. Then he made a self-conscious sound and looked aside, his inherent shyness returning. "But, for the moment, we should go. I know a place a few hours walk from here where we could build a fire with some safety. The air grows chill and it will freeze tonight."

"As you wish," Rhys murmured, but wouldn't let Luka's hands free until he tugged on them, the color rising in his face. After giving him an admonishing look, Luka crossed the glen and gathered up Rhys's shirt, holding it in his hands a moment before passing it to him. Rhys slipped it over his head and was enveloped in warmth, and the image of a bright fire and safety and love filled his senses. A flash of Luka's hearth.

The vision passed, though the heat remained, driving the chill from his bones. Luka had gone to the horse, rubbing its neck, whispering in her ear. He ran his hands over her sleek back, head bent in concentration. He rubbed each leg and staggered a little as he straightened.

"Enough," Rhys said firmly, going to him and putting a hand over Luka's. They were warm to the touch, as was the horse's coat despite the icy air. But there was a pallor in Luka's face now, his dark eyes drooping with exhaustion.

"You give too much," he reproached, concern making him sound impatient. Hurt touched Luka's face, and he turned, grasping the horse's mane in preparation to mounting. Rhys pressed against Luka, halting his movements.

"Look at me," he asked. Luka had a joyous nature, delighting in a sunrise, the song of a bird, a cup of tea. But there was a darkness in him as well, things from his past, terrible moments he wouldn't speak of, that woke him with nightmares. He'd sometimes brood for days afterward, and it took all Rhys's cajoling to tease a smile out of him. He would never willingly add to that burden.

Luka turned reluctantly, eyes downcast. Rhys tutted and put a finger under his chin, raising his face, and fell into his dark eyes straight to his pure, fierce soul. Love was a flame, all encompassing, his impetus. But doubt was there as well, and suffering. The terrible fear he wouldn't be enough to stop Aethan. Certainty that he wasn't enough to hold Rhys's affection.

Rhys moved his fingers to touch his trembling mouth and Luka's lips parted on a sigh. Rhys bent to give him a tender kiss. "I love you, Luka," he said firmly. "Believe that. Hold on to it, if you believe nothing else."

Luka drew a shuddering breath and nodded. His shy, sad smile ghosted on his lips, the one that made Rhys's heart pound, then he swiveled to grasp the horse's mane and swing with some difficulty onto its back. Rhys mounted behind him and wrapped him in his arms as Luka guided them from the glen, the forest growing dense and dark around them.

Chapter Six

Rhys stretched, weary from the long hours of travel. The mare was tired as well, head down as they plodded the barely discernable deer trail through the tall pine. Luka dozed, draped on the horse's neck. An hour ago, he'd leaned to the animal's ear and whispered something, then patted Rhys's thigh and gave himself to sleep.

The horse seemed to know where she was going, so Rhys relaxed, letting his mind wander. It had been cold like this the day Luka sent him from his side. He'd been scared, unbelievably hurt, with no knowledge of what he'd done wrong—why Luka no longer loved him.

Snow had sifted through the trees, stung his face, the trail growing darker, like this one, as he came off the mountain. Worn, heart sore, the scent of wood smoke from the village only served as a reminder of the warmth and love he'd found at Luka's hearth. He'd pulled the thick coat Luka had given him tighter against the chill air and thought of the embraces he'd never feel again.

Rhys huffed a laugh at the memory. He'd been so young. So lost in love with this man in front of him, who'd swept into that vile cellar like an avenging god to save him. Rhys had worshipped him, until Luka's diffident glances betrayed the love he tried to keep hidden, and Rhys finally saw him as a man, as lonely and vulnerable as himself. He couldn't help but love him in return, and one glorious night he climbed into Luka's bed and gave him his heart.

The trail turned, opening into a rocky space on the side of the mountain with the mouth of a cave gaping across the small area. The horse came to a halt and Rhys looked cautiously around, listening. Only the reassuring rustle of a small animal in the brush reached him and he swung to the ground. Luka sighed, coming awake, and Rhys helped him dismount, holding him close, hand on the small of his back when he landed.

Luka looked at him and gorgeous color flushed his cheeks, a self-conscious smile lifting the corner of his mouth as he glanced aside. Rhys chuckled, sure Luka had been dreaming of him while Rhys did the same, and delighted in the shiver that ran through Luka's lean body.

"We'll stay here tonight," Luka told him hurriedly and eased out of his arms. Rhys let him go, though he'd rather hold him a while longer. It had been five weary, lonely years, after all. He could be forgiven his need.

Luka patted the horse's shoulder, then found a large stick and scraped at the snow and ice near the trees. Understanding dawned and Rhys knelt beside him to uncover a patch of grass for the horse, who began nibbling on the tough sward before they'd finished.

They drank at a nearby spring then Luka rose and stretched. "Will you gather wood for a fire while I find us something to eat?" he asked, indicating fallen tree limbs on the edge of the rocky outcrop from past storms. "You may build the fire in the cave. There's a crack in the roof for the smoke."

"As you wish," Rhys replied, swallowing a sigh. Luka didn't eat meat, so it would be pinon nuts and a few berries, if they were lucky, when Rhys was hungry enough for a rabbit or two.

He gathered an armful of the smaller pieces of wood and crossed to the opening of the cave. He had to duck to get inside, but the space within was roomy with a ring of stone near the entrance holding remnants of previous fires. The floor was of fine sand and he sat, cross-legged, and stacked kindling inside the stones.

Snow fell lightly outside the cave and he sat back, hands resting on his thighs. He drew in a deep lungful of air to find his center, again, and serenity spread from his heart. When Luka had taken him from that cellar and brought him home, Rhys had been a wild thing, driven half mad with pain and abuse, nearly starved. Luka's patience and gentle words had calmed him. Luka had taught him to find the quiet space inside himself and from there gather strength.

Rhys went there now, peace settling over his troubled thoughts. He felt the power in the world around him and lured it inside. One of the first gifts Luka had given him was how to make fire. Rhys focused the energy in his hands, concentrated, then spilled it into the pile of sticks. Flames sprang to life, danced along the surface of the wood, and warmth soon filled the interior of the cave.

Once the fire was going strong, Rhys gathered larger pieces of wood to last them through the night. At one point, he looked into the shadowy forest, concern beginning to gnaw at him. Luka should be back by now. He chewed his lips then retreated to the entrance of the cave. If Luka didn't return soon, he'd search him out, dangerous as that might be. He added a log to the fire then went back outside. The mare stood nearby, shaking in the growing cold, and Rhys coaxed her closer to the fire where heat flowed from the cave's entrance.

The scrape of a boot on the edge of the outcrop sent his pulse hammering, and a relieved breath escaped him when firelight caught Luka's form approaching from the spring. For an instant he'd panicked, thinking Aethan had found him.

Luka met his frightened gaze. "For the moment, he is far away, my love," he assured him, his deep voice a welcomed sound in the gathering dusk, and Rhys smiled as he went to the fire. His tunic was pulled up, and he knelt, dumping out his findings. Rhys gaped at the pile of mushrooms, wild onions, garlic, frozen cranberries and crabapples, rosehip, cattails, and even a handful of black walnuts.

"Can you bring me a flat stone?" Luka requested and Rhys hurried to comply. The last of the light was going, the snow falling harder, and he hastened back to the warmth of the cave, kneeling by Luka's side. His stomach grumbled, and he gave Luka a sheepish glance.

Luka kissed him, his lips quirking. "I can't let my lover starve," he explained, and Rhys felt his face warm. He watched curiously while Luka placed the stone in the middle of the fire. Flames leaped up around it, sparks flashing into the sky, quickly going out. When the fire settled, Luka placed their meal on the stone to heat, shoving the cattail roots into the embers.

While they waited, Rhys took up several stones and cracked open the walnuts, adding them to the pile on the stone.

"Where did you find all this?" he asked, impressed. He hadn't noticed any of it while they were riding.

Luka shrugged. "I know where to look. Remember, I've spent my entire life in these woods."

Rhys stirred the fire, keeping the flames away from their meal. "Are you from Sweetbrier?" he asked cautiously, referring to the town below Luka's cottage Rhys had fled to after he'd left him. Luka rarely spoke of his past, though Rhys longed to know everything about him.

Luka was silent and Rhys despaired of him answering.

"No," Luka said abruptly, and Rhys sighed, wondering if he'd ever open up to him. He watched the fire until Luka picked up his free hand, kissed his palm.

"I'm sorry," he murmured, lips against Rhys's skin. "I don't mean to be secretive, but much of my past is too dark to speak of, too dangerous to know." He placed Rhys's hand against his cheek, covered it with his own, his gaze pleading when he spoke, "Rhys, all I've longed to do was move forward with you. Leave the tortuous web of my life behind. But all my plans are coming undone. All my choices seem wrong. I don't know—"

Rhys covered his lips with his fingers, halting the rush of words rising on a note of panic. "Stop, Luka. You needn't tell me any more. We are together now, and I am content with that."

Luka drew a shuddering breath. "No, my heart, there are things I should tell you now, though you may hate me afterward. But I swear I never knew the depth of my folly until this moment."

Rhys pressed their foreheads together, looking into Luka's eyes swimming with tears. "I am sure there are many things you have to tell me, but not tonight. We are both tired and worn. Please, Luka, let us eat and get what sleep we may. There will be time enough in the morning for revelations, if you still feel the need."

He kissed Luka's face, his lips, tasting his tears. Sitting back, he rubbed at his own eyes then plucked a cranberry from the stone, finally warm, and offered it to Luka, who opened his trembling lips. Rhys took one for himself, enjoying the tart, faintly sweet taste as it burst on his tongue. They ate their fill, Luka showing him how to scrape the cattail roots that hinted of potatoes when Rhys chewed them.

They shared the walnuts and Luka's mood seemed to lighten as Rhys teased him for the last bite.

"You're greedy tonight," Luka said fondly, and the love in his eyes made Rhys's pulse jump.

"Everything is delicious," he defended himself and scooped up the last mushroom. He fed it to Luka, his fingers lingering on his full lips as he watched the lovely color mount in his dusky cheeks. Luka took everything so much to heart, seizing blame where maybe there was none. Rhys kissed him once more. "Sleep now. Things will look better in the morning."

Luka appeared skeptical but gave him a slight nod. He sat up and dug in a pocket, pulling out several stones. He chose the granite, tucking the others back away. Rhys wondered what they were for. Luka never did anything without purpose.

Luka rubbed the granite between his hands, the stone the size of a small egg. "I found this by the spring when I washed our food. Would you mind banking the fire for tonight while I ward the cave?"

"Of course."

Rhys knelt up and stirred the glowing embers of their fire into a pile, adding a few large pieces of wood against it, then sat with his back to a nearby wall, feet toward the fire. He'd seen Luka ward their home with sage and sweetgrass. Widow Ravan used cedar. What would Luka do with a stone?

Luka moved to the center of the cave and took a slow turn around, banishing any malicious energy from the hollow. Raven had taught Rhys that much, explaining they wouldn't want to trap anything negative in with them when she warded a place. After several long heartbeats, Luka sat cross-legged on the sandy floor, a dark figure in the bright glow from the fire, relaxed, comfortable, as if he rested in his own home. Watching him, pride stirred in Rhys's breast. Most others he'd witnessed would strut around the area they warded chanting under their breaths, making grand gestures and filling the space with smoke that stung his eyes. It all seemed to be for show, their wards precarious at best.

It was never like that with Luka. He went calmly about his business, with purpose, and a reverence for the magic of the earth. He sat calmly now, his focus on the stone he passed back and forth between his hands as if weighing it, studying its structure, its essence. He did this for a long moment, then stilled.

The hair on Rhys's arms and the nape of his neck lifted, and he shivered. The air felt different, charged. His senses heightened. His cock stirred as well, and he sat forward, his heartbeat quickening. Witnessing Luka use his power never failed to arouse him.

Luka rose fluidly to his feet. Tucking the stone in a pocket, he held his hands open in front of his chest, palms out, and walked to the mouth of the cave. The air crackled as he stepped outside as if he pushed the ward wider. The mare snorted and stomped her front hoof as Luka approached her, but he spoke quietly to her and she settled, a shiver running over her when he placed his hands on her back. He stayed with her a moment, then left abruptly and hurried back to the fire.

"It's getting cold out there," he said, flashing Rhys a smile as he knelt, holding out his hands to the hot coals. He continued to shake, and Rhys sat back against the wall and opened his arms.

"Come here," he murmured. Luka hastened to comply, crawling between his knees to sit with his back against Rhys's chest. Rhys wrapped him in his arms, holding him close until he quit shivering. Once warm, Luka sighed and settled comfortably against him. Rhys kissed the top of his head, then moved him so he could undo his long braid and run his fingers through the silky hair. Luka practically purred, his eyes closing as he eased back against Rhys while Rhys continued to stroke his hair. It wasn't long before Rhys followed him into sleep.

Chapter Seven

Luka opened his eyes but held perfectly still otherwise, listening. What was it? The fire had died down to red coals, but it wasn't the growing cold that woke him, nor the hard stone under his body. It was dark beyond the fire's glow, and he sent a thought out to test his ward. Still in place. Rhys breathed steadily, a warm, solid presence at his back. A tiny smile lifted the corner of his mouth when Rhys gave a slight snort then breathed evenly again.

Rhys's muscular arms were still draped protectively around him, his thighs holding him snug. Luka had no desire to move, but the fire needed tending, and something had woken him. Easing himself from his haven, he shivered in the cold air heavy with the scent of wood smoke and pine. He stirred up the coals, thanking the flames for the warmth on his face and added several pieces of wood. The lonely howl of a wolf reached his ears, and he nodded at what had disturbed his sleep.

The horse moved restlessly outside the cave entrance, and Luka made his way with cautious steps across the dark floor to her. It felt colder out there, but the ward trapped heat from the fire and kept the animal from freezing.

"Easy, dear, I'm with you," he murmured, stroking her main. The wolf howled, sounding closer, and a hard shiver ran through the mare.

"He's hungry, yes," Luka granted, petting her. "But he can't pick up our scent through the barrier, nor see the firelight. We're safe here. Stay with us."

Rhys moved in the cave, coming awake, and in a moment joined them, delighting Luka with a kiss on his cheek. "What is it?" he asked sleepily, putting his arms around Luka from behind, his warmth seeping into him.

"There's a wolf hunting on the ridge—" A howl cut off his words and he chuckled. "As you can hear. I'm worried our friend here will bolt if it comes much closer."

Rhys nuzzled his ear. "Could you send your thoughts with her if she runs? Keep her safe?"

"I could." Luka paused, then turned so he could look into Rhys's eyes, deep wells in the darkness. "But I would rather stay with you, whatever happens."

Rhys made a contented sound, his sleepy face lighting, and he gave Luka a brief kiss. "Thank you. But you're growing chilled," he observed with concern, rubbing Luka's arms. "Come back to the fire."

Rhys took his hand and led him to the fireside. Luka sat cross-legged, putting his hands to the bright flames. Rhys knelt behind him and ran fingers through his hair, and Luka murmured his pleasure when he braided the long strands. It was a perfect moment, intimate. Luka wished they could stay there forever, then hastily took it back. It was never safe to make random wishes, especially inside a warding.

Rhys hummed softly, seeming content as he twined Luka's hair, and Luka dug in his pocket, choosing the rose quartz from the other stones he drew out. After tucking the remaining ones away, he held the quartz up to the fire, gazed at the tiny fissures in the pink stone. Beautiful despite its imperfections, the gem made him think of his heart and his deep love for Rhys. Of the mistakes he'd made but the firmness of his dedication.

Holding the walnut sized stone between his fingers, he passed it over the fire close enough to feel the sting of the flames, once, twice, until the quartz glowed from within. Luka clasped it in his hand and placed it over his heart. He let down his barriers, allowed his love to spill out. His chest swelled with emotion and he had trouble catching his breath.

He loved Rhys completely, his intelligence and kindness, his pretty mouth, his courage. Through the lonely years of his life, Luka had longed for a companion to share his hearth. To fill his days with laughter and sweetness. Someone who understood him. He'd never dared dream they'd share his bed. That joy was meant for others, not the reclusive, shy witch in his crude hut.

Joy filled Luka now, expanded, until Luka's body could no longer contain it. The tiniest sliver of his life force detached, burst from its bonds and entered the stone clutched to his chest. Luka couldn't stifle the soft cry of pain and elation that accompanied this release, and Rhys grabbed his shoulders, his concern and fear enveloping Luka.

"What is it? What's hurt you?" Rhys turned him, searching his face with a frantic gaze.

Luka shook his head, for the moment overwhelmed. He realized he was crying and wiped at his eyes with the sleeve of his tunic.

"It's nothing, my dear," he said, and laughed at his own absurdity when Rhys gave him an incredulous look. "I was thinking of how much I love you, and how sorry I am for sending you away like I did. If only—"

"Stop it," Rhys snapped, the sharp retort echoing in the cave, temper flashing in his eyes. "We won't speak of it again. You sent me away in good faith, to keep me safe. And when I reached the bottom of the trail, Widow Ravan was waiting for me. I didn't think of it at the time. I was young and had just been dismissed by the one I loved the most."

Luka flinched, but Rhys pressed on, "I realize now you had Ravan meet me that evening, and she took me under her wing at your request. You did the best possible thing to ensure my safety." He wiped a tear from Luka's face with a gentle thumb. "No more self-reproach. Every step we've taken in life has brought us here, together. It's all I've ever wanted."

"Dear heart," Luka said brokenly before Rhys pulled him close and kissed him, easing the pain in his chest.

Peace filled him and he kissed Rhys in return, feeling complete. Loved.

Rhys moved him back. "What's this?" he asked, touching Luka's fist between them.

Luka trembled. Would Rhys understand?

"It's for you," he said simply, opening his hand. The rose quartz glowed, then the light dimmed, went out.

"Lovely." Rhys picked it up, turning the gem over in his fingers. "Is it for luck?"

Luka hid his keen disappointment. "Among other things. It's a token. A little piece of me to keep with you always."

"Thank you." Rhys held it to the firelight, a pretty bauble, and tucked it away in a pocket. A sudden yawn took him, and he laughed. "Sorry. I need to sleep. Come with me?"

Rhys settled back against the cave wall and Luka sat between his legs again, curling on his side against his chest. There was a sharp ache inside him, a reminder of his torn soul. But in time he would heal. Rhys's heart beat steadily under his ear, his arms held him close, and it was enough.

He didn't remember falling asleep, but sunlight flooded the cave when next he opened his eyes. He blinked at the dark apparition standing over them, then bolted upright.

"They come," she warned, then the vision of Widow Ravan dispelled as if it had never been there. Luka scrambled to his feet, heart pounding as he frantically checked his ward. Still firm. But would it hold?

"Rhys, get up," he said urgently, keeping his gaze focused on the cave entrance and the stony outcrop beyond. Rhys rose instantly and came to his side, and they moved to the edge of the barrier as one. The mare's ears were pricked, and she moved restlessly, her attention on the forest beyond.

"I didn't think they'd find us so soon," Rhys confessed, and Luka winced at his dismay. But then Rhys clenched a fist, his gaze darting around for a weapon, bolstering Luka's own courage.

"I am with you, Rhys, whatever happens," he promised, his heart hot. These were the men who'd abused and tormented Rhys for uncounted years. They would pay.

"No, Luka," Rhys said unexpectedly and put his hands on Luka's shoulders, turned him so they faced each other. He searched Luka's eyes and Luka wondered what he saw. Rhys gave him a tender smile. "You're the gentlest man I've ever known. I won't have you do violence on my account."

"I won't let them hurt you," Luka said fervently, his resolve unshaken.

"I am a grown man," Rhys reminded him. "And have spent many years taking care of myself. Without you."

Luka dropped his gaze to the stones at his feet. "Of course."

Rhys tutted and put a finger under Luka's chin, raising his face. He leaned closer and brushed Luka's lips with his own. "I've been alone, but that doesn't mean I wouldn't rather have enjoyed every moment of that time in your company." He pressed their lips together before Luka could answer, untangling the knots of pain in his chest.

The scrape of a hoof on stone had them springing apart, though Luka reached instinctively for Rhys's hand, reforging the bond they'd shared years ago. He would need Rhys's strength as well for this.

Lorin stepped out of the tree line leading a roan, with Aethan following, still mounted on his own horse, though he slid from the saddle immediately. He handed Lorin the reins and sauntered toward them over the rocky outcrop. Morning sunlight glinted on his dark hair and highlighted his handsome features, while Luka and Rhys remained in shadow. Good. Luka would take every advantage given.

No doubt sensing Luka's ward, he stopped several steps from it, hands on hips as he surveyed them, squinting in the sun's glare. His gaze slid to their clasped hands, and he raised a brow. "Did you fuck him last night?" he asked Luka conversationally, as if they sat at morning tea. "He's such a hot, tight hole."

Rhys flinched but Luka gave his hand a quick squeeze.

"Your words mean nothing," he answered dryly, giving no weight to the hateful utterance. "What do you want here?"

Aethan immediately hid his surprise at his response and straightened, dropping all pretense. "I want what is mine. I want the Well of Hope."

"Hope belongs to the world, Aethan. What you want is to control it."

"And why not? Others squander hope on banality. 'I hope it rains today.' 'I hope my husband returns from market before dark.'" He looked at Rhys and sneered. "'I hope Father doesn't come to my room tonight'. All a waste of something so powerful."

"Perhaps, but hope is not yours to give or withhold. Go back home, Aethan. You will never find the Well."

"Then I will take Rhys. Perhaps his torment will change your mind." Without warning, Aethan motioned toward them, and Luka held his breath, bracing as a wave of power smashed against his warding. It wavered, shimmering in his sight, but held. Sweat broke out on his brow with his effort to sustain it as Aethan took a step closer, hands held up, palms facing them. The sorcerer was strong. *Too strong?*

Rhys tightened his grip on his hand, adding his strength, inviting Luka to take what he needed. He wished then that Rhys was far away from him, safe. Happy. But it was too late for that. Aethan narrowed his eyes to glittering slits, a single drop of sweat working its way down the side of his face. Lorin put a hand on his shoulder and Luka shuddered under the strain of holding the ward. Rhys let out a small sound of pain, bruising his heart. *Rhys shouldn't be here!*

He put thoughts of Rhys from his mind, closed his eyes on Aethan and Lorin standing opposite. The ward became everything. It solidified under his concentration. Aethan's breathing grew labored, but Luka put that aside as well. He *became* the ward, putting himself between Rhys and the men who would hurt him, unbreakable. In that moment he knew, without doubt, he was the stronger. The knowledge was thrilling and terrifying.

But Rhys whimpered, though Luka could tell he'd tried to stifle it. Luka looked at him, saw his own body standing immobile beside Rhys's beloved form. Rhys had his head down, but he glanced up as if sensing Luka's attention, and Luka gasped at the agony lining his sweet face. He was taking too much!

Instantly, he dropped the ward, and the sudden release of energy staggered the men facing them. In that moment of confusion he grabbed Rhys's hand and urged him on the mare.

"Run," he directed, already turning to face the others.

"Not without you," Rhys said fiercely, holding out his hand to help him mount.

There was no time, Aethan had already recovered.

"Go!" he shouted, and the horse bolted under his touch. Rhys sent him a frantic glance over his shoulder, then ducked down to avoid a tree limb as the mare crashed into the forest along a narrow game trail. With a shout, Aethan and Lorin sprang to their own mounts and gave chase, Lorin flashing Luka a look of hatred as they passed him.

Luka shivered as silence settled on the outcrop. "Be safe, my love," he murmured and closed his eyes, sending an image to the mare of a haven to make for, if they could stay ahead of Aethan. It sickened him to think of Rhys once again at the monster's mercy, but Rhys now carried a piece of Luka's heart. Luka would find him.

Chapter Eight

Luka passed his hand over the coals of the fire, whispering a final word of gratitude as he drew its light and warmth into himself. Once the ashes were cold, he chose a stout walking stick from the fallen branches on the edge of the clearing and started on the trail after the others. Heart sore, he played over the morning's events in his mind, agonizing if he'd made the right decision in sending Rhys from his side. But how else could he have protected him? He could have held the ward, but Rhys would have suffered for it. As it was, he'd already taken too much of his strength.

A deep hoof print in the mud on the side of the trail made his heart thump, and he sent his thoughts swiftly to Rhys's mount. The mare ran smoothly, the path Luka had chosen for her clear in her mind. Luka dared not look at Rhys on her back, not willing to burden him with his fear and longing.

"Be safe, dear heart," he murmured, and staggered at the sudden wave of love and concern that washed over him. Rhys had sensed him! Luka ached for the day they could be together in peace and plumb the depths of Rhys's power.

As it was, he sent his own love back then turned his thought to the men following Rhys, content with the distance still between them. Nevertheless, he quickened his pace, building speed, faster and faster until he fairly flew over the game trail. He thought he might fly, if he picked up his feet. But he had never tried it and now was not the time to experiment. He could keep this pace for several hours before he would need to rest. Then he sighed, knowing it still wouldn't be enough, and sent a plea out on the wind for aide.

Quieting his mind, Luka gave himself to the chase, allowed his body to work on instinct, assessing the path ahead and adjusting accordingly. It had frightened him the first time he'd done this, lost to the nearly animalistic pleasure of speed and freedom, not sure he could come back from the euphoria.

He didn't slow until his breathing came in gasps and his lungs burned. Returning to himself, he became aware of the ache in his body, muscles strained. Thirst was a driving need. The endless pathways stretched out before him and he cast around—there, a tiny spring a quarter of a league ahead. He stumbled on, his hazy vision finally clearing as the welcome trickle of water caught his ear. A lush glen opened on the right, the snow that had fallen earlier still clinging in the deep shadows.

Luka went to his knees on the edge of the glen with a soft cry of pain and a mumbled word of gratitude before drinking his fill of the sweet water bubbling from the spring. Its coolness eased his fiery throat, expanded from his chest to his limbs, leaving him shivering. Exhaustion slammed into him and he couldn't catch himself and toppled to his side, where he gulped in the thick air, pungent with damp earth and grass and pine, giving him life.

Sunlight filtered into the glen, and he blinked at the interlacing limbs sheltering him. A robin landed overhead, dancing along the tree branch. Needles rained down on him and Luka closed his eyes. Sleep licked at his senses, seducing him, and a groan was pulled from him as he pushed up into a sitting position.

"Are you at our meeting place?" he asked softly, banishing the pain of his tired limbs from his mind.

Nigh onto immediately an answer floated on the air. "I'm close." He waited patiently for the voice to continue. "But I sense you are still far from here." The next message came at a longer interval. "I sent Paddy for you."

Luka listened, but there was no further communication and he was too spent to reply. But Ravan's message filled him with hope. She would soon reach Oak Knoll, where she would find a safe place for Rhys, should he make it that far. And she had sent one of her swiftest horses for Luka.

He climbed to his feet, closed his eyes until the dizziness passed, then picked up his walking stick and started on the trail once again. His clothing was damp from the grass, bits of moss clinging to his tunic. Usually, he would make things right with a whisper of a thought. Dry his clothes. Remove the ache from his bones. But it had been a grievous few days, and his soul still needed to heal.

He chewed his lips as he shuffled along the muddy path, growing more anxious with each step. Would he have any strength left once he caught up with Aethan? He realized with dismay how slow he was moving and picked up his pace. Not the speed from earlier, that was beyond him, but enough to bring sweat to his brow, his heart pounding.

Even this proved too much, and within the hour he stumbled to a stop, tears of frustration stinging his eyes. "Damn it."

He caught himself up, widening his eyes in panic, and quickly snatched the thought back.

"Forgive me," he croaked, his throat once again raw and burning. He spread out his arms, opening himself, searching. The forest had gone silent, a held breath. But in a moment a breeze rustled through the trees. A bird chirped. Insects hummed. He staggered under the overwhelming relief that filled him. How could he have made so careless a demand? He'd once...

Old grief and crippling regret bowed his shoulders, but he drew a shuddering breath and moved forward on the trail. He couldn't change the past. Could never make up for what he'd done with a foolish wish, once upon a time. What he'd come close to doing a moment ago. He could only guard his thoughts and do his best.

He'd only taken a few shuffling steps when the clop of a horse's hooves brought him again to a stop. The path ahead darkened, overhung with tree limbs and twisted vines. Was it a friend who approached? An old enemy? Either way, he was too weary to fight, and leaned heavily on his walking stick with both hands.

In less than a heartbeat, a stallion burst from the trees, all pitch-black coat and fiery eyes. Luka snorted a laugh. This was Paddy? Leave it to Ravan to come up with such a ridiculous name for this magnificent animal. Lithe limbed, powerful, the horse stopped before him, his breathing only slightly labored though he'd come a far distance for him. Luka rubbed his nose, slid a caressing hand down his proud neck.

"Thank you," he murmured, and pulled himself painfully onto the stallion's broad back. The animal turned about and Luka hastened to curl his fingers in his thick mane, ducking low as the muscles bunched beneath his thighs, and Paddy sprang down the trail the way he'd come, swift as a hawk. Magic twined around the stallion, familiar, comforting, and Luka gave in to his exhaustion, letting the quick motion nudge him toward the sleep he desperately needed. He wouldn't fall.

He dreamed. A woman rode a white horse down the muddy main street of Oak Knoll, back straight, head lifted as her green eyes dispassionately took in the doors being shuttered against her. A blood red cloak flowed from her shoulders like a queen's mantle, a ruby at her throat. Rosehips were twisted in a circlet on her silver hair.

A tender smile touched Luka's mouth. Of course, Ravan would dress in her finest clothing and boldly enter a village who shunned magic in any form, who would gladly take a knife to a witch, given the chance.

"Is he there?" Luka asked and held his breath, trembling with hope.

Ravan tilted her head as if to listen. "No. I sense him near, though danger surrounds him." She paused. "Go to him, Luka. I will be here when you need me."

"I owe you my thanks—"

"See to his safety," Ravan interjected, sharp enough to cut. "He is my pupil as well as yours, Luka. I would see no harm come to him."

Luka nodded, and the dream shifted. He found himself in a misty glen, the air cold, the moss damp. The mare stood to the side, head down, foreleg bound in cloth. Luka glanced around, fear slithering along his spine. Rhys sat with his back against a boulder, chin resting on his drawn-up knees. He didn't appear aware of Luka's presence until he stood before him, then he looked up, face lined with fatigue and pain.

"We almost made it," Rhys said, voice tired, the damp air muffling his words. "But then the mare slipped on a pinecone and fell hard. Bones weren't broken, thankfully, but she limps and I will not ride her further."

"And you?" Luka didn't breathe, his trepidation hanging between them.

"Unharmed. But Luka, I'm afraid. Aethan is closer now. I sense his corruption on the air."

"Hold on, Rhys. I am coming."

Rhys nodded, then closed his eyes and leaned his head back against the stone. Luka sat beside him. Rhys was chilled, having torn his sleeves for the binding on the horse's leg, and Luka gathered him in his arms, Rhys's head on his shoulder. But after a short time, Rhys stirred and eased back to meet Luka's troubled gaze.

"You need to go, my heart. Sleep. You will need your strength when you catch us up."

"I don't want to leave you alone," Luka protested, though he knew the wisdom of Rhys's words.

Rhys cupped his face, gave him the softest of kisses. "You are always with me," he murmured, then nudged him away. "Go now."

Luka gasped as he jolted awake, disoriented, until he realized the stallion still moved beneath him, taking him closer to Rhys with each swift step. A half grin sprang on his face.

"You have grown strong, if you can compel me," he said to Rhys, though the man could no longer hear him. Pride and love stirred in his heart, but he firmly put that aside, closed his eyes, and willed himself to sleep without dreams this time.

Chapter Nine

The sound of hooves reached his ears and Rhys raised his head from where he sat against the boulder, instinctively checking his ward. Holding, though he knew in his heart he was no match for Aethan. But it would keep that bastard Lorin out. Aethan was demanding, thorough. But Lorin was purposefully cruel, delighting in Rhys's pain when he took his pleasure in him.

He would one day kill them both.

Rhys sighed, knowing such thoughts would distress Luka. His lover held all life sacred, to be treated tenderly, with care. Rhys had never seen him harsh to any living creature. He even thanked the river for water and the fire for its warmth. Rhys loved him completely but could never be that man. His anger was all that had sustained him through the nightmares he'd endured as his father's prisoner.

Rhys covered his face with his hands and shuddered with the horror of it. After his mother had died, Rhys had survived, loading crates for the shop keepers in Moss

Hollow, assisting the butcher and blacksmith, running errands. But Aethan had come for Rhys's mother, and on finding Aliya long dead, took Rhys instead. He'd spent months in that damp cellar, beaten, starved, repeatedly raped by a man who should have nurtured him. And when Aethan had him captive once again, after he had left Luka, Lorin had joined in, taking him separately or together, seeing how far they could torment and torture him until he broke. He'd clung to his anger as a lifeline, enduring the pain and degradation, plotting his revenge.

"I'm sorry, Luka," he whispered now, clenching his hands into fists. "There's no forgiveness in me."

The horses came to a stop at the edge of the glen, but he didn't look up, gathering his strength. There was a push against his ward. A stronger one, then Lorin swore at him in fury, instantly followed by Aethan's mocking laughter. Rhys came close to feeling sorry for Lorin. Rhys had endured Aethan's biting derision as his captive. But to live with it day in and day out, without reprieve, as Lorin did? It could drive a man...insane.

"Still not as strong as your brother, Lorin? Not surprising, given how weak your mother proved. Kaelyn was always a disappointment. It might have been a mercy had she died giving birth to you."

Even though directed at his half brother, Rhys was shocked by his callous, cruel words, and let his ward slip. Not much, and he hastened to reinforce it, but it was too late. Lorin followed Aethan into the glen. Rhys focused his gaze at the moss under his feet, managing not to flinch when Aethan crouched in front of him. Lorin loomed over them both.

"Where's your witch?" Aethan asked as if this were a pleasant conversation in front of the hearth. Then he made a clicking sound with his tongue. "I remember, he sent you out as a distraction, gambling I'd chase you, leaving him free to do as he will. But I would have thought he'd find a way to be with you now. Has he grown tired of you already? Spoiled goods? Or did you prove too much for him? I like to think I...improved your skills."

He ran a finger up Rhys's thigh and Rhys batted his hand away, lurching to his feet. "Don't touch me."

"Ho, feeling feisty, are we?" Aethan's lip curled. "Or is fucking that pretentious witch giving you airs? Perhaps you need to be shown your place. Shall we each take an end, front and back? My cock up your ass, Lorin down your slim throat?" He licked his lips. "You make such delicious sounds when we take you like that."

Rhys knew Aethan was baiting him but couldn't stop the surge of fury that left him shaking. Enough. He gathered his strength, meaning to attack Aethan with all he had, even if it killed him. But a sudden spark of heat against his hip gave him pause. Distracted, he slid a hand in his pocket, drew out the pink stone. It was warm to the touch, glowing faintly with an inner light. Beautiful.

"Who gave you that? Never mind." Aethan scowled at the gem. "Luka's always been a fool." He made as if to snatch the stone, but Rhys pulled it out of reach. "Keep it, then, for all the good it will do you," Aethan snarled, but kept his gaze on the rock until Rhys slid it back to his pocket.

He held the stone in his fingers a moment longer. Did this mean Luka was close? Clearly he'd wanted Rhys not to attack the others. He'd better hurry, then. Aethan would grow tired of talking soon enough and then Rhys would need to protect himself. He'd be damned if these men took him ever again.

"What did you mean when you said Luka used me as a distraction?" he asked, desperate to give Luka more time.

"Exactly that. Luka is cunning. I imagine while we've been chasing you, he's set all kinds of machinations in motion."

"But still you chased me."

"Of course. I wasn't ready to fight the witch. With you in our possession, I won't need to."

"Luka won't stop because of me."

Lorin snorted, reminding Rhys he had two sorcerers to deal with. "Luka's besotted with you," he said in disgust. "He would never leave you in harm's way."

"Be silent, Lorin," Aethan snapped, temper a hot flash in the cold air. "I'm talking with your brother at the moment."

Lorin clamped his lips shut, but fury smoldered in his blue eyes as he gazed at Aethan's back. Rhys wondered how Aethan couldn't feel it, but then concluded Aethan didn't care.

"As I was saying," Aethan continued, "Luka wouldn't hesitate to use you to gain his ends." His voice dropped to a harsh whisper. "I've seen it before."

Rhys swayed, the discordant tones of Aethan's voice winding in his head, the words playing incessantly, laying seeds of doubt. Could it be true? Luka had abandoned him once, sent him away to fend for himself, uncaring what befell him at Aethan's hands. There was nothing to keep him from betraying Rhys now.

Sickened, Rhys peered between his lashes, and caught Aethan's triumphant smirk before he hid it away behind a concerned look. *Bastard.* But Rhys didn't dare reach out for Luka, though he could feel him drawing closer. He only needed to hold on a little longer.

"What do you mean?" he asked, putting a quaver in his voice as if he had begun to doubt Luka. *Never!*

Aethan put a conciliatory hand on his arm, forcing Rhys to suppress a shudder of revulsion. The man claimed to be his father, and yet all he ever received was pain and humiliation at his hands. He looked up and saw Lorin avidly watching, and a sudden thought occurred to him. Luka's magic was pure, a gift from the earth. But Aethan and Lorin's sorcery was a dark, corrupt thing. Was the horrific act of incest the final key to twisting magic to their terrible purpose?

The thought made him feel powerful. If he could somehow use this knowledge to his advantage...

He looked down at Aethan's hand on his arm. "Tell me."

"Despite what she might have said, I loved your mother. Aliya was a delight! A dark-haired beauty. Wild thing in bed—" Both Rhys and Lorin hissed at this and he shouted with laughter. "Easy, boys! Kaelyn was the same." He looked between them and a smile curled his lips. "I only now notice. You each have Kaelyn's fair complexion and Aliya's deep blue eyes." His fingers idly caressed Rhys's arm. "But it is my seed that put the fire and magic in your blood."

Rhys exchanged a glance with Lorin and saw his own fury mirrored in a face that could be his own. He hoped his emotions were better hidden.

"What does this have to do with Luka?" he asked, surprised he could speak in so level a voice.

"Why everything, my dear. While I was making love to Aliya, Luka was enamored of her as well. I speak the truth," he said in reply to Rhys's quickened breath. "Did he never tell you? He was Kaelyn's guest at the manor, for his health, she claims. Whatever the reason, he couldn't keep his eyes off Aliya. It became embarrassing, the way he marked her steps when she passed.

"Finally, it grew wearisome, and I took Aliya for myself, to spare her the undesired attention. It was ludicrous how hurriedly Luka abandoned her after that. Stealing away in the night without a word to anyone. And when she left us shortly afterward to a life of want and degradation, where was Luka? I think he knew all along where she lived, the squalor in which she raised you. Why didn't he help her? Or you? What kind of love is that, after all? He discarded your mother back then, and now you. Why do you stay with him?"

Rhys couldn't answer and unclenched the fists he held only when his hands started to ache. Aethan lied, but there was a grain of truth in there somewhere.

"Luka loved my mother?" he asked, voice hoarse, playing for time. But he definitely had questions for Luka when they met up.

"Did you never wonder why he chose you, Rhys? Out of all the people he's known in his long life? And he is old, my dear, trust me. My father spoke of him as a contemporary, a witch of extraordinary power. I caught a glimpse of him at Father's table when I was a youth, and he was as timeless and handsome as he is now. Ageless. Why would someone like him choose you, unless as a reminder of a lost love?" He glanced at Lorin. "We all make do."

Bleak despair flashed over Lorin's face, replaced by a mask of cold indifference. Rhys's heart clenched. How young was Lorin when Aethan first sought his bed? His mother had died of consumption when he was but a child. How long after before Aethan gave in to his dark, unspeakable desires?

Aethan made a sudden move, kissing him hard. Rhys's first instinct was to shove him away in revulsion, but he couldn't fight both him and Lorin together. *Luka, hurry!*

In that instant, footsteps pounded across the glen, and Aethan was plucked from him and held at arm's length, Luka's hand fisted in his tunic. Luka was a flame in the mist, magic surrounding him. "Do not touch him," he said, voice low, dangerous, vibrating in the cold air, setting Rhys's teeth on edge.

Aethan gave a shaky laugh. "Why, Luka, I—"

"Never again." It was a command, sharp as a blow, and thunder rumbled overhead. This was more than magic. Power surged under Rhys's boots, thrummed in the air around them. Luka *compelled,* and the earth itself answered. Rhys watched Luka, pride and fear surging inside his breast. Lorin seemed terrified, while the color drained from Aethan's continence. He appeared shaken to the core, shocked.

Time hung suspended on a knife blade, a heartbeat of deadly peril, then Aethan nodded his proud head, hatred in his eyes. "As you wish." Luka released him and he drew a breath, confidence returning. "But why do you bother, Luka, when Rhys clearly despises you?"

Luka tilted his head, curious, while Rhys's heart thudded.

"Can't you see it? I told him about Aliya." Confusion swept Luka's face. "Don't you remember? You loved her and then abandoned her when she needed you the most. And now you abandon him."

Luka swiveled to Rhys, lips white, eyes pleading. "That's not how it was. Let me explain—"

"No," Aethan interjected. "I won't let you speak and bewitch him with your words. You left him and Aliya to starve. There is no defense for that. No forgiveness."

Fire flashed in Luka's brown eyes, answered once again by thunder. Lorin stepped closer, and the air crackled as he and Aethan gathered forces. Rhys shivered. Death was near, breathing over his shoulder. What could he do? Luka, his gentle lover, would kill to defend him. He couldn't let him do that.

Desperate, he shoved his hands in his pockets, gathering his own strength, and felt the stone Luka had given him. He drew it out, turning it over in his palm. It felt warm to the touch, softly lit as if it sensed Luka's presence. Aethan caught sight of it and his harsh laughter grated over Rhys's taut nerves. Luka looked from Rhys's face down to the gem, and pain darkened his eyes.

"Oh, my dear Luka, your expression!" Aethan crowed. "Beyond priceless. To think you had given the man your heart, and he not know the value of such a gift."

Rhys made a confused sound and Aethan looked at him, his smile beyond cruel, his voice dripping spite when he spoke, "Didn't you realize? Luka tore out a piece of his essence, his soul, and shoved it into the gem so you could have his heart always. But it is more than a token of affection. It is his talisman to you. He would come to you, wherever you were, should you need him."

He turned his gaze on Luka who stood, head bowed, looking defeated. "Of course, he would not want such a gift from a man who condemned his mother to deprivation and a painful death."

Rhys stared hard at the gem resting on his palm. How he must have inadvertently hurt Luka, not understanding the precious gift he'd been given. But death still hovered at his shoulder, mirrored in Aethan's wild, glittering eyes, Lorin's hatred, and Luka's clenched hands at his sides.

"No, I wouldn't want it." He tipped his hand and watched, aching, as the jewel dropped to the mossy ground. He ignored Luka's soft sound of pain and stepped forward, pushing the stone in the mud with his boot.

"I'm leaving," he muttered, choked with emotion, and shoved through the men, heading for his horse. He felt Aethan and Lorin at his back but didn't pause. *Luka!* He gave a quick glance over his shoulder, but Luka didn't watch him. He'd left the glen, heading down the trail the way he's come, damn it all.

Chapter Ten

Rhys put a hand on the mare's shoulder and sighed. He felt her exhaustion, the pain in her foreleg. If he ran, he wouldn't get far on her before the others caught him up. And Aethan wouldn't stop this time, taking what he wanted from Rhys and leaving him to die.

Aethan called their own horses over and paused before mounting at the sound of pounding hooves. Luka broke into the glen, tucked low on the stallion's back, hand outstretched. Rhys's heart leaped as Aethan and Lorin dodged to either side. He sprang forward and gripped Luka's hand as he passed, swinging up behind him.

The stallion didn't break stride, darting into the trees, forcing Rhys to duck or risk a low branch sweeping him off his perch. They traveled only a short distance, though, before Luka made a sharp gesture with his hand toward several boulders and the horse swerved off the narrow trail, coming to a halt behind them. Luka made a sweeping motion this time, a ward between them and the trail.

Rhys caught his breath. What he'd just done should have been impossible. A ward took time…

Within moments, the sound of hooves drew close. Rhys held his breath as Aethan and Lorin galloped past without a glance, hastening down the trail as if Luka and he still rode ahead of them. They waited in silence, then Luka nudged the horse forward.

Rhys stopped him with a hand on Luka's thigh. "Wait, please."

Luka paused, his gaze on his hands twined in the stallion's mane. Rhys had felt him shaking as they rode but put it down to the cold air. He could tell now that Luka had been weeping, his breathing ragged in the silence.

"Luka, look at me," he asked, hurting for him.

Luka shrugged. "We should go."

Rhys would have none of that. He wound Luka's silken braid in his hand and gave it a slight tug. "Look at me," he said again, and waited. At last, Luka sighed and shifted to face him. Tears wet his dark skin, making his eyes luminous in the weak winter light. Rhys leaned to him, brushed his lips with his own, and felt Luka's gasp.

"I don't believe a word Aethan has said," he assured him, aching to have Luka pull him into his arms.

Sadness filled Luka's eyes. "Some of it is true," he said, "I—"

Rhys stopped his words with a soft press of lips. "Once we are safe, you can tell me your truth. Luka, trust me. Whatever it is, we will work it out together. And then you will fuck me."

Luka gave a startled laugh, gorgeous color flushing his skin, a reluctant grin tugging the corner of his mouth. Rhys gave him an arch look. "That is, if you still want me…"

"Always," Luke replied fiercely and pulled Rhys into his arms. Mist clung to the trees around them, but Luka's body was warm, and Rhys snuggled close while Luka kissed him over and over, urgent, fiery caresses that turned his blood molten.

Rhys put a hand on Luka's thigh, felt the muscles tense, and wished there was time to undo Luka's braid and spread the silken mass around them as they made love. Instead, he tightened his grip on his hair and pulled his head back, feeling Luka's moan against the lips he pressed to his exposed neck. The rich odor of cold, damp earth filled his nostrils, but over that Luka's clean scent stirred his senses, a green meadow and sunshine. Rhys gently sucked the rapid pulse in his throat, drawing another moan from him. Luka had always been so responsive to his every touch.

Luka eased back with such reluctance Rhys's heart stumbled. "We should go," he said, making it sound more of a question than a suggestion.

"Take me somewhere safe?" Rhys asked, running a finger up Luka's thigh, thrilling at his sharp breath. "But my horse…"

"Will find her way without harm," Luka promised. He faced forward and leaned to whisper in the stallion's ear. The proud creature threw its head up, snorting. Luka twined his hands once again in its long mane and lay over his neck. Rhys hastily slipped his arms around Luka and crouched down as the horse sprang into a fast trot. They crossed the path they'd been following and dodged into the trees on the other side, surely guided by Luka's magic.

"Try to sleep," Luka instructed kindly. Rhys took that as an invitation to nestle closer, resting his head on Luka's back. The movement of the horse and Luka's warmth guided him toward sleep, and if Luka murmured a spell to aide him into dreams, he welcomed it.

The dreams were pleasant at first, scenes from his childhood. Playing in the creek below their hovel. Picking fruits and herbs for Mother's preserves. Walking with her to the top of the hill to watch the sunrise. But then they changed, growing dark. Mother's cough worsening. Her strength ebbing. The long dark night of her passing.

Rhys had wept, grief and a deep sense of loneliness settling its heavy burden on his young shoulders. But a hand had rested there as well. Widow Ravan, sharing that terrible vigil with him. He remembered now, she'd been there for days with her herbs and smudges and remedies, then guided his mother into sleep and peace as she slipped away. Funny how he'd forgotten that.

Or been made to forget. There was something else, *someone* else in the room, that last terrible night. Rhys concentrated. Candlelight flickered off the grim walls he and Mother had decorated with branches and dried flowers. The scent of sage and eucalyptus hung heavy on the air. A figure hesitated in the doorway and Ravan rose instantly to go to him.

"You mustn't be here," she whispered fiercely, but Rhys could still hear them in the dead silence of the cottage.

"I know. I'm sorry, but Aliya..." the man stopped, sounding heartbroken, his pain and fear thick in his voice. "He's alone now."

"You can't help him. You'll only bring danger to him if you stay. Aethan will find him through you, given time. Go now, Papa. I will protect him."

The stranger's breath caught on a broken sound and Rhys glanced across the room to meet dark eyes in a face twisted with grief. Startled, the man widened his eyes, and shock ran through Rhys...

He jerked awake and grabbed for Luka to keep from falling.

"Careful, my heart," Luka murmured, sounding half asleep himself. They both straightened, Rhys putting a hand at the small of his back and stretching his spine and shoulders, while Luka ran a hand over his face and stifled a yawn. The stallion had his head down, moving at a slow, steady pace in the gathering dusk. Evening approached and lights appeared through the trees. Rhys was glad when they left the forest and saw the village of Oak Knoll climbing the hill before them, the cluster of oaks at its center rising above the houses.

"Are we staying here?" he asked hopefully, the scent of woodsmoke and cooking meals floating up to them. He ached head to toe and would give anything for a bath and warm bed. Preferably with Luka.

Luka's breath caught as if he knew Rhys's thoughts. Emboldened, Rhys pressed against his back, running his hands up Luka's thighs.

"I want to be with you," he murmured and nuzzled Luka's neck. Luka didn't reply and Rhys eased back. "Unless it's not safe here?"

Luka looked at him helplessly, longing and uncertainty warring in his dark gaze. *Damn it.* Aethan had placed the doubt of Rhys's affection in his mind. He'd find a way to be rid of both he and Lorin if it was the last thing he did in the world.

Luka faced forward, and a sigh escaped him. "It's safe enough," he replied and nudged the stallion forward. Rhys hurt for him. Determined to prove his love and desire, he moved Luka's braid aside and placed a kiss on the nape of his neck and thrilled at the shiver that ran through his lean body. Chuckling, he continued to kiss his neck, along his jawline, until Luka turned his head and met his lips. His lips were cold, but his mouth was warm and inviting, hungrily returning Rhys's kisses.

"Enough!" Luka pushed him back with a laugh. "Can we at least wait until we're indoors before you try to seduce me?"

"As you wish," Rhys agreed roguishly and ran a finger down Luka's back, exalting in his hard shudder. His body responded, and he moved closer, trapping Luka between his legs. Luka's desperate moan was music, but he grabbed Rhys's wrist as he reached around to take him in hand.

"Not yet, darling. Please," Luka urged. "I would have you safe first."

Rhys smiled, content for the moment, and straightened. They approached the town's main road, and he looked around curiously. Attractive cottages and shops lined the thoroughfare with the welcoming lights of a tavern spilling out into the gloom. There were few people out as the snow thickened and night wasn't far off, the small cluster in front of the tavern paying them no mind except for a cursory glance as they passed.

A thought occurred to Rhys, and he put a questioning hand on Luka's arm. "Are you from Oak Knoll?" he asked. Luka didn't answer immediately.

"Yes, once upon a time," he finally admitted. Rhys pressed his lips together when he didn't expand his answer.

"I hope someday you'll trust me with your past," he said, and pulled away, but Luka grasped for his hand, kissing his fingers.

"Forgive me," Luka begged, sounding close to frantic, pushed to his limit. "I've tried to protect you, only to fail time and again. You deserve to know, though the telling will be hard—"

Rhys hastily squeezed his hand to halt the rush of words. "Hush, my love. I shouldn't have asked." He berated himself for causing Luka distress. "I'm exhausted. My thoughts muddled. You owe me no explanations."

Luka drew a troubled breath but said no more as they approached the oak grove at the center of town. Before they reached it, he guided the stallion down a narrow side street. Firelight flickered in the windows of the few cottages they passed, but it had grown dark and silent around them, the cold sting of snowflakes on their skin.

They halted before the last cottage, set apart from the others. The yard was pitch dark and only a faint glow under a shuttered window attested the dwelling occupied. Rhys slid immediately from the horse's back, more than glad to stop moving for a time. Luka was slower in alighting, staring a moment at the cottage, body held rigid, until he gave a sharp nod and dismounted.

Rhys made to lead the horse to the small outbuilding he spotted behind the cottage, but Luka stopped him with a hand on his shoulder. "Go inside, please, where I know you'll be safe. I'll be in shortly."

Rhys hesitated but Luka pressed his lips into a stubborn line.

"Very well," he gave in, but watched as Luka walked around the cottage, the horse trailing obediently. In a moment, a light appeared as Luka lit a lamp in the makeshift stable and rubbed the stallion down while it nibbled at feed in the trough.

Chewing his lip, uncertain, Rhys turned his gaze on the cottage. It seemed older than the other dwellings on the road, made entirely with fitted stone. He smelled wood smoke and sweet grass rising from the tall chimney, and maybe fresh-baked bread, making his mouth water. He climbed the steps to a narrow porch, and paused, magic prickling against his skin. A ward, then, but one that would allow him to enter. It felt somehow familiar, and he pushed the latch on the door and eased it open.

Chapter Eleven

A spontaneous smile rose on Rhys's lips. The room within was warm and welcoming, bright with candles and a merry fire on the hearth. Something bubbled in a cast-iron pot, smelling gloriously like a savory stew. A table was set with fresh bread and butter and honey, along with a pot of tea. Rhys could have wept, only then realizing how worn and anxious he'd become.

"Are you going to let all the heat out of the cottage?"

The last of Rhys's tension eased from his shoulders and he hurriedly shut the door behind him. "Well met, Ravan," he said, bowing to the witch who stepped out of a dark corner with a bowl of apples in her hands.

Raven set the bowl on the table as she hastily passed it, then pulled Rhys into a tight embrace. He barely heard the words vehemently whispered in his ear, but the horror and growing dread eased its hold on his heart, and he drew the first easy breath he'd taken in a long time. Tears filled his eyes, and he made no move to hide them. After Luka had sent him away, Widow Ravan had been his ally, even when his pride wouldn't allow him to accept her help.

She put him back in one of her abrupt moves, sniffing at her own tears. "I wasn't sure you'd make it," she confessed, then drew a deep, steadying breath. "Well, you're here now and dinner's ready."

"Thank you—"

Ravan waved off his words, going to the fire. "Luka asked for my help. Of course, I came. How is he?"

Before he could answer, the latch on the door rattled and Luka entered in a rush of cold air and snow. He shoved the door closed against a brisk wind and stomped the caked ice from his boots before turning to them. "The storm's growing worse." He took in the room and his face lit with a smile. "This is delightful. Ravan, thank you. I'm nearly starved and half frozen."

Luka crossed to them, giving Rhys a shy smile as he walked by him to embrace Ravan and place a kiss on her forehead. Rhys studied them. In his dream, Ravan had called him Papa. But that couldn't be so. Silver already overtook her light hair, her face worn though still pretty, while Luka seemed much younger. Rhys had thought him thirty years old at most, body well-built and virile.

He tore his hungry gaze away from him to look at the fire, hoping Ravan hadn't caught the longing in his eyes for a soft bed and Luka's arms. A smile twitched his lips as he wondered if Luka was aware he planned on seducing him that night.

Ravan clapped her hands like a young girl, regaining his attention. "Now that we're all safe, please, sit down. There's much to discuss."

They took a moment to wash with some water simmering at the hearth, Rhys salivating from the delicious smell of stew wafting from the pot over the flames.

"Let me serve you," he asked, reaching for the ladle.

Ravan returned his smile. "I feel the exhaustion in you. Go and sit with Luka. But there *is* something," she continued with a sly wink. "You can make us breakfast."

"My pleasure, madam." Rhys sketched a bow, heart light with joy and a peace he hadn't felt in what seemed an eternity. He'd often brought in eggs from the barn and made them breakfast while Ravan mixed her potions nearby. Those had been happy days, despite the ache of loss that never left him. He wished now that he had accepted her offer of a room back then, rather than live on his own in the rough lean-to he'd built outside of town, and spent most of his lonely nights, until he'd gotten work at a farm... But pride had always been his folly.

He took the chair beside Luka at the table and saw the yearning in his gaze before Luka glanced away, blushing slightly, making his heart skip. Ravan handed them full bowls, the aroma intoxicating, and settled with her own opposite them. Hungry as he was, he waited while the two witches closed their eyes and soundlessly thanked their beloved earth and sky for this safe haven and warm hearth and the food set before them.

In a moment, Ravan handed him a plate of bread and butter and honey and took up her spoon. "Luka, can you tell me now what has transpired? I think you owe me this much."

Rhys watched him. Candlelight glinted on the strands of silver in his long braid, but he sat up, body as vigorous as ever, eyes keen, intelligent, beautiful. "Most of the story you know," Luka began. "But I would like to hear from Rhys how he'd come to be in Aethan's hands again."

Rhys swallowed his mouthful of stew at the expected question. He'd wracked his brains for any reply that wouldn't wound Luka, but finally concluded that the truth was the only answer he could give. Luka would know it, otherwise.

"When I left you, Luka, I was lost. I didn't know what I had done wrong, that you would send me away like you did. I had somehow lost your love that was everything to me." He ran a finger through the condensation on his water goblet, laughing a little. "I was barely eighteen and heartbroken and felt life had lost all beauty." He grieved a little for the young man he'd been, once again alone in the world. Luka's sound of hurt was a slight balm for the painful memory.

"Ravan met me at the bottom of the trail and took me in as her apprentice to learn her ways of magic. But it ate me alive to be a burden, doing nothing to earn my keep save for a few chores around the cottage." He went on despite Ravan's muttered protest. "I built a shelter for myself outside town and did whatever odd job needed doing, whatever put food in my belly, finally laboring for a nearby farmer, Calan Dunne—

"You know him?" he asked when Luka growled in his throat.

"Only that he is a brutish man," Ravan put in angrily before Luka could speak.

Rhys shrugged. "He wasn't kind and worked me to the bone. But I had a meal and warm bed every night—"

"And no friends and no chance of making any," Ravan interrupted again. "You should have stayed with me. I could have kept you safe—"

"I couldn't ask that of you," Rhys countered, leaning toward her across the table. "Aethan had found me once before. Without Luka's protection, it was only a matter of time before he unearthed me again."

Ravan visibly paled and quickly glanced at Luka. Rhys turned to him as well, wishing he could take his words back. Luka's eyes were downcast on the bread he was crumbling between his fingers, lines of suffering etched on the profile he kept to Rhys while his chest rose on a quavering breath. He wouldn't look at Rhys and Rhys hurried to finish his tale.

"I was out late one night last summer, chasing an errant goat through the woods, when I walked into Aethan. Lorin was with him and I had no chance to escape. They never said how they'd found me. Why would they look on some isolated farm outside Sweetbrier? However, they had done so, and locked me in that room you found me in, Luka, for their…amusement. At first, I made many attempts to escape, but the punishments were painful, and I at last gave up." He couldn't help but add, "There was no one out in the world who cared what became of me anyway. Except maybe Ravan," he added, to be fair.

He waited, but Luka didn't speak, though there was a glimmer of tears in the corner of the eye he could see. Luka had hurt him deeply, but he never realized until now how angry he still was at the man.

"I answered your question," he said quietly. Luka flinched and rubbed the tears from his eyes with an impatient gesture.

Ravan put out a hand in protest. "You mustn't blame Luka, Rhys. This is my fault. I was charged with watching you. And failed. I didn't even realize you'd been taken. I recognize now I must have been bespelled. Whenever I felt for you, I was filled with reassurance and peace. You were safe. But that was obviously not so. I failed—"

"Enough, Ravan," Luka said. His tone was soft, but an instant silence fell on the room. Pressure built in Rhys's ears as the earth took a breath, then sound burst back in, the fire crackled loudly after the utter quiet.

Rhys turned to Luka in concern. "You've set a ward. How… Are they near?"

Luka lifted a shoulder in a half shrug. "They won't come this way."

Ravan thumped her hand on the table, making them both jump, and Rhys drew a quick breath at the fire in her green eyes. "That isn't a ward. Papa, what did you do?"

"I will keep him safe," Luka vowed, and set his lips in a grim line. The fire crackled in the sudden tension between them.

"That isn't an answer. The earth...shifted. What did you do?"

Luka gave her a defiant look. "I made a wish."

The color drained from Ravan's face betraying her fear, and Luka's expression softened. "It was a little wish, honey. Nothing to shake the foundations. I merely turned their thoughts from Oak Knoll. We need rest, Rhys especially. I've guaranteed we'll get it."

Ravan clearly wanted to argue but shook her head instead. "You know the danger of this, so I'll say no more. I only worry for your safety."

"I know and thank you for your concern." Luka drew a deep breath and turned unexpectedly to Rhys. "You have questions."

Rhys scrambled to gather his myriad of thoughts. "Too many to express," he said with a slight laugh, and watched, dismayed, as Luka's expression turned wistful. He nodded, coming to a decision. "But I don't want to hear any answers until morning. We're tired and anxious. Let's eat this delicious meal, sleep, and gather back here tomorrow."

Luka smiled faintly. "You wish to spare me. You needn't. I deserve your anger, and much more."

Ravan made an exasperated sound. "Enough, Luka. Listen to the boy. There will be time enough in the morning for recriminations."

Luka laughed aloud, and Rhys's heart hurt for the desperate tone underneath. "As you wish."

They ate in silence for a moment, then Luka took Rhys's hand under the table and Rhys's swirling thoughts calmed. He raised their hands, kissing Luka's knuckles. "I love you," he said, searching the dark eyes fixed on him. "We'll get through this," he continued and saw a fire kindle in Luka's gaze.

"I love you too." Luka held Rhys's hand against his cheek.

Ravan dropped her spoon in her now empty bowl and rose to her feet, giving them a wry look. "Now that that's settled, I'm going to my room. For the rest of the night," she added plainly, and winked when Rhys gaped at her. Giving a merry laugh, she left the table, picking up a candle and book off a nearby shelf before disappearing through one of the doors in the far wall. Rhys caught a glimpse of firelight in a cozy room before they were left alone.

He turned to Luka and saw the dark blush on his face, but also the heat smoldering in his gaze on him. Rhys rose and leaned over him, bent to nibble at his lips.

"Why don't you attend to the fire while I clear the dishes?" he suggested, and Luka nodded helplessly, his gaze on Rhys's lips. Warmth flooded through Rhys, making his cock stir.

"The fire?" he said more firmly. Luka stood, snatching a kiss as he passed Rhys, his eyes flashing. Joy combined with the lust licking Rhys's senses. He loved ordering the powerful witch around, up until the point Luka took control and drove him mad with his touches and teases, fucking him gloriously.

He hastily cleared the table, taking a moment to carry the butter down to the root cellar. He'd left it out to spoil once upon a time, and Ravan had boxed his ears. Keeping the lesson in mind, he washed the dishes using the simmering water from the hearth and Ravan's soap, fragrant with herbs, before joining Luka on the rug before the fire.

Rhys took a moment to look down at him. Luka sat cross-legged, compact body held loosely, belying the intense gaze in the soulful eyes he raised to Rhys. Firelight played over his handsome features starting an ache in Rhys. He found nothing more erotic than to see his own pale skin twined with Luka's mahogany limbs, their fingers woven, Luka's dark hair spread around them mixed with his light tresses.

A flame ignited in Luka's eyes and he reached eagerly for Rhys, pulling him into his arms. Rhys straddled him, kissing him repeatedly while he undid the string in Luka's hair and slowly unwound his braid, sliding the soft strands between his fingers. Luka moaned against his lips and Rhys slipped his tongue into the warm depths of his sweet mouth.

He pulled back, pressing their foreheads together. "Take me to bed," he demanded, staring into Luka's dark eyes, and saw love and lust flare, then settle into smoldering passion.

"As you wish," Luka answered and slid his hands under Rhys's ass, pulling him against his hardness. Joy burst in Rhys's chest. Luka's obviously forced politeness betrayed his tight control of emotions running rampant under the surface. Rhys would soon have the pleasure of pushing him beyond his restraint and watching him come apart.

"I love you," he declared, and smothered Luka's answer in a deep kiss. He untangled from Luka's arms and rose to his feet, drawing Luka up with him, kissing him as he led him by the hand to the open door in the far corner of the room, his pulse racing in anticipation.

Chapter Twelve

Luka paused on the threshold to the bedroom, taking in the bed, bright with quilts, and the heavy oak furniture. He'd made the furniture himself a lifetime ago, from a lightning struck tree in the yard. Coals glowed in the small fireplace set in the wall to the right, heating the room, and his face warmed, knowing Ravan was on the other side. But she had set wards, as he would, and no sound would pass between the walls. The thought alone made his heart jump and rush.

Rhys still held his hand, his smile curious, a teasing light in his eyes. Love was there as well, and need, and desire seared along Luka's nerves.

"Stand by the bed," he instructed, though they both knew it was a command. He'd waited long, intensely lonely years for this moment, never sure he'd have Rhys in his arms again. And in the morning, he'd answer questions that might drive them apart. He only had now, this room and this man who held his heart.

Rhys crossed to the bed, body lithe, firelight turning his hair to burnished gold. He was beautiful and Luka's chest ached as his love overflowed.

"Take off your clothes," he said, heart pounding, when Rhys faced him. Rhys drew a sharp breath, flushing under Luka's gaze, but pulled his tunic over his head. The warm glow of the fire caressed the sleek muscles of his chest and stomach, and Luka's mouth went dry when he bent to undo his boots and pull them off, the muscles of his back rippling with the movement.

Rhys straightened, and a smile quirked his full lips when he unlaced his britches. Luka smiled in return, knowing his love shown in his eyes, but he forced his gaze away. There were things to do first. He went to the fireplace and knelt to stir up the coals and add another log. Pausing, he thanked both the fire and Ravan for the warm room as the heat from the crackling flames kissed his skin. He thought of Rhys standing naked behind him and bowed his head, overcome with the joy spilling through him, and thanked the very essence of life for the gift of Rhys's love.

Wiping at the tears forming in his eyes, he rose and picked up the bundle of sweet grass and sage Ravan had left for him along with a black raven feather. Bending, he lit the bundle at the fire. Sweet smoke rose in the air, and he straightened, inhaling deeply. His thoughts cleared, the fear and anxiety from the past few days dropping from his shoulders. He rounded the room to the right, using the feather to waft the smoke into the corners and along the walls.

Rhys watched him and Luka could feel his love and pride and mounting hunger. His cock grew heavy, but he ignored it, finishing the room. Once back at the fire, he walked purposefully up to Rhys, who raised his chin, brave and lovely. Luka kissed him gently, savoring his soft lips. Then he stepped back and used the feather to direct the sweet smoke along Rhys's body and under the feet Rhys raised.

His hands shook as he set the smoldering bundle in a waiting dish on the bedside table, knowing he'd soon have Rhys in his arms. He noted the small vial of oil beside the dish and his blood heated, stinging his face, though he should have expected Ravan's thoughtfulness. Going to the center of the room, he drew another cleansing breath and brought his closed hands up to his chest. He focused his power, intention clear in his mind, then opened his hands, palms out, and sent the energy outward to encompass the room in a barrier not even Aethan could break through.

"A ward, Luka? I thought Aethan couldn't find us."

Luka looked at him, and something in his gaze caused Rhys to flush a gorgeous red. "I want no interruptions," he murmured, and walked up to Rhys, stopping shy of touching him. "Undress me."

Rhys's blue eyes darkened, and a sensual, deliciously naughty smile spread on his face. "With pleasure, Witch," he replied, voice husky, but instead of touching his clothing, he cupped the back of Luka's head and tugged gently on his hair until Luka tilted his head back. Rhys's gaze raked his face, and it was all Luka could do to not ravage the sweet mouth so close to his own.

Rhys brushed their lips together, warm, soft, tempting. Luka held himself still, felt Rhys's breath of a laugh. Then Rhys moved back and lifted the tunic over Luka's head. Luka shivered as warm air caressed his skin, teased his nipples. A crease appeared between Rhys's brows. "I wish I could see you better."

Luka's heart jumped, and he sent a thought to the fire. The candles around the room lit one by one until light played across Rhys body, glittered on the drop of moisture gathered on the head of his erect cock. Luka groaned, licked his lips, and forced his knees not to buckle, though he ached to have Rhys in his mouth.

He started when Rhys ran tender fingers along the deep scars on his chest. They'd never spoken of them and now was not the time.

"My pants?" he managed, silently urging Rhys to hurry before he lost control. Rhys knew him well, and while Luka always attempted to drive him to a fever pitch of need, Rhys did the same to him, toying with the knot, brushing his straining cock. He finally had them undone and Luka let them slip down around his boots.

Rhys knelt and undid the laces, and Luka put a steadying hand on his shoulder as Rhys removed his boots and pants, pushing them out of the way. Rhys looked up, and Luka gasped at the passion on his face, making him bewitchingly lovely. Unbidden, Rhys licked Luka's cock, making it jump, and Luka lost his breath when soft lips closed around the tip. Rhys moved, gradually drawing him into his mouth, and a moan was pulled from him as his dick disappeared between his lips, the contrast of his dark flesh and Rhys's white skin shatteringly erotic.

He gently moved his hips, and the moist heat and pull of Rhys mouth sent waves of pleasure spiraling through him. But at this rate Rhys would have him coming and that wasn't what he wanted at all. Not yet.

Gently caressing Rhys's golden head, he eased back, and Rhys let his dick slide from between his glorious lips. Rhys looked up, eyes bright, face flushed, and licked his swollen lips, making Luka groan again. He wanted to push inside him, right now, and spill into his lover's body while Rhys came in his hand.

Instead, he pulled Rhys up into his arms, kissing him over and over, ravaging his lips of their sweetness. Rhys stepped tight against him, slipping a hand between their bodies to grip both their cocks, stroking them together. Luka permitted the unparalleled pleasure for a moment, then gripped Rhys's wrist, nudging him back.

"On the bed," he said thickly, breathing hard, hovering on the edge of orgasm. Rhys nodded, though he gave Luka one last squeeze before complying, mischief and lust flashing in his eyes. Rhys stretched out on the bed, hair spread on the pillows, firelight playing across his porcelain skin. Luka came undone; the love swelling in his chest came close to choking him. Never in his life had he thought he'd have such a beautiful lover, intelligent and kind and brave, and the faults that made him human made Luka love him all the more.

He climbed onto the bed, but instead of taking Rhys in his arms as he ached to, he crawled to the back of the bed and sat at Rhys's feet. Rhys rose up on his elbows and raised a questioning brow.

"It will be difficult to fuck me from way back there," he observed and flexed his ass, making his cock jut skyward. Luka laughed, joy once again running through him.

"Stop being naughty and lie still," he said sternly, though he could feel the wide grin on his face.

Rhys watched him a moment then dropped his head back in surrender. "Do whatever you'd like," he said, sounding a trifle breathless.

Luka looked up the sleek body, the white thighs and beautiful cock waiting for him, and swallowed hard. Gathering the energy not being used on the ward, he picked up Rhys's foot, kissed the bottom and ankle, and then did the same to the other. He moved with intention along his legs, each kiss on Rhys's body an invocation for protection.

The lush balls and cock in its nest of golden curls distracted him and he licked and sucked at them, taking Rhys into his mouth before letting him slip out. Thrilling at Rhys's whimper of need, he came close to swallowing him down again, but he wasn't finished. He continued on, his arms beginning to shake as they held him suspended over Rhys, his energy practically spent. But he couldn't help pausing at Rhys's pale nipples, licking and teasing them until Rhys squirmed beneath him. Chuckling, he moved to each side, kissed Rhys's fingertips, palms, arms, the slim column of his neck.

Luka took his time on Rhys's beloved face, kissing his eyes, the eyelids fluttering against his lips, his ears, the forehead tasting of sweat. He looked deep into Rhys stormy eyes to his fiery soul and blessed that as well, Rhys's sharp breath ringing in the room. Heart full, he softly kissed his plump lips and Rhys's breathing turned ragged.

"Please, Luka, I can't... I'm on fire! I need to come," he pleaded.

Luka gave a broken laugh and heard the strain in his own tones, "So do I."

He stretched to reach the small vial of oil on the bedside table, then moved back to straddle Rhys's thighs. Rhys's body shimmered with sweat as did Luka's, and he tasted salt when he licked his lips. Rhys stared at him, eyes wide, wild, and Luka's hands shook, making it hard to remove the cork from the vial. He accidentally spilled some on Rhys's thigh, but shrugged and dipped a finger in the fragrant oil. He nudged Rhys's thighs apart and at long, long last, rubbed his finger against his hole. A hard shudder ran Rhys's body with the contact, a deep moan escaping him, and delight surged through Luka. *So responsive!*

A finger wasn't enough. He scooted back, pushed Rhys's legs up and apart, and pressed his tongue against that warm opening. Rhys gasped, clutching at the quilts as Luka pushed harder, sliding his tongue in. Rhys's thighs fell open in surrender and Luka fucked him with his tongue, Rhys shaking beneath him. Rhys's balls pulled up and Luka moved swiftly, removing his tongue and replacing them with a slick finger. Another, and Rhys cried out as a fingertip slid over that spot inside that drove a man wild.

Luka swallowed Rhys's engorged cock to the root, pushed his fingers in deeper, and Rhys bucked, sobbing Luka's name as he came. Luka greedily swallowed, licking at him until Rhys whimpered, tossing his head helplessly on the pillows.

Rejoicing he'd made him come, Luka released his dick to look at him. Rhys lay boneless, eyes closed, an expression of bliss on his face, sated. Luka worked steadily in him, mesmerized by his dark fingers disappearing into his pale body. He ached to have his cock in there, the muscles hot and tight around him.

Leaning forward, he plucked Rhys's nipples with his free hand, pinching lightly then harder the way Rhys liked it. He licked at his dick again, thrilling when he at last hardened. *Now*. Removing his fingers from Rhys, he oiled his dick, stroking it a few times, pleasure rippling through him.

Rhys opened his eyes, wonder suffusing his face. "Luka, what did you do to me? I feel more alive than I ever..." He took in Luka palming his dick and his eyes widened. Moving on the bed, he hooked his arms under his knees and pulled his legs up and open.

"Now, Luka," he said hoarsely. Luka surged forward, sliding easily into him, groaning as heat and flesh engulfed him. Rhys pulled him into his arms and Luka buried his face in his shoulder, overcome with the beauty of the moment. They fit together perfectly, as if Rhys had been made for him. He laughed a little at the absurdity, but then he moved and pleasure exploded in him, driving all thought from his mind. They rocked together, Luka stifling his groans against Rhys's neck. Rhys thickened again, crushed between their bodies, and in a moment gave a guttural moan, and Luka felt the warmth of his come between them.

Luka thrust again and again into him, grown desperate, sweat dripping from his brow, and only by degrees became aware that Rhys stroked his hair, his back, his words becoming clearer, "All is well, Luka. We're here, together. You can let go."

His orgasm ripped through him and Luka cried out in joy and pain as he came, his love and the anguish of the long years without Rhys spilling from him. He trembled when it was over, overcome, and Rhys kissed away his tears, holding him close, secure.

"I love you," Rhys told him firmly.

Luka let out a quivering breath and rolled to his side, pulling Rhys snug against him. "I'm sorry," he said, finding it hard to meet Rhys's gaze. "I hadn't meant to lose control like that—"

Rhys's shout halted his words. "Luka, you were amazing! Never apologize for showing your love to me."

He stretched and laughed in delight. "What did you do? All my senses were heightened. I felt the lightest of your touches. Every inch of your girth—"

"Rhys!" Luka laughed, somewhat shocked by Rhys's candor, but his heart sang at the mirth and fondness shining in Rhys's blue eyes. He rose up on his elbow to look down at him and couldn't help brushing a thumb across the wide mouth that could give him so much pleasure. Rhys smiled in such a way his heart thumped with gladness.

Rhys gave a sleepy yawn, but then a frown grew between his brows, and Luka wondered where his thoughts had wandered. "I'm sorry I lost the stone you gave me," he said at last, the vexed tone directed at himself.

Luka laced their fingers together, bringing Rhys's hand up to kiss his knuckles. "It's not lost at all," he murmured, and laughed out of happiness at Rhys's wondering look.

Chapter Thirteen

"Where is it?" Rhys hurried to sit up, and Luka turned to reach over the side of the bed for his clothes, pulling the pink quartz from a pocket. He held it in his palm a moment, warming it. Pain flared inside him, his wounded soul not quite healed. But he would give all he was for Rhys, if need be. He reinforced his intention and handed the stone to Rhys, emotion practically choking him.

Rhys took it reverently, held it cupped in his hands so that the faint glow within shown on his face. "It's beautiful, Luka. I'm sorry I didn't know what it signified when you gave it to me. Will you tell me about it?"

Luka lifted his shoulder in a shrug, then sat up straighter at Rhys's frown. He was right, this wasn't a time for evasion. He drew a breath, weariness creeping over him, but he put it aside and gave Rhys a smile, his love spilling over.

"I love you," he began, voice throbbing as he spoke through the emotions holding him captive. "I have since the moment your gaze met mine in that dank cellar, brave and strong and beautiful." He tenderly ran a finger along Rhys's chin, needing to touch him, thrilling at the soft blush in his skin, knowing he'd caused it. "I had no expectations you could love me in return."

"You were my dream," Rhys told him, and went on despite Luka's snort. "In my lonely bed at night, weary and hurt, I'd long for someone to find me, stronger than Aethan's cruelty and darkness." He moved to put his lips against Luka's ear, his breath sending a pleasant shiver over him. "But I didn't know you'd be so handsome or have such gentle eyes." He dropped his gaze. "Nor have such a delicious body—"

"Rhys! You're teasing when I mean to be serious."

"My pardon." Rhys turned his head, kissing him. "Please, go on."

Luka couldn't resist another kiss, Rhys's full, sweet lips a definite distraction.

"But you did love me," Luka continued. "You woke me up, brought me to life. Reminded me what happiness is. The stone is a symbol of my love, and a talisman."

Rhys picked up the pink gem, holding it to the light of a nearby candle. "Aethan said you imbued it with a piece of your soul. Is this possible? Never mind." He gave Luka an arch look. "I believe there is nothing beyond your skill."

Luka enfolded Rhys's hand holding the stone in his own. "A small part of my life's energy is in there, though you have all of my heart."

"But why? Luka, who am I for you to do this for, but the son of your enemy?"

"No, my love. You have never been that to me." Luka again kissed Rhys's fingers twined with his own, and his heart thumped. He could never see the erotic contrast of their light and dark skin and not be affected.

"It's true I find great pleasure in your body," he continued, and flushed hotly when Rhys's eyes kindled, and hurried on, "But more than that, I see your soul. Pure and bright and true. You steal my breath and leave me trembling with your fierce courage, untarnished by the horrors you've suffered. Tempered and unfaltering."

Rhys stared at him, then moved to grab the back of his head and pull him into a kiss, wild and passionate, making his blood surge and rush. Tears stung his eyes, overcome with love for Rhys in his arms, his heart singing, grateful and humble, sending broken thoughts of gratitude to the universe who gave him such a gift.

"Hush, dearest," Rhys murmured, stroking his hair, and Luka became aware he was sobbing once more and fought for control. Rhys must think him a fool.

"I'm well," he muttered, pushing up, but turned his gaze away from Rhys's searching eyes. "I'm more tired than I realized."

Rhys pulled him back down, rolled to face him. "Of course, you are. You've expended more energy than anyone should." He wiped Luka's tears with a tender thumb, kissed his eyes and lips. "Sleep now, my sweet witch. Between you and Widow Ravan, we're as safe as we can be."

A wave of exhaustion washed over him, and for a brief moment, Luka wondered if Rhys had bespelled him, but then a welcomed sleep claimed the last of his thoughts. He dreamed sporadically, but they were pleasant wanderings, forgettable, and each time he woke Rhys was there, holding him, the room snug and warm and safe.

Morning sunlight met him when he woke the last time, more refreshed than he should be, and he smiled, feeling the echo of Rhys's joy leave him with the last tendrils of sleep. The pillow beside him was empty, but he took a moment to snuggle in the quilts, Rhys's scent lingering in the bedclothes. Images from the night before played in his mind and he felt his cock waken. He laughed, heart happy, then bit his lips. Ravan's patience would give out if he asked for the morning as well.

With a sigh, he climbed reluctantly from the bed and drew on his clothes. He could willingly spend the rest of his life in that room with Rhys, but there was much to be done before they could find such peace again. Allowing his eyes to close, he thanked the earth and sky for the gift of last night and the coming day, then firmed his lips, picked up his boots, and strode purposefully from the room.

He stopped in the doorway, his lips curling into a spontaneous smile. He'd expected to find the others grim and brooding at the table. Instead, Rhys stirred a pot over the fire, the scent of warm oats and herbs filling the air, while Ravan stood at the table, laughing at something he said while she kneaded dough for bread. They both glanced at him as he entered the room and the love and concern in their eyes filled his heart to bursting. Composing his features, he walked over to them, his face warming with the heated look in Rhys's eyes.

"You finally woke up," Ravan teased, deftly shaping the dough into a round loaf. "There's tea in the kettle, if you'd like."

"Permit me," Rhys offered, pulling a mug off the shelf over the fireplace and pouring him a cup. Their fingers touched, and Rhys smiled into his eyes and leaned forward to give him a tender kiss. Desire sparked along Luka's nerves and he forced down a groan. Rhys wasn't as circumspect, his moan intensely erotic against his lips. If Ravan wasn't present...

"But I *am* here," she said drily, and they broke apart, Luka smiling into Rhys's flushed face. Ravan sighed, her tone regretful when she continued, "I'm happy you found each other again, truly. But this is not a honeymoon. We have serious matters to see to."

Rhys gasped, her words clearly taking him by surprise. Warmth spread through Luka. He'd never suggested Rhys stay with him always. That would be more joy than he deserved. But Rhys's unexpectedly shy glance, the way he pressed his teeth against his lips to hide a grin, suggested...

Luka's heart pounded, and he cupped Rhys's face with his free hand. "When this is all over," he murmured, and kissed him, a promise. An oath. Rhys drew a shaky breath when Luka released him, his eyes shining, then he shook himself, sending an apologetic glance to Ravan.

"The porridge is ready," he said to the room in general, sounding breathless, and turned to stir the pot once again. "Would you care for some? Ravan?" he asked when Luka nodded.

Luka set his tea on the table then returned, the bowl warming his hands when Rhys passed it to him. Rhys touched his arm when he would have carried it to his place, and with a sly glance at Ravan busy putting the bread dough in an oiled pan, he added a pinch of cinnamon to Luka's porridge from one of the clay pots over the stove. Luka exchanged a grin with him. Ravan was jealous of her spices. He took the spoon Rhys handed him, snuck one more kiss, then crossed the cozy room to take his chair.

Rhys joined him with two more bowls. He helped Ravan clean the flour from the tabletop while Ravan cleared her ingredients and set the bread in the hearth to bake. Luka was discomfited when they took chairs opposite him when they finished, blue and piercing green eyes settling on him. He had trouble swallowing the porridge now tasteless in his mouth.

Raven pushed her graying braid over her shoulder and picked up her spoon, stirring her bowl while Rhys ate with appetite. She asked after a moment, "Rhys, you have questions for us?"

Rhys stilled, then carefully put down his spoon, sitting back in his chair to take in both of them. His gaze turned troubled and Luka told him encouragingly, "Go on," though his heart thumped.

Rhys looked between them and laughed self-consciously. "I don't know what to ask first."

Ravan tapped the side of her bowl, the clay resonating a pure tone that vibrated through Luka, making his shiver. "You wish to know if Luka is my father."

Rhys nodded, wide eyed.

"He is."

Rhys continued to stare at her, his look turning puzzled. Luka held his breath. His story would be told soon, and the old grief, never far from the surface, was nothing compared to his fear Rhys would walk away from him.

"I see no resemblance," Rhys began.

Luka answered forcefully, "She looks like her mother."

"Oh."

Rhys continued to study Ravan and Luka could see the questions hovering on his lips. He looked at his daughter as well. Ravan's complexion was slightly darker than Rhys's, as if she spent more time in the sun, and her hair was once as golden as Rhys's own. She'd been a fairy child, growing wild in the woods, and Luka's greatest joy.

Ravan smiled at him. "Then she must have been beautiful as well as brilliant," she stated, and Luka's heart lightened at her teasing.

"She was that," he answered fervently, and took the hand Ravan held out to him across the table.

Rhys drew an unsteady breath and looked right at him, uncertainty and the fear of loss in his eyes, and Luka's heart squeezed when Rhys gathered his courage to ask, "Where is she?"

The old grief rose up, tightening Luka's chest, and he was unable to answer. To his horror, he watched Rhys's eyes darken with pain, though he pressed his lips together, making it clear he would wait for Luka's reply. Luka had never loved him more.

"She left us," Ravan said for him, and went on despite Luka's faint protest. "She said her name was Loralyn. She'd wandered out of the forest one night, a beautiful, wild thing, a broken dove who collapsed on Luka's doorstep. He took her in, tended her. She had a malaise that lingered for many days. They loved. I am the result of that. But the day of my birth, while Luka gathered wood to keep the house warm for us, she slipped away, perhaps back into the forest. Luka searched, but there has been no sign of her since."

Luka stared at his and Ravan's clasped hands, her brittle tone tearing at his heart. He felt Rhys's gaze but couldn't meet his eyes. Not yet. Not until it had all been said.

"There's more," Rhys guessed in the charged silence.

Pressure built in Luka's ears as if the very air awaited his reply, but the words he needed wouldn't come. The snap of the fire shattered his nerves.

"There is," Ravan answered when it was clear Luka couldn't. But he softly pressed her hand, swallowed the lump in his throat, and tentatively raised his eyes, to be seized by Rhys's burning gaze.

"She was beautiful," he explained quietly, desperate not to wound him. "A wild, magical thing. A creature of the woods. She captivated me, tender and sweet, and took away my loneliness. When she left... I couldn't..."

Luka broke off, dropping his gaze to the tabletop. What he'd done next had been terrible, unforgivable, and he couldn't bear to see aversion creep over Rhys's face.

"Tell me," Rhys urged, and his compassion broke Luka's heart.

Ravan took up the story. "The villagers say that Luka searched the forest every day for three weeks. Then, on the night of the full moon, he entered the grove of oaks at the heart of town. They say they heard thunder, saw flashes of light, though the sky was clear. Then the earth roared and shook, an earthquake that leveled most of the buildings. Many were injured, though none fatally. They saw when Luka came out of the trees that his face glowed. He spoke to no one, and in the morning he and the child were gone."

Luka gave a painful laugh, his life's tragedy measured out in a few brusque words. If he could go back... No. He let go of Ravan's hand and clutched his own together in his lap, then raised his eyes once more to Rhys. Rhys's face was pale, lips firm, eyes flashing fire.

Rhys moistened his lips, his expression gentling. "What did you do, my sweet witch?"

Luka's heart lurched. Rhys called him that when he loved him the most. "I was beside myself with worry," he said, trying not to plead, desperate for his understanding. "Keep in mind, mine was a lonely life, few friends. Most people were afraid of the dark-hued witch who did magic they didn't understand. But Oak Grove was where my wandering feet led me, and the oak trees still whispered in my ear.

"Loralyn was a gift, filling my home with life and laughter and moments of joy. I was beside myself when she left. I scoured the forest for days on end, not eating. Not sleeping. I left my infant daughter in the care of my neighbors. There was no sign of her. In desperation, I went to the grove, and I..." Luka stopped, afraid to say the next words.

"What, dear heart. Tell us," Rhys urged.

"Yes, Papa. You never have said what you did to cause the earthquake," Ravan prompted. "Or was that coincidence?"

Luka sighed, shame burning through him. "I made a wish," he confessed, and cringed at the utter silence that met his words.

Chapter Fourteen

Rhys looked at Luka's bowed head and fought against the shock caused by his confession. He needed to think clearly. Luka would bear the misery of the world on his shoulders if they let him, and Rhys refused to allow that to happen.

"Was it such a terrible wish?" he asked, keeping any hint of accusation from his tone.

Luka seemed to hunch further into himself. "I couldn't find her, and I...couldn't be alone again. I went to the grove and abased myself and asked for... hope."

Rhys sucked in a breath, thoughts racing.

Luka raised a haggard face. "The earth gathered all the hope it had and put it in my keeping. Me, who had made so selfish a wish."

"The Well of Hope."

Luka finally met his gaze. "Yes."

Rhys wouldn't let him look away, searching the stormy brown eyes across from him. Luka's near despair broke his heart.

"This is why Aethan pursues you so relentlessly," Ravan observed, breaking the tension between them. Rhys sent her a distracted look, not wanting to take his eyes off Luka. "The sorcerer is powerful, yes, but he more often than not manipulates others to carry out his machinations. I understand now why he's come himself. He wouldn't want to entrust such power to anyone else."

Luka put his face in his hands. "And I have endangered both you and Rhys, the two I love most in all the world." He drew a breath then sat up, squaring his shoulders. He dropped his hands, a look of determination settling on his face. "So be it. It's past time I stop running from the fate I set in motion so long ago. Ravan, will you aide me?"

"A moment." Rhys put up a finger when Ravan pushed back her chair with a hard scrape over the wooden floor in preparation of rising. "You said I may ask questions. I have one more." He looked squarely at Luka. "Where does my mother come into this story?"

A gentle expression touched Luka's face, making Rhys's chest tighten with a mixture of emotion: pain and love and a sharp fear of what he might learn. Ravan glanced between them and rose to her feet.

"I know this part of the tale," she said, her tone compassionate. "Papa, I will go into town and make preparations." She squeezed Rhys's shoulder as she passed him, and Rhys wasn't sure whether to be comforted by the gesture or terrified. He watched as she went to the fire and removed the loaf of bread, then she crossed the room and drew on a cloak. The door sounded loud when she stepped outside and closed it behind her in a rush of cool air, leaving them in silence. Warmth and the scent of freshly baked bread surrounded them as they looked long at each other, then an unexpected smile spread on Luka's lips.

"You seem unsure, my heart," Luka murmured, his tone infinitely tender.

"Did you love her?" Rhys asked, voicing the question he most feared the answer to.

"I adored her," Luka answered promptly and reached across the table to take Rhys's hands and hold them tightly. "After the earthquake, I tried to help, but the people of Oak Knoll hated and feared me. I feared for my life and Ravan's, and fled with her into the forest, half out of my mind with grief and loss. Looking back, I realized Loralyn had bewitched me. The few months I had with her seemed more of a dream than anything real.

"But at the time, I was bereft, rootless, lost. It was mere chance that Lady Kaelyn stumbled upon us one day while out riding. She took us to her home and fed us and gave me a bed. I think that was the first night I'd slept in months."

"And Mother?"

"I had barely stepped inside the manor when Aethan's character was revealed to me. I am aware of the others in the world who use magic, but Aethan had always been on the edge of my thoughts, his true power and darkness hidden until then. Mama had warned me long ago of those who corrupt power for their own selfish use, naming them sorcerers and necromancers. I have met several of them in the past, and have worked to keep them in check, to protect the innocent. I have made enemies…

"Aethan is the culmination of their dark knowledge, twisting and expanding what he has learned until none rival him. A deadly sorcerer. I would have left his home immediately, afraid for my daughter's wellbeing, but Alliya took Ravan into her heart, hiding her away from Aethan, keeping her safe. Aethan never realized she was within his grasp.

"I stayed with them only a few months, until my health returned, and then stole away in the night with Ravan to Sweetbrier and my cottage on the hillside. Whatever Aethan might have told you, I had left the manor long before he turned his dark appetites toward Alliya. Believe me, if I had known her plight, or the depths of Aethan's depravity, I would have returned to her aide, but she never called to me."

"And you never checked on us later," Rhys said quietly, needing to hear the reason for that as well.

"I couldn't! Aethan had found out about the Well. I don't know how. I had to keep my whereabouts hidden from his sight, and his spies are everywhere. If I had gone to Alliya after she'd fled to the village, he would have found me, and her through me. I concealed your cottage and sent Ravan in my stead, to do what she could. But Aethan is jealous of power and watches her as well, though he does not know of our relationship, and she couldn't go as often as she would have liked."

Luka rose and rounded the table, slid to his knees beside Rhys. "I am sorry for the poverty you and Alliya suffered. I sent what I could, through Ravan, but I haven't much myself... If I could, I'd undo the past. But all I can do is move forward. Can you forgive me, Rhys? Will you come with me?"

Rhys looked into the beautiful eyes gazing up at him, saw his love and regret and the deep, terrible loneliness so much a part of him. His heart clenched, and it took a moment for him to speak, a bleakness touching Luka's expression as he waited that made him panic.

He rose to his feet, pulling Luka up with him as well. "I will go with you, my love, wherever you lead." A trifle taller, Rhys could look down into his face, the warmth of Luka's muscular body wrapping around him. Luka moved to kiss him, but Rhys raised a hand.

"One more question," he said, biting his lip at the uncertainty that flashed in Luka's eyes. "If Ravan was an infant when you met my mother, then her age would be around my own. So why does she seem a much older woman? Older than yourself?"

Luka shrugged. "Ravan's talent to change her appearance comes from her mother. Why she chooses this persona, I have never asked. She married young, deeply in love with her woodsman husband. Perhaps when he died, she lost all interest in romance."

"And you, Luka, who appear so much younger?" Rhys asked softly and watched a blush creep into Luka's face at his scrutiny. Handsome and compelling, he surely couldn't be more than thirty years?

"Do you truly want to know?" Luka asked in a whisper.

Rhys gently cupped his chin in preparation of kissing him. "I'm curious by nature, dearest, but if you'd rather not tell me..."

Luka moistened his lips, eyes wide, vulnerable. "I was a young man when the trees in the grove were but acorns." A forlorn smile twitched his lips. "But I do not have Ravan's ability to change my guise. This is my true appearance, for good or ill."

Rhys caught his breath and his heart surged at a sudden thought. "And through all your long years and all the people you've met, you've chosen me," he said in awe, and ran a thumb over Luka's trembling mouth.

"Always," Luka answered fiercely and moved, pressing their lips together, and Rhys gloried in the passion behind it. That such a powerful witch could want him... He nudged Luka toward the bedroom they'd shared last night, but Luka halted, laughing a little, eyes flashing with emotion.

"I want nothing more than to go in there with you, my heart, but there's no more time. I can't keep Aethan out forever, and there's one more task to perform before we can leave."

"What is it?"

Luka didn't reply immediately, instead crossing the room to the door leading to Ravan's bedroom. "Come with me," he said, motioning Rhys to follow. Inside, Rhys found a room very much like the one he'd shared with Luka, though vibrant color splashed across quilt and pillows and throw rugs. Crystal glittered on the dressing table in the warm glow of the hearth, the room fragrant from lavender and eucalyptus hanging in the rafters.

Heavy clothes and two thick, brightly colored cloaks were laid out on the bed for them. Luka was already dressing, pulling the warmer garments over the ones he already wore. Rhys did the same, gathering up the cloaks when they exited.

"Will you fill the waterskins?" Luka motioned toward the pail of water at the sink. Rhys filled the two flasks hanging on a peg by the stove while Luka took a sack to the cellar, emerging with apples and cheese and last night's stew in a crock. He wrapped the freshly baked bread in cloth and stowed that in the bag as well.

Rhys hesitated when they met at the outside door, looking back at the cozy rooms. "Will we say good-bye to Ravan?"

"She's meeting us at the grove. Come, Rhys, we must hurry."

Rhys followed him, questions once again swimming in his head. But Luka's sense of urgency kept him quiet as they left the cottage, Luka firmly shutting the door, and hurried up the muddy road. The sun shone brightly, though the air was crisp, and Rhys put his face up to its light, his fearful mood easing.

The streets were strangely quiet, but as they neared the center of town, shop keepers left their doorways to watch them pass, their expressions less than friendly. Rhys remembered the earthquake and stepped closer to Luka. Luka carried no weapons, but Rhys dropped a hand to his belt and the long knife he'd borrowed from Ravan's kitchen.

The wide road inclined steeply to the oak trees, the town falling behind them as they climbed. Rhys sweated under the heavy clothing and it was a relief to reach the top. Ravan waited under the ancient oaks in a patch of sunlight and Rhys's lips twitched with a smile he daren't show her. She looked every inch the witch she was in the rich, red cloak, jewel at her throat, the cold, proud way she carried herself. No wonder the villagers were intimidated into silence below.

"Everything is ready, Papa," she said solemnly when they came up to her. Luka set the sack he carried down beside her. Rhys noticed two horses waiting under the wide limbs of the trees, the stallion they'd ridden yesterday and another with a pure white coat. His attention swiveled back to Luka when he touched his arm.

"Stay here with Ravan, please," Luka requested. "This shouldn't take long."

"I can go with you," Ravan put in, her tone suggesting they'd argued this out before.

Luka gently shook his head. "No, my dear. It wouldn't be safe for you. And if I—" He broke off and lifted Rhys's hand to his lips. "Stay safe, my love," he murmured.

"Luka!" Rhys tried to hold on to him, heart inexplicably thumping as fear coursed through him. *What was happening?* But Luka shook his head and turned on his heel, disappearing under the thick, low limbs before Rhys could stop him. All too soon the gloom under the trees swallowed him up.

Chapter Fifteen

It took all of Luka's courage to walk under the trees and leave Rhys behind. Ravan was safe. Aethan was the stronger, but it would be a bitter battle, one Aethan had no reason to engage. But Rhys had been in his hands twice now. Luka knew deep in his heart that the third time would leave Rhys broken, a shadow of himself. Aethan would have no mercy for the man who held Luka's heart.

But there was nothing he could do at the moment but follow the lines of energy to the center of the grove and what waited for him there. Ravan had earlier called up the spirits for him, but she didn't have the power to speak to them. Only he could do that, a gift from his mother. He knew little of his father, an entity more spirit than man, his mother claimed, before she too walked into the forest, leaving him alone in the world.

Luka drew in a lungful of the cold air growing thick under the heavy branches of the old trees. The earth was covered in the mulch of hundreds of seasons, sunlight struggling to reach through the twined limbs overhead. The rich odor filled his senses, and he touched the trunks as he passed them, feeling the rough bark under his fingertips and the life surging from the earth, spreading through the thick, tangled grove.

His heart beat madly as he approached the small clearing at its center. The earth was bare of leaves there, revealing a thick layer of moss sparkling with dew in the sunlight. A withered trunk, as tall as himself, stood at its center, twisted and burned by lightning. Luka couldn't guess its age.

He drew a breath and stepped from beneath the oaks into the circle. Instantly, silence descended, approaching painful. Gone was the whispering of leaves, the faint rustle of insects. The sunlight remained, but there was no warmth to it. The air was no longer cold. All that remained was the earth firm under his feet and a faint glow emanating from the tree standing once again whole and alive before him.

Luka dropped without hesitation to his knees, fear an icy blade in his chest. He'd been there once before, long ago, and destroyed a town in his hubris. The utter quiet pressed on him and he laid himself out on the moss, arms extended in supplication. The tree glowed from within, growing brighter, a door opening...

No! He shouldn't be there. No man should. Last time, something had reached from that horrible threshold and tore at his chest, trying for his heart. The price of his foolish wish. Terror raced circles in his mind, and he opened his mouth in a soundless scream as the doorway widened, madness gibbering on the edge of reason...

"Hush, sweet boy. I'm here."

The chaos in Luka's mind slowed. He became aware of gentle hands brushing his hair off his face wet with his tears. Familiar arms held him close.

"Mama?" His voice was a mere whisper, or maybe a thought in his head. There was no response, and he trembled as he looked up into the face bent over him. He lost his breath, but then struggled up with a cry of joy and disbelief, clinging to her like a child. Her black hair fell in a silken curtain around them. There were tears on her beloved face, her complexion as dark as his own. Fondness and peace filled her rich brown eyes, along with the unconditional love she'd always given him.

"Are you real?" he asked, choked with tears, then a terrible thought came to him and he straightened, holding desperately to her hands. "If your spirit is here, then you must have left me," he stated, grief tightening his chest.

A tender smile touched her lips. "My darling boy, I left my earthly vessel long ago, but you know this, in your heart." She placed her hand on his chest.

Luka swallowed a broken sob and let his mother pull him back into her comforting arms. He called to mind the terrible spring day she climbed from her sick bed. He'd been a young boy, afraid of being alone. But she had to leave, she'd said, and walked into the forest without looking back. He'd made up stories in his head afterward, during the long, solitary evenings by the fire, that she had gone away to be healed, and joined his father, and one day they would come home...

She kissed the top of his head now, kissed his face. "I'm so sorry, sweet Luka. I tried to prepare you."

"I know. I didn't want to believe you." Luka drew a steadying breath, clung to her for another, wonderful moment, but then sat up. He laughed a bit when she brushed his tears away with her fingertips as she'd done when he was a child.

"Why are you here?" he asked, holding her hands, needing to touch her.

"You have come to return the Well of Hope," she answered. "I have been sent with the reply, an emissary, if you will, as a gift for your true, loyal soul." The note of pride in her voice broke his heart.

"And the answer?" He looked at their clasped hands, afraid to hear her words.

"You know this as well. It is not yet time. Hope is still needed until you have faced what is to come."

"Mother... What if I am not strong enough?" he whispered, voicing his greatest fear.

She pressed a kiss to his forehead, and he panicked. He couldn't say good-bye and lose her...

"Perhaps you are not, my sweet, gentle boy," she conceded, but then her smile turned brilliant. "But you are not alone, Luka. Never alone," she reminded him, her love spreading around him like a heated blanket, comforting, secure.

"Luka?"

The voice came from the edge of the grove, and Luka felt the moment his mother left him, tearing a hole in his heart. But he pushed to his feet. The glow in the ancient oak faded, a door closing, and he drew a quivering breath. Rhys waited for him under the trees. He crossed the short distance. Rhys spoke to him, but he couldn't hear, the silence of the clearing muting his words. But his gestures, body language, the urgent plea in his face, all spoke of love and concern.

Sudden anger burned through Luka. He'd lost so many of those he cared for. His dear parents. Loralyn. So many lonely years waiting for...something. Waiting for Rhys. He'd be damned if he let Aethan destroy the happiness within his reach.

He didn't make the vow lightly, knowing what he risked, the chance of being reunited with his parents and those he loved in the life beyond this one. But he was done being afraid. He couldn't go back to the life he'd led up till now, one of hiding, obscurity. He'd deal with Aethan.

A coldness settled in his heart, grim determination. There were those who'd aided Aethan, spied for him, betrayed Rhys to him. Luka would hunt them as well. Rhys would be safe, whatever the cost.

"Are you ready, Aethan?" He sent the thought out into the world, then stepped out of the mossy circle straight into Rhys's waiting arms. Rhys tried to speak but Luka smothered his words in fervent, glorious kisses, needing his taste, touch, the scent of him. Rhys laughed a little at his vehemence, eyes shining, when Luka finally released him.

"Did you find what you needed?" Rhys asked him softly, touching Luka's face. Then he shook himself, concern replacing the fondness in his expression. "Forgive me for interrupting. Ravan sent me. She says Aethan is near…"

Luka grabbed his hand before he could finish speaking and set off at a fast pace through the trees. He'd lingered too long, putting them all in danger. Rhys asked no more questions, gathering their few supplies while Luka spoke with Ravan.

"Thank you for taking us in," he said, holding her in a tight embrace, his heart full. "It meant everything to me."

Ravan brushed impatiently at her wet eyes. "I love you, Papa. I would see you happy." Her gaze slid to Rhys waiting with the horses and turned back to him. "Were you successful?"

"No. It seems I must carry the Well until the end."

Ravan paled. "What does that mean?"

Luka took her hands. "I spoke with your grandmother," he said, his elation and grief heavy in his voice. "She died long ago, when I'd hoped…" His voice cracked.

"You hoped to see her again," Ravan supplied gently, pressing his hands in sypathy.

"Yes. I didn't realize it, but I'd hope she'd walk out of the forest one day. Come back to me. But it was a dream…" He stopped as his terrible sadness threatened to crush him with its weight, but he shoved it away, drew a deep breath. "But I have you and Rhys now. When this is all over, Aethan defeated, there will be no more hiding. We can live as a family, as we should."

"I would like that above all things," Ravan assured him, tears on her face.

Luka held her close, his beautiful, strong daughter, then put her from him. "You'll take care?"

"Of course. Aethan has no quarrel with me. I'll meet you at the appointed time."

Luka nodded, emotion once again tightening his throat. But he wouldn't think of defeat. He joined Rhys at the horses. Rhys had already mounted, the bag of supplies on his back. Luka picked up the sack Ravan had readied for him and paused at the stallion's head, rubbing a hand along his proud neck. "Thank you for bearing me," he murmured, then clutched a handful of the black main and swung onto his back. There was no saddle or bridle, Ravan's mounts didn't need them.

He glanced over at Rhys and his blood surged, heat sweeping through him. Rhys wore the cloak Ravan had given him, royal blue, matching his eyes. The sun landed on him, glinted in his golden hair, making him seem some faerie prince. Strikingly beautiful.

Rhys handed Luka his own robe, but Luka shook his head at his questioning look, not realizing he'd been staring until Rhys blushed and glanced away, though a pleased smile quirked his lips. Luka swung his heavy cloak around his shoulders, a deep burgundy, and snorted at the fine material. If Ravan wanted to draw attention to them, she'd succeed, though he felt a fool in the ostentatious garment.

"Do not worry. I have packed less colorful cloaks for you if needed, Papa. Be safe," Ravan urged them, and Luka nudged his horse over to her, placing a hand on her head.

"I love you," he told her, then straightened and requested his horse to gallop, refusing to think it might be the last time he'd see her. He wanted to send her home, keep her safe. But Ravan would simply laugh at him and do as she pleased. He grinned at the thought, fiercely proud of her. Rhys followed him, coming up beside him when the road opened out. They didn't speak until Oak Knoll was far behind, the canopy of the oak trees disappearing from the horizon.

"May I know where we're going?" Rhys asked after some time, glancing at him. Luka could see more questions hovering on his lips, Rhys refusing to give them voice, trusting him.

"Toward Sweetbrier. I need to speak with the farmer you worked for," he replied, shivering at the unaccustomed coldness inside him. Someone had tipped Aethan off to where Rhys had been living. He had to discover who, if he wanted a life with Rhys after...

"And then?" Rhys nudged their horses closer. "What is your plan, Luka?"

"We'll go to Ash Swale," he replied carefully, studying Rhys's reaction. Rhys drew a sharp breath, eyes widening with dread. Good. His fear might be enough to save him. Then Rhys firmed his lips, nodded, and pulled his cloak tighter about his shoulders. Luka followed suit, settling in for the long hours ahead.

Chapter Sixteen

Rhys chewed his lips, uncertain. They'd traveled many leagues that day, and as evening approached, Luka searched for a place in the woods they could fortify for the night. There was something wrong with him. Rhys had sensed a change in him when he'd come out of that circle in the oak grove, growing stronger as the day progressed. A distance, as if Luka cut off a part of himself.

He'd have none of that. Luka was often led by his fierce, passionate heart, willing to put himself in danger for those he loved. He had something planned, something Rhys wouldn't condone, and strove to hide it. Rhys would confront him with it that night before Luka did something they'd both regret.

Luka drew the dark stallion to a halt and studied the boulders in the small clearing they'd entered. Pride and love stirred in Rhys as he watched him. He could feel the power in him, the strength in his taut body. Noble and beautiful in the long cloak Ravan had lent him. He marveled again that such a man could love him, the bastard and plaything of his enemy.

"Luka?" he whispered, throat tight.

At first, Luka seemed not to hear him, but then turned, dark eyes glittering in the fading light. "What is it, dear heart?"

Rhys rode up next to him, leaned and clasped the back of his neck, pulling him into a kiss. Somehow Luka always tasted sweet, a heady wine to his senses.

"I love you," he said firmly. "We'll make camp and eat. Afterwards, we'll discuss what's weighing on your mind."

Luka blinked, and his lips twitched in a reluctant smile. "You seem sure of yourself."

"I know you, my witch. You'd bear the world on your shoulders. I won't allow it."

Rhys held his breath. There'd been a flash of temper in Luka's handsome eyes. Had he pushed too far? But then Luka blushed and glanced away, seeming shy.

"As you wish," Luka yielded. He took another look around the glen. "We'll stay here tonight."

Rhys slid from the mare's back, taking the time to rub her down with the cloth Luka handed him. Tall trees surrounded the glen, the scent of pine and rich soil and fern thick in the cold air caressing his face. Luka did the same with his mount, then left Rhys to lead them to the small spring in a corner while he went over to the boulders.

Rhys scratched the mare behind the ears while she drank, his boots sinking into the thick moss, then did the same to the stallion, who snorted and bobbed its head, shaking him off.

"Thank you for carrying us today," he murmured to them. "After I've fed our sweet witch, I'll warm the grain Ravan has packed for you."

He left them, then came to an abrupt halt halfway across the glen, a thrill shooting through him. Luka stood at the tall boulders, hands held in front of him, palms out, and Rhys closed his eyes, letting the wave of power wash over him. He knew Luka felt uncomfortable in the lush robe Ravan had provided him, but it suited him, the rich burgundy complimenting his dark complexion.

He peered through his lashes, moistening his lips. Luka stole his breath, powerful and beautiful. He would have gone to his knees for him then, taken his thick cock in his mouth. But Luka needed to be wooed, though he didn't realize it, a service Rhys was more than willing to perform.

"Are we safe?" he asked, coming up to him.

Luka cocked his head as if listening. "I think so. Ravan has put them off our trail, though it is temporary. We'll need to be on our way by dawn."

Rhys nodded, and couldn't help but touch his hand as he passed him, having spotted dried limbs on the edge of the glen, perfect for starting a fire. Luka gave him that shy smile again, and Rhys stopped to kiss him, grateful he had the right to do so.

Dinner consisted of leftover stew and Ravan's bread. Luka had paused, head bowed, to give his thanks, and Rhys's chest expanded with the love he felt for this good man. After eating, Luka rinsed the few dishes in the spring while Rhys built up the fire and fed the horses. It had been a cold day, and he feared the temperature might drop below freezing during the night. He thought about staking the horses close by, then concluded any of Ravan's creatures would have enough sense to stay near the fire's warmth.

He returned to the fire and watched Luka walk to the edge of the glen, no doubt checking his warding. Seeming satisfied, Luka started back and Rhys hungrily watched his lithe, strong figure as he approached. Last night had been amazing. He'd always enjoyed his time with Luka, his sure touch, gorgeous cock, but their lovemaking had been overshadowed by Aethan's cruel use of him. But it seemed last night, as Luka caressed him, he'd gathered all the hurt and humiliation and horror of Aethan's attentions, and washed Rhys free of them with his lips and tongue and murmured blessings. He could meet Luka now with a whole heart, unhindered by nightmares.

Luka appeared thoughtful as he came up to the fire, then caught Rhys's stare. Rhys thrilled at the dark blush that flooded his face. But even as their eyes met, Luka's gaze slid away. Rhys's heart pounded. Time to find out what was going on with his secretive witch. He allowed Luka to crouch across the fire, stir the embers before adding more wood against the growing darkness, but didn't remove his focus on him.

Luka squirmed and at last looked up. "You have questions?"

"Yes. You're concealing something from me. What is it?"

Displeasure once again flashed in Luka's dark eyes. He wasn't used to being challenged. But Rhys wouldn't let it lie. This was too important. Gathering his courage—Luka could be formidable when angry—Rhys pressed. "What is bothering you, my love?"

Luka shrugged, but then his lips twitched as if he realized it was a childish gesture. "If I appear preoccupied, it's because I'm worried about keeping you safe and keeping the Well out of Aethan's hands."

"There's more to it than that," Rhys countered, and held his breath.

Luka raised a brow, giving him an aloof look, a barrier going up between them. "I don't know what you mean."

Rhys leaned toward him, the heat of the flames uncomfortable on his skin. "I think you do."

Luka growled in his throat and stood. "Believe what you want. I'm going to bed."

He marched past Rhys, who scrambled to his feet, boot slipping on the moss covering the glen. They'd build the fire close to the boulders, creating a warm pocket in which to sleep. Luka reached the tall rocks as Rhys came up to him, and he turned, thrusting out his arm. His hand landed flat against Rhys's chest, keeping distance between them.

Rhys grunted at the impact, widening his eyes with surprise. He knew Luka was strong, muscles lean and toned. He'd licked them often enough. But there had been a strength in that push he hadn't expected. Nothing magical. But Rhys was young and strong, sure he was an easy match for Luka. But now... If they were to grapple, he was no longer certain he'd come out on top. Somehow, that thought thrilled him to the core. He wanted one day to be at Luka's mercy, held down by that powerful body, unable to free himself...

The firelight reflecting off the rocks highlighted their features. Luka must have read his expression, sucked in a breath, though he only said, "Let me be, Rhys."

Rhys shivered at the warning in his voice. "No."

He took a step closer, forcing Luka to drop his hand or push him away. Thankfully, Luka lowered his arm, allowing Rhys into his space, though he wouldn't meet Rhys's searching gaze. Rhys cupped his chin and Luka clenched his jaw.

"What is going on, Luka?" he asked softly, studying his averted face, willing Luka to look at him. "There's a...a coldness in you I've never sensed before. It's been growing since you returned from the oak grove. I'm worried for you."

Luka's exhale came out on a sigh. "You needn't be concerned. I know what I'm doing."

Rhys forced his chin up. "No, I don't believe you do."

Fire flashed in Luka's rich brown eyes, temper flaring. Rhys moved closer, forcing him against the stone wall. He still held Luka's chin and placed his free hand on the rock beside his head, trapping him with his body.

"Tell me," he demanded, staring into Luka's glittering eyes.

Luka drew himself up, body trembling with fury against Rhys. "No."

Rhys shivered. This was it. He was no match for Luka, either physically or in the use of magic. Perhaps love could win out over both. That Luka could brush him aside like a gnat and simply leave, there was no question. Would he hurt him? No, though he could so easily shred his heart.

The fire crackled behind them, cold air pressing on his back. One of the horses shifted. A small animal rustled in the nearby bushes. Firelight played on Luka's face, carved mahogany, and his dark eyes glowed, proud and angry, devastating.

"Tell me," Rhys urged roughly.

Luka raised his chin, eyes narrowing to smoldering slits. Power surged in him, flowing into Rhys where their bodies touched. It swept through him like fire, bursting into his mind like a spike. He winced at the sharp pain, tears springing into his eyes.

"Tell me," he forced out. He pressed his forehead to Luka's, both slippery with sweat, and fell into his eyes. Anger and fear and stubborn pride swirled hotly around him, though love was mixed throughout. Rhys pushed deeper, ignoring the agony building in his head. There was something... He came against a barrier of ice, a locked door.

"Don't," Luka whispered in his mind, a command, a plea. Dread.

Rhys felt the moment Luka pushed back, driving him from his thoughts. Frantic, Rhys threw himself against the ice, and screamed as the terrible cold seared into him, freezing his limbs, his heart, lungs. He couldn't breathe! His body collapsed, his mind swirling in a vortex of exquisite pain into darkness.

He was back instantly, slamming into his body with a cry that scorched his throat, leaving it raw. Luka held his sprawled body, head bent over him, and a tear splashed against his upturned face.

"I'm well," he whispered and struggled to sit up, wincing at the pain pounding in his head. Luka pulled him against his chest, pressing fingers to his throbbing temple. His pain eased, though his body felt beyond exhausted.

"Why didn't you stop?" Luka asked him in anguish. Tears choked his voice.

Rhys pushed away, climbing to his knees, and Luka dropped his arms to his sides, looking defeated, miserable. Rhys cupped his cheek, felt him flinch, but didn't let go. "I saw what you had planned."

Luka tilted his head back against the boulder, hands clenched on his drawn-up knees. "I won't let them hurt you. Never again," he said defiantly. His defiant gaze challenged him.

"You would kill them," Rhys said carefully.

"If I had to."

The admission shocked him, though he had seen that dark thought, buried in ice. Angered, frightened, he nudged between Luka's knees, grasped his hands to pin them against the stone. "You will not," he said forcefully, glaring down at him.

"I will, if I have no other choice." Luka set his lips in a stubborn line. They stayed like that a moment, gazes clashing, then Rhys's shoulders slumped as all emotion left him, except one of profound sorrow.

"You cannot kill for me, Luka," he said. Begged, his heart aching that his beautiful, gentle witch would have such thoughts. Something shifted in Luka's eyes, the piercing light fading.

"Why, Rhys, if it is to protect you?"

Rhys's heart stumbled at his uncertainty. "Because, my dearest witch, you are all that is good and pure. You hold life sacred above all else. I would not have you go against your nature. I would rather die myself than see it happen."

"No," Luka said brokenly, and dropped his gaze. "You can't leave me...alone."

"I never will," Rhys promised fervently. "We will find another way to deal with our enemies."

Luka let out a shaky breath and nodded. Rhys smiled slightly and bent to kiss Luka's tears from his eyes. He became aware of how they sat, Luka against the wall, Rhys between his legs. He moistened his lips and Luka's breath caught. The heat of his body crept into Rhys, and then fire scorched through him when mischief glinted in Luka's eyes and he dropped his knees open in clear invitation.

"Oh, you don't fight fair, witch," he murmured and eased into Luka's embrace, relishing the feel of his solid body against him. But he also felt Luka's exhaustion, in both body and mind, and quieted the riot of his blood. He kissed him once, the soft brush of lips, and groaned, wanting to drown in him. Luka held on to him when he pushed away, and he gave a breathless laugh. "We're both beyond tired and need to sleep," he explained. "Let's see what the morning brings?"

Doubt flickered in Luka's eyes, but maybe it was the firelight, because he smiled and kissed the tip of Rhys's nose. "Very well." He moved to sit up, but Rhys pushed him gently back.

"I'll take care of the fire. Sleep now," he suggested, and waited until Luka wrapped in his cloak with a sigh and settled against the stones, head pillowed on his arms.

Rhys crossed to the fire, banked the coals, and added several larger pieces of wood. The horses stood nearby, heads down. Night had closed around them, a dark cold wall on the edge of firelight. Rhys checked Luka's ward. Still strong, even after all the energy he'd expelled that day.

"My witch," he murmured, heart full, humbled. He wanted in that moment for all of it to be over, that they could forget about the Well of Hope. Find a home to share and live together in peace. But Luka had taught him the dangers of wishing.

Instead, he clenched a fist. "We'll end this soon, darling," he said, and joined Luka against the stones.

Luka looked up at him, eyes unreadable in the flickering light. Rhys tucked his cloak tight and lay down beside him, smiling as Luka rolled to his side, pulled Rhys close, and nestled his head on his shoulder.

"Goodnight, my heart," Luka whispered, reaching for his hand.

"Goodnight, sweet witch," Rhys said, and let sleep take him.

Chapter Seventeen

Rhys woke, shivered, and reached for Luka's warmth, frowning when his fingers grazed solid rock. Where... He snapped his eyes open and hurriedly sat up. Predawn light glittered on a dusting of snow and the footprints marching across the glen, joined by horse hooves, and both disappearing into the trees. *Damn.* Did he have to tie Luka down?

The thought made his lips twitch. As if Luka would hold still long enough for that. And Rhys had been bound and abused often enough not to find any appeal in it. Unless...it was Luka tying the knots. It scared him sometimes how much he trusted Luka.

He climbed to his feet and stretched muscles gone stiff with cold, then shook the snow from his cloak and went to the fire. The wood Luka had added before he'd left had burned down to coals. He must have been gone at least an hour. He'd also left the larger pack behind, the one carrying most of the food and extra clothing.

Bits of ice stung his face and Rhys glanced upward at the gray sky, promising snow.

"We could have traveled together," he muttered, his breath a puff of white smoke. Out of sorts and more than a little angry with Luka, he stomped out the coals with a heavy boot. He then slung the pack over his shoulder and went to where the white mare nibbled frozen blades of grass on the edge of the glen.

He scratched behind her ears. "Let's find him," he told her, and swung onto her back, adjusting the pack to a more comfortable position as she headed along the trail Luka and the stallion had left in the snow. Rhys frowned as the trees closed in around them. Chances were, he needn't worry about Aethan and Lorin finding him. Luka wouldn't have left him on his own if they were near.

"But you shouldn't have left me," he stated, holding on to his anger to keep the worry at bay. He didn't fear for himself; his enemies couldn't do more to him than they already had. But they could drive Luka to kill, and that was intolerable. His gentle soul would be destroyed.

The air grew colder under the trees as the morning progressed, and Rhys hunched into his cloak as sleet stung his exposed skin. He recalled the first time he'd seen Luka, sweeping into that cellar like some avenger warrior of legend, all light and fury. He'd been Aethan's prisoner for months on end, allowed in the upper story on occasion, but mostly held in the cold stone and moldy underground.

He'd tried to escape many times, caught and punished. But the last time had been a living nightmare. Chained and beaten to his knees, Aethan raped him brutally and whispered in his ear, revealing for the first time their relationship. Dark despair took him, and he had wished for death before Luka found him.

He'd been sitting at the table, chained to the wall by his neck, shackles on his wrists. Footsteps on the floorboards overhead confused him. Aethan had left, maybe for a couple of hours, or days, leaving him with a mug of water and some bread he shared with the rat in the corner growing braver. Was he back so soon? A shudder ran through Rhys. If the monster, his father, touched him again…

A scream rose in his throat when the trapdoor opened with a scrape and thud, and footsteps descended the rickety stairs. But then a stranger came into view, dressed simply, dark skinned, with the most beautiful face Rhys had ever beheld. Youthful yet full of wisdom, dark hair in a braid, with deep brown eyes filled with compassion and sorrow and a swift anger on seeing him.

The man crossed the room in a wave of power, breaking the chains binding him with a touch, his hands infinitely gentle when he helped Rhys to his feet and out of his prison.

"I'm Luka," he said in low, rich tones that vibrated through Rhys as he aided him to mount the horse waiting outside. Luka swung up behind him, quieted his fears with a soft word and touch. Rhys slept, and didn't wake until evening was far advanced, and he looked curiously from the horse's back at the humble cottage they stopped before, with its herbs and roses growing wild in front. A warm fire waited inside, and Luka assisted him to the hearth, stirring up the coals and adding wood while Rhys sank thankfully onto thick blankets.

His face had heated when Luka sat back on his haunches and his thoughtful gaze traveled over him.

"I can offer you a bite of stew in a moment," Luka murmured. "But a wash first, I think."

He moved closer, and Rhys sucked in a breath when he removed his filthy stockings. "I don't think…"

"I sense there are wounds on your body that need attending. Be at peace. I mean you no harm," Luka told him and continued to undress him, his expression turning grave when he saw the welts and bruises covering Rhys's chest and back. His touch was firm, impersonal, though color stained his cheeks when he removed Rhys's breeches. He used a soft cloth dipped in water simmering on the hearth, fragrant with sage, to wash the grime from his body. Rhys cried out when he cleaned the open sore on his neck.

"Forgive me, Rhys. I'm being as gentle as I know how."

Rhys gave him a close look. "You know me?"

Luka lifted a shoulder. "I dreamed of you, your anguish heavy on my heart when I woke. I felt I knew you, and, of course, came for you."

"And left me again," Rhys muttered now, brought back to the moment by snow falling from a tree limb, striking his face. Some slipped under his hood and down his neck, and he swore under his breath, shivering. Unable to ignore his hunger a moment longer, he slid off the mare's back and led her to a clear space between the trees. He fed her a handful of grain, then took a packet of dried meat and a few apples for himself and sat with his back to a nearby boulder.

"Luka, where are you?" he asked, looking up into the gray sky, snow slowly sifting to the ground around him. He didn't expect an answer but became aware of a warmth spreading against his side. Searching his pockets, his fingers brushed against something hard, and he pulled the pink quartz from a pocket, glowing softly, heating his hand.

"You are thinking of me, as I am you," he murmured, and brought the rock up for a soft kiss. "Know this, my witch. Whatever you have planned, I will catch up before you can carry it out."

Something moved in the brush across the glen, drawing his gaze. Slipping the gem away, he leaned forward, trying to glimpse... The ferns parted and the sweetest face appeared, a pixie, with large green eyes and hair a wild flame around her head. The woman stepped forth, clad in a thin sheath of gold and brown despite the cold. Rhys drew in a hard breath. She was a creature of the woods, her magic washing over Rhys in a heady wave, her beauty captivating him.

She moved toward him with lithe grace, wild and free as a fawn, her eyes glinting mischief as she approached. Rhys found he couldn't move, except to lean back helplessly against the stones as she knelt beside him, and her hand burned where it rested on his thigh. She tilted her head and his senses swirled.

"I haven't seen you here before," she said in a voice like the chime of a bell, sending a pleasant shiver through him, hardening his cock. Perilous and tempting, she leaned into him, the pink tips of her breasts visible through the thin garment she wore brushing his skin, his blood burning.

Rhys fought the enchantment, knowing the dangers of the Fae to mortals.

"What would you have of me?" he asked, voice choked with the effort to speak.

The creature made a sound of delight and sat back, clapping her hands like a child, smiles wreathing her plump lips. Rhys hungered to taste their sweetness and bit hard on his tongue to clear his head. A pout formed on the wicked mouth and he closed his eyes, blocking out the bewitching sight.

"Stop it," he demanded, hating how weak his voice sounded, how his body responded to the sensuous creature.

"Open your eyes," she countered.

Rhys's eyes flew open to find his vision filled with her large green eyes, brilliant as gems, looking into him, brushing against his points of pleasure, pain, loneliness, with promises of love and carnal delights beyond his imagining. His thoughts narrowed to the feel of her lush body against his and the ache in his cock.

A groan of frustration and anger escaped him, and he shoved her off, scrambled to his feet, to lean, panting, against the boulder. The lovely sprite gazed at him in surprise, and then the fever in Rhys's blood quickly withdrew as she rose and took a step back, giving him room to breathe.

"You are strong, pretty one. Luka had chosen well," she murmured, running fingers down his arm as if she couldn't help the intimate gesture, a sensual creature by nature.

"You know Luka?" Rhys asked as his sluggish thoughts cleared.

She shrugged a bare shoulder. "He passed through here earlier today. I caught a glimpse of you in his mind. You're as beautiful as he pictures you."

"And why have you come to me?" he pressed. The mystic creatures of the forests rarely mingled with humankind. He didn't trust her, sensed danger in her casual mention of Luka. What web had Luka become entangled in?

"I have a message for your beautiful witch."

"Tell it to me."

The creature's full mouth lifted in a smile and she slanted Rhys a sly glance, green eyes glittering. "I've been entrusted to deliver it myself." She looked Rhys over, and the tip of her tongue touched her lips. "You may travel with me, if you desire."

Rhys nodded curtly, clenching his teeth, angered by his body's response to her nearness. She played with him, teased at his senses, and would leave him in the blink of an eye, bereft and longing, her enchantments woven into his very being.

"I will travel with you," he said at last, and sucked in a breath at her brilliant smile. He was most likely a fool but wanted to keep her with him and perhaps warn Luka before the beautiful nymph sprang on his shy witch, perhaps weaving her spells around him before Luka had time to put up a ward against her.

The thought troubled him, as did the unexpected prick of jealousy. Seeing no alternative, he gathered up his pack, stowing the extra food, and climbed back onto his horse. The woman laughed up at him as he held out his hand to help her mount, and she sprang lightly up in front of him, a warm, vivacious body in his arms.

"I'll take you to your precious lover," she said gaily, and threaded slim hands through the mare's white mane. "Hold on," she warned, and bent to whisper a word to the horse. They were off, a streak of light in the dark forest, and Rhys wondered at the power and magic surrounding them.

Chapter Eighteen

Luka slid from the stallion's back, keeping a hand on his shoulder as they stood on the outcrop of rock and gazed at the farm below, the lights of Sweetbrier a short distance away. This was the land Rhys worked before Aethan had taken him. The memory of his bright spirit lingered in the air and soil, gathered at the barn behind the moss-covered house.

The sun was lowering into evening, casting a pale light over the winter landscape. Ice filled the cracks in the stone under his feet, the fine layer of snow beginning to harden as the temperature dropped once again. Luka sighed and sat cross-legged, gazing unseeing at the valley filling with shadows. He missed Rhys.

The stallion moved off, finding a patch of grass on the edge of the forest. Luka huddled into his cloak as familiar loneliness crept over him, somehow heavier today. A slight wind carried the scent of smoke and cooking things to him from the village and an ache started in his heart. He longed to be home, snug in his cottage with a fire crackling on the hearth, Rhys beside him, holding his hand.

It had been his fault both times Rhys had been taken by Aethan. He should have done more to keep him safe. Done better by him and Aliya.

"But I thought my absence would keep his attention from you," he explained to Rhys's image in his mind and wiped at his tears before they could freeze on his skin. But he had been wrong, as he'd been so many times in the past, while others paid the price of it. Perhaps that was why his mother had left him. Why Loralyn had returned to the forest, leaving him alone. Rhys would go, sooner than later. Even Ravan...

Light appeared in the farmhouse below against the growing darkness and Luka climbed laboriously to his feet, stiff with cold. He needed to confront the man who'd betrayed Rhys, to somehow find a way to undo Aethan's web of spies around him, if his lover was to be truly free. He clutched a small grain of hope to his heart that Rhys would forgive him, but he would do whatever he must, to ensure his safety.

Before he could start down the slope under the bluff, the stallion neighed and threw up his head, while joy and panic swept Luka. Rhys was there. How... Small matter. Luka had to hurry. He scrambled down the rocky hill with a silent plea to the earth to guard his steps. Rhys would try to stop him, and Luka could not allow that. He reached the valley floor safely and started across the wide field toward the farmhouse, barren now in winter, crusted with ice and fresh snow that crunched under his boots.

He walked with purpose, gathering his energy close, the lump of ice in his heart spreading. He'd meant to stalk the man, ferret out his secrets, but with Rhys so close... Bursting into the house in a wave of power and terror, wrench the answers he needed from his enemy, by any means, seemed the only course.

He stumbled to a halt, brought up short by the cold fury seething in his chest. This wasn't like him. But he had never loved this desperately before. Perhaps—

A form sprang out of the darkness and slammed into him, knocking him off his feet. He landed with a heavy grunt, pain knifing up his back. The man grappled with him, but with a supple twist of his strong body, Luka rolled him over onto his back, instantly pinning his hands above his head. His opponent struggled, but Luka held firm, and couldn't help the smug grin that touched his lips.

"Let me up," Rhys muttered, squirming to break Luka's hold. Then he stilled, chest heaving, and something flared in his eyes. Luka was instantly aware of how he lay sprawled over him, a knee between his thighs; groin, hips, chests pressed together. Rhys moved, a sensuous stretch of his body, and Luka was vaguely alarmed at how he roused at having Rhys helpless beneath him, at the mercy of his slightest whim.

The world darkened around them, but Luka could plainly see Rhys's face, so close. He knew Rhys stared at his mouth, and heat swept him when Rhys moistened his lips, an open invitation. A moan was pulled from him, lust and need, and he lowered his head, touched his tongue to the sweet velvet of Rhys's lips. They parted, and Luka groaned again and slid into the honeyed heat of his mouth, kissing him long and deep. Rhys sucked on his tongue and Luka felt the pull on his cock. In answer, he pressed his knee against Rhys's responding hardness.

Luka drew back, breaking their kiss, and scrambled to collect his surging senses. Rhys blinked at him, a trifle dazed, fire in his eyes, mouth parted and moist. He looked wanton, utterly desirable. But Luka couldn't make love to him in the frozen mud. Could he?

He pushed up, laughing under his breath, and pulled Rhys to his feet with him. "I can never resist you," he confessed, and brushed his thumb over Rhys's lips, swollen from their kisses.

"You don't have to," Rhys assured him as he straightened his clothing. He rubbed his wrists and Luka gave him a look of dismay.

"I'm sorry—"

"Don't you dare apologize," Rhys cut off his words with a sharp gesture. "I rather enjoyed being dominated by you. In fact—" He stepped closer, making Luka's heart pound. "—we need to explore this further. Would you like it, Luka? Me enthralled, powerless, while you take your pleasure in me?"

Luka stared at him, finally remembering to breathe while his pulse thundered in his ears. "You're distracting me," he accused, made awkward and shy by Rhys's boldness. He'd been gentle with his lover, knowing his past, but perhaps Rhys needed more from him. Once again, Luka longed to be home, Aethan's cruelties a thing of the past, and search out all the ways to bring Rhys to ecstasy.

He drew a deep breath, determined to create this future for them.

"Why have you followed me?" he asked, and then widened his eyes. "Who brought you here so swiftly? I had several hours lead."

Rhys's smile left his face. "We'll discuss you abandoning me later." He tilted his head, and Luka followed his gaze up the hillside to where the horses stood, dark silhouettes in the dusk. A figure shimmered beside them, and Luka frowned, unable to touch its magic.

"She stepped out of the woods, saying she's come with a message for you," Rhys explained, and put a hand on Luka's arm. "I'm not entirely sure I trust her."

"Then you are wiser than most. How did she appear to you?"

"Her hair is a flame. Wild green eyes. Surely, an enchantress of some power."

Luka nodded. He'd known a woman like that, once upon a time. He searched Rhys's face, saw his faint blush. Of course. Very few mortals could resist the Fae. Had they... No, he wouldn't ask, and pushed the sting of jealousy from him. The slam of a door inside the cottage brought him back to the matter at hand.

He took a step toward the dwelling, but Rhys tightened his hold on his arm. "You will not harm him, Witch."

Hot blood scorched Luka's face at his tone, dismayed he'd caused Rhys to mistrust him. He gave a curt nod in place of a reply, keeping his face averted. The cold spot inside him had melted in the burning shame tightening his chest. He strived to be a good man but had gone against his very nature when he'd contemplated harming another living being. If Rhys eventually left him—and he had no reason to think otherwise—it would be his own doing, nothing more than he deserved.

The farmhouse was lost in shadows, but firelight flickered in a window, oddly comforting, where Luka expected to find apathy and decay. Rhys led the way, climbing the steps of the wide porch, and gave the front door a sharp rap with his knuckles. Luka was disconcerted by his brashness, then remembered Rhys knew the farmer, had worked for him in the past. Rhys would have issues of his own to work through with the man.

They waited. Silence greeted them—then the creak of a board, the fumble of the latch. The door swung inward and a large man filled the entranceway, backlit by the fire. The axe in his hands lowered but was held at the ready. He looked them over, a flicker of recognition in his eyes as they landed on Rhys. With a grunt and jerk of his head, he motioned for them to enter and crossed back to the fire crackling on the hearth.

Luka glanced at Rhys, but his expression was unreadable as they stepped into the cabin, and he closed the door behind them. They took a moment to remove their muddy boots, and Luka shivered, missing the warmth of his cloak as he hung it on a peg by the door. The room was still cold, the fire having only been lit a short time before, and they crossed the barren floor, thankful for the heat of the burning logs and the worn woven rug laid out before it.

The farmer stood to the side and set the axe against the wall at Rhys's raised brow.

"Why have you come?" he asked gruffly, firelight glinting in his red hair, his gaze sliding to Luka and back to Rhys, who clenched his hands.

"I worked myself near to death for you, Calan, to be beaten and starved in payment. Then you sold me to Aethan. I would ask you why." Rhys's cold tone chilled Luka.

Calan gave him a contemptuous look, a sneer curling his hard lips. "What do you have to complain of? Your work was slovenly done, and Aethan paid me far more than your worth. Be grateful you had a roof over your head, Rhys. Who else would have taken you in, without experience or someone to vouch for your character? I got the worst of the deal, to my thinking."

The two men glared at each other, and Luka studied the farmer. Calan's face was handsome in the firelight, powerful body evident despite his rough garb. He disarmed Luka. He'd expected the man to be cowardly, easily manipulated by Aethan's subversions. But Calan was proud and clearly no one's fool. His gaze was intent on Rhys, dismissing Luka for the moment, leaving Luka free to peer into his heart.

Luka sucked in a hard breath. Pride and anger played on the surface of Calan's mind as he fenced words with Rhys. But underneath was fear and a sorrow that burrowed deep. Love and unbearable pain twisted his heart, leaving it raw and bleeding. But why...

"You have a son," Luka stated, and Calan's indrawn breath was a hiss of pain. Silence fell on the room, eased only by the snap of the fire.

"I don't—" Calan's voice broke, and he covered his face with his work-worn hands. He backed to the wall, a shuddering sob escaping between his fingers. "I won't deny him," he forced out, and choked as if the words caught in his throat.

Luka's heart squeezed, and he glanced at Rhys, whose pitying look was tempered with caution. Catching Luka's gaze on him, he shook his head. "I know of no such person," he said softly. "I never saw a child on the farm."

Taking a calming breath, Luka let his glance travel the somber room. A low couch faced the hearth, the pillows bunched as if the man habitually slept there. A solid table and two chairs sat behind it in the shadows. A cup and plate rested on the mantel along with several unlit candles, the remains of Calan's dinner in a pot over the fire. It was a sparse room for a solitary man. And yet...

A woolen cap rested on a hook beside the mantle. Drawn to it, Luka took the soft hat in his hands. Instantly, the image of a boy, thirteen or fourteen years, sprang to his mind, laughing up at his father. Playing in the nearby creek. Bringing in the cow from the pasture.

He closed his eyes, a tear slipping through his lashes. "Aethan?" he murmured, not to call the sorcerer, but he sent a tendril of thought out in search of his malignant presence. Luka took a sip of air, nauseous. Aethan's dark essence saturated the wood of the cottage down to its foundation. Luka opened his mind further, finding traces of him in the surrounding fields and outbuildings as well. His hold on the land and its caretaker was strong, too much for Luka to break. It remained for Calan to do so himself.

Calan staggered from the wall with a wounded cry, lurching over to grab the cap from Luka's hands, shoving him aside. "Don't touch this! How dare you—"

"Peace," Luka told him.

Calan stared at him, the anger gradually leaving his face until only sorrow and anxiety remained. He crossed to the couch and sat, hands between his knees, rolling the cap around and around.

Luka's heart ached for him. "How long has he been gone?" he asked gently, though he could guess the answer.

"Months before Rhys came to work for me," Calan said heavily, eyes on the fire, though he glanced up at Rhys's low sound of pain. "Aethan said he'd be returned once I took Rhys in and reported back to him. He didn't keep his word," Calan ended, impotent rage thickening his voice.

"Are there any others, like you, who watch for him?" Luka pushed, senses heightened to catch any stray thoughts of treachery.

Calan jabbed a hand through his thick hair. "Perhaps, but they are unknown to me. Please go. I have endangered Tarian's life by speaking with you."

"I have masked our presence," Luka assured him. "Aethan will not know we've been here." He took a step closer, the pain and hopeless fear from Calan washing over him. "Can you tell us where your son is?"

"There is a cottage in the forest outside Sweetbrier—"

Rhys gave a strangled cry, his pain slamming into Luka before Rhys brutally checked it, and stood, face turned as he fought for control. Luka watched him in dismay, dread creeping through him. He feared to ask the next question.

"Has he been held there long?"

Calan shook his head. "He was moved around, though he is there now. Aethan tortured me with the knowledge, warning me to stay away. I tried to rescue Tarian once, the first month he was taken. Aethan sent me three of his fingers in retaliation. I haven't tried since."

Luka held perfectly still as the full horror of what Calan claimed sank in. How had he not known Aethan had taken another prisoner? Rhys's suffering had been the tolling of a bell in his head, insistent, striking his heart. Perhaps because Luka had already been involved in his life?

He drew a troubled breath. Aethan was indeed strong if he could hide Tarian from him. He met Rhys's vicious, tortured gaze, and for a moment the weight of his failures crushed him. But he set it aside, accepting there would be a reckoning one day.

"We'll set him free," he promised Rhys's unspoken plea.

Chapter Nineteen

Rhys gave a sharp nod, face pale, jaw clenched, the fire in his eyes reinforcing Luka's resolve to rescue Calan's son. He glanced at the farmer, and the terrified hope in his expression came close to breaking him.

Calan rose, Tarian's cap clenched in one hand, and his voice shook when he spoke, "You would do this for me? Why, when I have betrayed Rhys to his enemy?"

Rhys answered unexpectedly, fury lacing his words, "No one carries the blame here except Aethan." He held Luka's gaze until the knot of pain around his heart loosened. "Calan, you will take us to this cottage you speak of."

Calan's fear spiked. "I dare not. If we should fail... Aethan would murder Tarian before my eyes, in payment." His thick chest heaved, undone by the panic surging through him.

Luka immediately put a hand on his arm, feeling the muscles tense and bunch while a shudder ran his strong body. "Be at peace. We will find Tarian and return him to you."

"But Aethan—"

"Had better keep his distance," Rhys hissed through his clenched teeth.

"Aethan will have no knowledge of our presence until we are far away. He will never know of your involvement in this," Luka assured him.

"How will I explain my son's sudden appearance?"

Luka dropped all pretense, the conviction of his words echoed by a rumble in the distance. "I will not allow Aethan to bring any more pain to this world."

Rhys's breath caught behind him while Calan's dark eyes widened with awe. He took a step back and swept Luka a low bow. "My lord. I am at your service. If it is your wish, I will go with you..."

Heat rose in Luka's face, embarrassed he had lost control, if only for an instant. The power in him was not his, but a gift of the earth and nothing he should display. He was not a man for others to follow.

"There is no need, Calan. But send your good wishes with us."

Luka turned toward the door, to be stopped by Calan's hand on his shoulder. "It is late, my lord. Will you stay? There is food, and blankets for your comfort tonight."

"No. My impulse is to hurry. You will know soon enough if we succeed."

He passed Rhys with a nod, not meeting his gaze, and fetched his cloak from the hook by the door and stomped into his boots. Rhys did the same, and they exited the warm farmhouse. Rhys gasped at the cold and instantly Luka swiveled and pulled him into a close embrace, kissing his face and his wet eyes.

"I am so sorry, Rhys. Will you stay here until I return? You should not have to go back to that terrible place."

"And you, my sweet witch, are not going there alone." Rhys's tone was firm, and Luka eased back to look at him. It was fully dark now, though the light from the moon shone on his face, and Luka could clearly see the stubborn set of his lips and the anger smoldering in his eyes.

"Do not do anything imprudent," he warned, feeling the recklessness in his lover.

"I will see that boy freed," Rhys said firmly. "Will you call the horses?"

Luka sighed and sent a thought into the night. The stallion's bray rang through the darkness and soon hooves thundered across the field in a sharp crack of ice.

"Where is the Fae?" Rhys asked, a frown between his brows when the horses drew up without their bright companion.

Luka shrugged. "The woodland folk do as they choose. She will find us, if that is her whim."

They mounted and Luka led them across the farmland to the road heading for Sweetbrier. As much as he desired Rhys to stay behind, safe, it felt good to have him riding at his side again. He slanted him a look to find Rhys's eyes on him, and his pulse quickened. Rhys nudged their horses closer together, reached out to grab the back of his head, and pulled him in for a kiss.

Luka clung to him and tasted Rhys's sigh in his mouth. Rhys bunched a fist in his cloak over his breast when Luka eased back, halting him.

"You can't leave me like that again," Rhys admonished, sounding more drained than angry, shaking him a little. "It serves little purpose. You know 1 will follow."

"I suppose you will," Luka acknowledged, and smiled at Rhys's glower, barely discernable in the dark, adding boldly, "Perhaps you are meant to be with me always."

Rhys's breath was sharp in the quiet and he clenched his hand tighter in Luka's cloak, leaning close. "Toy with me, Witch, and I will pull you to the ground and fuck you right here, no question."

Luka shivered, part lust, but mostly regret for Rhys's turmoil. "I am sorry, dear heart. You would have tried to stop me had I stayed with you. I came here in hatred and wrath to extract the truth from one of Aethan's puppets, only to discover he was another victim of the sorcerer's practiced cruelty. I'm grateful you stopped me from doing something I would regret all my life."

Rhys grunted, abruptly releasing Luka. "Perhaps you will have more trust in me in the future."

Luka nodded, finding nothing to say. They traveled in silence, lost in their own thoughts as the night deepened, moonlight making it possible to trot the horses at times. At intervals, they'd stop to rest and managed a few hours of sleep while the moon set. Dawn found them approaching the sleeping town of Sweetbrier, which they skirted to the east, climbing the steep trail through the thickening woods to the cottage where Rhys had been held captive years ago.

Luka's heart grew heavy as the sun rose, and the trail became clear to read. No one had traveled that way in days if not weeks, and he nudged the stallion to a quicker pace, concerned with what they'd find ahead. In moments they came to the cottage and drew rein, Luka taking an anxious breath. The dilapidated structure appeared the same as he remembered, moss on the roof, saplings crowding the moldering walls. The air of neglect and decay sent a shudder of revulsion through him.

They dismounted and cautiously approached the sagging porch. Luka wrinkled his nose at the scent of rot as he sought for Aethan's presence.

Rhys halted at the broken steps, his voice sounding choked when he spoke, "Is there a ward, Luka? I have a great loathing to go inside."

Luka drew his brows together in concern. "There is, though it is in tatters. Aethan's abandoned this place."

Rhys visibly paled, and Luka pressed his lips together, bracing for whatever waited inside. Setting each foot with care, they climbed the steps and crossed the porch, Rhys hissing when nausea struck them as they passed through Aethan's ward. The door proved to be ajar and Luka pushed it open against the uneven floor within, not wanting to think what its unlocked state implied.

They waited a moment for silence to settle, Rhys's uneven breathing a knife in Luka's chest. Luka would have spared him this nightmare if he could. The trapdoor leading to the cellar was thankfully closed, and Luka purposefully lead them to the door on the opposite wall, praying to find Tarian there instead of the place of Rhys's intense suffering. This door proved unlocked as well and Luka peered inside, allowing his eyes to adjust to the morning sunlight filtering through ragged curtains.

The bed drew his gaze instantly, and a cry left his lips. Aching with pity and fear, he approached the still form sprawled on the filthy sheets, willing Rhys to remain at the door. Tarian lay unmoving, naked, eyes sunken, lips cracked and bleeding. Bruises and open sores ran his too-thin body, bluish with cold, and he surprised Luka when his chest rose and fell on a shallow breath.

"Fetch water," he said urgently, noting the empty bowl beside the table. How long had he been without the life-giving liquid? He nudged the tortured lips open with a gentle finger and winced at his partially swollen tongue. Perhaps two days. Luka placed a hand on his chest, felt the racing heartbeat, the quick breaths he took.

"Tarian?" he murmured, brushing the dull hair from his forehead, tangled from sweat that had dried days ago, the brilliant red still striking against his pale skin. Returning footsteps thumped across the cottage and Luka slid an arm under the trembling body, lifted Tarian slightly. Without a word, Rhys joined them and tilted the water flask to Tarian's lips, allowing him a trickle of water.

Luka's heart jumped when Tarian coughed and his long lashes fluttered against his waxy skin, parting on eyes the color of a summer sky. Confusion and pain swam in those light depths, and he clutched feebly at Luka's arm, obviously disoriented and dizzy from severe dehydration.

"Easy, Tarian. We're friends," Rhys said huskily as he offered another sip from the flask with an unsteady hand. Tarian whimpered and chased the flask with his lips when Rhys pulled it away. Rhys made a sound of pain and Luka quickly cupped his face with his free hand, forcing Rhys to meet his gaze. That Rhys saw himself in the tortured boy was evident in his anguished expression, and Luka's heart bled for both of them.

"Peace, dear heart," he murmured, caressing Rhys's pale cheek. He rarely entered another's mind, but this time sent a tendril of thought to Rhys, asking to share his pain. Tears gathered in Rhys's eyes, and he nodded, then let down the barriers in his mind. Love flooded to Luka, and then by slow, poisonous drips, the awakened terror and pain of Rhys's torment passed to his heart. Luka sent compassion and his deep love in return and saw with gratitude when the horror left him and Rhys drew a ragged breath.

Rhys gave him a tremulous smile and turned his head to kiss his palm. Luka sighed, taking a moment to settle Rhys's pain with his own, then shifted to Tarian. This would be harder. The boy appeared to have been fed, only recently abandoned when Aethan gave chase to Luka. He would need water and food and safety to recover. But it was the horror crawling in his mind that troubled Luka. It had taken Rhys months of Luka's tender care before the black despair lessened and Rhys could sleep without nightmares. They didn't have that kind of time now. Aethan was closing in.

Rhys gave Tarian one more swallow of water, then Luka eased him back on the bed. Tarian watched him with a frantic gaze and Luka turned to him fully, placed his hands on either side of his head.

"Let me help," he urged and pushed gently into his mind. Tarian resisted and Luka waited, hoping…

Tarian's walls unexpectedly dropped, and Luka fell into horror, pain its merciless companion. Aethan kept at him with his small tortures of fingernails and teeth, the agony of his cock. The relentless assault of nightmare and brutal visions and bursts of indescribable pleasure tearing his mind apart. Luka cried out, the onslaught overwhelming, too great to bear. But Rhys placed a hand on his shoulder, a reminder of love, and Luka swallowed down the anguish pouring from Tarian until the last bitter drop fell into his heart.

Luka gasped, pulling away from Tarian. Climbing to his feet, body in agony, he stumbled to the window and stared blindly through the tattered curtains while he suffered Aethan's torments. His tears flowed, and Luka let them fall, knowing it would be some while before the horror and clinging dread eased from his soul, though he had little time to spare for it.

Chapter Twenty

Rhys watched Luka, longing to go to him, hold him in his arms. Why had Luka done that? Rhys had felt the tremendous power gathered to him. Had seen the terror and bewilderment leave Tarian's eyes while Luka trembled and wept, at last stumbling to the window, hunched with pain, not allowing Rhys a glimpse into his thoughts.

Tarian groaned, struggled to sit up, and fell back with a gasp, chest heaving with exertion.

"Don't be afraid," Rhys told him, smoothing the tangled hair from his face. "You are safe. We won't harm you."

"I know," Tarian said on a breath of pain, his gaze going to Luka, and an expression of awe touched his features. Rhys studied his face. Healthy enough, despite the ravages of dehydration. He would heal.

He eased off the bed but touched Tarian's hand at his panicked look. "I'm going to the other room for a brief moment."

A flush rose in Tarian's face and he pressed his swollen, bloody lips together as if embarrassed by his fear. Rhys gave his hand a reassuring squeeze. He shot Luka a glance, but he still had his back turned to them. With a sigh, Rhys exited to the main room of the cottage. A pail of water rested on the hearth, cold, with a layer of dust floating on its surface, but Rhys didn't have time to warm it. Tucking several towels under his arm, he then lifted the pail and returned to the bedroom.

Tarian watched him with wide eyes as he crossed to him, the color mounting once again in his cheeks when Rhys dipped the edge of a cloth in the water and washed the tears and blood from his face and neck. Ignoring Tarian's distress, he worked his way down the young man's body, rolling him to his side at one point to remove the filthy sheets.

Luka joined him as he finished, carrying clothing he'd found in a trunk against the wall draped over an arm. They helped Tarian dress, and the young man sat on the side of the bed, pale and shaking, when they'd done.

"We can't stay here," Luka warned, voice throbbing with compassion as he gazed at Tarian.

"I can travel," Tarian told them with a proud tilt of his head, though pain whitened his lips. Rhys smiled for the first time that long night, silently rejoicing Aethan hadn't broken the lad's spirit.

Luka left them briefly and came back carrying a pair of worn boots. "I found these by the front door," he said, showing them to Tarian. "Are they yours?"

At his nod, Luka knelt by the bed and slipped wool socks over Tarian's slender feet. Color rose in Tarian's face, his lips parting, as Luka bent over his task, working the boots on and pulling the laces tight. Rhys saw the moment Tarian's gaze turned adoring. Not that he could blame him. Luka's braid had come loose and soft tendrils of dark hair caressed his earnest face, making him appear young and vulnerable in the muted daylight.

Luka stood, warmth in his rich brown eyes as he held his hand out to Tarian. "Can you stand?" he asked, unaware of Tarian's regard. Tarian set his feet firmly on the floor and pushed to a standing position. He stood tall as Luka, though thin as a willow, and swayed as he clutched Luka's arm for support.

"I'm well," he said in short order, straightening. Luka nodded, then removed his cloak and settled it on Tarian's slumped shoulders.

Tarian's blue eyes widened in disbelief and his fingers fumbled with the clasp at his throat. "My lord! I can't wear this."

Rhys's heart clenched, realizing only the thumb and second finger remained on Tarian's left hand, the rest a mass of twisted, ugly scars. He wondered if they hurt him.

Luka drew a ragged breath and put his hands over Tarian's, halting him. "Peace. It is simply a cloak. I have another."

"But..."

Tarian shot Rhys a distressed look, and he stepped forward, touching his shoulder as he bent to his ear, "Wear it until you are warm, Tarian. You can exchange it with Luka later."

Uncertainty and returning fear clouded Tarian's sky-blue eyes pleading with him. "How do you know me?"

"Your father sent us," Luka put in, and Tarian started and tensed under Rhys's hand.

"My father?" Horror dawned on his face. "Then he knows what Aethan... What he...did." A sob broke from him and he covered his face, his shame palpable. Luka made a hurt sound.

Rhys squeezed Tarian's shoulder, again putting his lips to his ear. "Your father only cares to see you safe. Believe me, we will make Aethan pay, have no fear of that." He continued when Tarian quieted, "And you are not the only one Aethan has had."

Tarian jerked his head up and Rhys nodded grimly at his shocked expression. A shudder ran his slim body, and then Tarian raised his head, setting his lips in a firm line. "Tell me what I can do."

"First, we will take you home and ease your father's fears. After that, we will see," Luka told him gently, though his tone was firm. There would be no argument.

Rhys looked Tarian over, noting the tremble as he held himself upright. "Can you walk?"

The pale, ravaged lips pressed together once more and Tarian took a step forward, only to gasp with pain and swoon. Rhys caught him before he could hit the hard floor.

"Poor child," Luka murmured, choked with compassion, but there was anger simmering below the surface, banked fury.

Rhys swept Tarian up in his arms and followed Luka as he exited the room. Luka stalked across the cabin and outside, calling the horses as he passed the threshold. He took Tarian from Rhys, then handed him up after Rhys had mounted. Rhys looked at him, but Luka wouldn't meet his gaze, going instead to the porch to retrieve their packs. He handed one to Rhys and pulled his coat from the other, sliding it on.

"Luka?"

Luka shook his head once, and energy crackled in the air around them. Thunder rumbled. Rhys caught his breath. He'd seen Luka angry before, but never like this, cold and dangerous. Luka walked back to the cottage, stood before it, hands up, palms facing inward. The air shimmered, pressure building until Rhys found it difficult to breathe. Then Luka turned his hands to the cottage, and with a whoosh it ignited, instantly engulfed in flames. The horses snorted and stepped back as heat and embers flowed over them.

Luka joined them, face impassive, eyes glittering, and mounted the stallion without a word, turning to gallop into the trees. Rhys watched the cottage burn, heart pounding, then settled Tarian in his arms and followed

Luka, more frightened by this act than anything Luka had done previously.

They traveled in silence, Luka keeping a fast pace, but after some time he slowed to a walk, head lifted as if listening. Rhys came up beside him, shifting Tarian against his shoulder.

"What is it?" he asked as Luka chewed his lips, a sure sign of worry. The familiar sight calmed the panic that had been growing in his chest.

Luka looked at him, and sorrow fell over his features. "I must apologize. I lost—"

"Don't you dare," Rhys practically growled, chest hot with emotion. "That was a place of pain and unimaginable suffering. If you hadn't burned it, I would have gone back and done it myself."

They stared at each other, then Luka nodded. His gaze dropped to the young man in Rhys's arms, brow wrinkled with concern. Rhys sighed. Did Luka have to take on all the pain of the world?

"He breathes, Luka. He will heal," Rhys assured him kindly.

Luka gave him a tentative smile and reached a hand to him, only to pause, hand frozen midair as a wail sounded on the wind, a soul lost. Rhys's heart ached with the pathos of it, grief and utter despair. Tears burned his eyes, and he nudged the horse forward, needing to find her...

Luka touched the mare, and they halted. Rhys rounded on him in fury, but Luka gazed into the thicket of trees ahead, and Rhys's anger dropped from him as if it had never been. What was going on? It was as if another had plucked his emotions. Confused, he put a hand on Luka's. "What is it?"

Luka sighed and shifted on the stallion as if settling a burden on his shoulders. "Come out, Fae," he called sharply in the cold air. "Your tricks won't work here."

Silence fell on the forest, and then a soft laugh, infinitely sweet, floated on the air, and a woman, bewitchingly beautiful, the fae he'd seen earlier, stepped onto the path in front of them. Her sheer gown fluttered on a breeze Rhys couldn't feel, bewildering his senses. The creature's green jeweled eyes fell on him and his heart thumped, cock stirring as she licked ripe lips.

Luka moved impatiently and Rhys shook his head, coming out of a spell he hadn't felt her cast.

"Enough, Loralyn." Luka's voice was hard. "Why are you here? What would you have from us?"

The fae glided up to them, graceful, lovely, and walked between the horses, putting a hand on Luka's thigh. Rhys saw him flinch, face paling, though the pain was promptly submerged.

"I have come to warn you, of many things," Loralyn said, her voice music. She tilted her head, her hair a flame in the gray morning, and Rhys blinked, bemused by the magic that was part of her being.

"But why you? Why now?" Luka challenged, his dark face impassive, giving nothing away.

The fae hissed in quick anger. "We have much to discuss, my love. But not here. Aethan comes."

Startled, Rhys shot a gaze to the trail. "Calan—"

"Is safe." Loralyn glanced at him and Rhys gasped as her beauty struck him anew, captivating, bewildering, causing his blood to heat and rush. He forgot his duty to Tarian unconscious in his arms, his love for Luka beside him. Lost in the glittering eyes that drew him in...

"Loralyn," Luka snapped, and the fae turned her head, breaking their connection. Rhys clenched his teeth, realizing his danger. He would be no one's plaything. Never again.

Luka gazed down at the fae. "What do you propose?"

"I will take you to a place of safety. Then we will talk."

A look edging despair crossed Luka's face, but he nodded once, and took the hand the woman held out to him, pulling her up in front of him on the stallion. She twined her hands in the animal's long mane, bent to whisper in his ear, and they bolted into the trees, swift as an arrow from a bow. The mare's muscles bunched between Rhys's legs. He hunched over Tarian and they followed, quick and sure, the fae's magic flowing around them, keeping them from harm.

Rhys lost track of time as the forest swept passed, and fought off sleepiness and the bright, glittering dream on the edge of his senses. The fae would have to look elsewhere for her amusement.

He risked a peek at the stallion ahead. Luka sat stiffly while the fae glanced over her shoulder, laughing in his face. Rhys knew her now. Loralyn. Luka's wife, who'd left him long ago. And broke his heart. Rhys clenched a fist. He would keep his head with the enchantress, for both their sakes.

Chapter Twenty-One

The horse slowed, drawing Rhys from the dream of summer fields and Luka clasped in his arms on a bed of wildflowers. The scent of sweet alyssum and lilac followed him, and he blinked in confusion at the tall pine surrounding them, the flakes of snow drifting through their branches, coating the floor of the small glen where they halted.

The fae laughed, the tinkle of bells, and Rhys sighed wearily, swinging from the saddle, lifting Tarian down with him. Luka slid from the stallion and clutched its side as he swayed, exhausted. Rhys's heart clenched, aching to go to him. But the fae was there first, springing lightly to the ground to wrap an arm around his waist.

Rhys scowled at a prick of jealousy and carried Tarian to a cluster of rocks near the center of the glen. The lad stirred, looking at him in confusion, and Rhys instantly set him on his feet, though he kept a hand on his elbow.

"We're safe here," he answered Tarian's panicked gaze, hoping it was true.

Tarian drew a quick breath and eased down on a rock, pulling Luka's cloak tighter against the cold air. "Perhaps," he murmured.

Rhys followed his gaze across the glen. The fae danced among the trees, a glimmer of light, and Rhys felt the energy as she set a ward around them. Luka came over to them, gave Rhys a tired smile, and dropped down beside Tarian. He unslung his pack from a shoulder and foraged, handing Tarian a packet of dried fruits and nuts. Hunger flashed across Tarian's face, but he had the wisdom to eat slowly, nibbling on small pieces while his starved body adjusted.

"I'll start a fire," Rhys offered, and placed a hand on Luka's shoulder when he would have risen. "Rest, sweet witch. I'm capable of gathering wood on my own."

Luka gazed up at him and Rhys fell into the depths of his beautiful eyes, to be surrounded by warmth and love and the joy of a true friendship. Deeper, to the hunger and longing never far from the surface. Beyond, to a desperate, remembered loneliness the fae had stirred up.

Rhys smiled and caressed Luka's face, brushing a thumb over his lips, which parted on a gasp. He picked up his hands and placed a kiss on each palm. "You have my heart," Rhys assured him, and saw tears glitter in Luka's eyes before he dropped his gaze, color flooding his cheeks. Satisfied, he shot a gaze across the glen to the fae on the edge of the trees.

"You won't hurt him again," he vowed under his breath.

It didn't take long to gather wood. Clearing a space of snow near Luka and Tarian, Rhys then knelt and lit the kindling with flint and the edge of his knife while the fae knelt across from him, watching curiously. Once the shavings caught, he added larger pieces of wood, and sat back when Loralyn motioned with her hand and the fire engulfed the pile.

He inclined his head and Loralyn clapped her hands merrily. "We work well together," she exclaimed in her musical voice, and Rhys hated that he felt flattered by her praise.

Luka sat forward, hands held out to the crackling flames. "What do you have to tell us?" he asked abruptly, eyes on the fae. Loralyn pouted, then dropped all pretense, leaning toward Luka earnestly. "Annalise has sent me."

The fire snapped in the silence. Tarian looked between them with concern dawning on his youthful face, but Rhys waited, hurting for Luka but knowing the wisdom of not interfering.

"Why would she do that?" Luka asked at last, face impassive.

"She says it is time." Loralyn gazed at each of them, and for a moment appeared uncertain. "Where is Ravan? I had hoped to see our daughter."

Luka flinched and anger rose in Rhys.

"Tell us, Fae," Rhys snapped. "It's time for what? And why should we believe Luka's cherished mother would have anything to do with you?"

Loralyn turned her green eyes on him and Rhys's breath caught in his throat, the muscles constricting, strangling. He glared at her, refusing to back down. If Loralyn didn't know he would die for Luka, she did now.

"Fair questions," she said, turning back to Luka. Released, Rhys sucked in air, throat bruised, while Tarian rubbed Rhys's back. His blue eyes were wide with fear, but anger lingered there also, directed toward the fae. Very good. His loyalty remained with Luka, when it could so easily have transferred to the magical creature.

"Loralyn?" Luka prompted, and Rhys shivered at the coldness of his tone.

Temper flashed on Loralyn's lovely face. "While you've been rescuing strays," her eyes flicked to Tarian, "Aethan has been tearing the world apart to find you. He's bound creatures of both earth and air to his will in his search. Your mother protects her forest but sought me out, knowing I could find you when no one else has been successful."

Rhys narrowed his eyes. More manipulation? The creature seemed full of deceit, yet perhaps she told the truth in this instance. More than likely she still had a connection to Luka, damn her. Rhys blinked, the jealousy knotting in his guts a surprise.

"And her message?" Luka pressed, clearly growing impatient. Rhys gave a silent cheer and accidently caught Tarian's eye, and they exchanged a look of triumph. Their witch wouldn't be fooled by the clever enchantress.

Loralyn glowered at them, eyes flashing. "She says you can no longer delay, Luka. It is time to go to Ash Swale and do what you must."

Luka paled but nodded his head in acceptance. "Thank you, Loralyn," he said, and dropped his eyes to the fire as if dismissing her.

Loralyn pressed her lips together, controlling her anger. "Annalise has bound me to see you safely to the swale." She rose gracefully to her feet. "Sleep now. I will watch. We must be on our way in a few hours."

Rhys wanted to protest but Luka gave him a slight shake of his head and he swallowed his words.

"That would be kind of you," Luka acknowledged, and sighed, the strain of the past few hours seeming to catch up to him. His hands shook as he reached for more wood for the fire, and Rhys touched his arm.

"Permit me, Luka. Please, lay down now. We can all use the rest."

Luka gave him a grateful smile and moved back slightly from the bright flames, rolled in his cloak, and lay facing the fire, head resting on his hands. After a slight hesitation, Tarian did the same, head near Luka's feet. Rhys stood and added more wood to the fire. He was hungry and felt sure Luka would be the same, but that could wait until after they'd slept.

He didn't want to go to Ash Swale, that mire of dangerous footing and toxic air. A haunted place, where no animals lived. Where the earth had turned itself inside out.

He lay down facing Luka, and after a time, allowed a smile to play on his lips. Luka appeared to be at peace, his face relaxed in sleep, his beautiful mouth partially open. Rhys had the sudden urge to kiss him, part his lips further with his tongue and taste his warm sweetness. He sighed, closing his eyes. It may be a long while before he had that pleasure again.

Dreams took him instantly, confusing, wild, a swirl of light and color, though it seemed only moments when he roused again. He lay still, eyes closed, enjoying the feel of fingers threading his hair, soft lips pressed to his. *What?* He opened his eyes, then scrambled to sit up, pushing the fae from his arms. She laughed merrily, plump breasts pressed against his chest, arms twined around his neck.

"Leave me be," he said angrily. He glanced at once at Luka and found his brown eyes on them. His expression gave nothing away, but a hot blush crept up Rhys's face anyway.

Loralyn hopped to her feet and clapped her hands. "Up! Up. Time to be going."

The sun was far advanced, leaving only a few hours of sunlight in which to travel. The horses trotted to them, rested and fed, and it took mere moments to douse the smoldering fire, shoulder their packs, and mount. Rhys held his hand out for Tarian, but Loralyn flitted between them and swung up in front of Rhys, nestling back against him.

Luka ignored them, mounting the stallion and assisting Tarian up in front of him. "Shall we?" he asked without glancing at Rhys. The fae nudged their horse into motion and the stallion followed behind.

Chapter Twenty-Two

Luka tore his gaze away from Rhys on the mare. Loralyn perched in front of him as she guided them through the forest. They had run for a while and now walked to rest the horses. He hunched in his cloak against the cold, grateful for the warmth of Tarian's slight body in front of him. Loralyn leaned back on Rhys's shoulder, laughing up into his face while Rhys shook his head. Luka told himself he was glad he couldn't see his expression. Loralyn was lovely, enchanting.

He was surprised he felt nothing for her, after loving her so intensely. But that was the way of the fae. She'd played with him for a while and then forgot him. But she had given him Ravan, and for that, the emptiness and pain that had followed had been worth it. And the enchantment she had cast over him was no more.

She turned her attention to Rhys now, and who was Luka to deny him the pleasure? Loralyn had filled his days with happiness, his nights with passion. Rhys deserved a little joy in his life, after all his suffering. And when she was done with him, Luka would be there to comfort him in his loss. If Rhys would have him, a poor substitute.

Tarian moved restlessly, his words bitter when he spoke, "Why do you allow it, my lord? Clearly she is set on beguiling him."

Luka shifted on the stallion to give him more room as Tarian turned toward him. "Rhys is free to make his own choices. As are you," he added, continuing their discussion from earlier.

Tarian swiveled to look him fully in the face, then his gaze darted away just as quickly. "I believed that, at one time. But now... After what Aethan did..." Distress thickened his voice, "I tried to fight him, lord. I promise I did. But he was cruel—" Tarian broke off, jerking away to bury his face in the stallion's mane, his mutilated hand hiding a wet cheek.

Luka's heart clenched with pity, his mind racing as he tried to find the words to comfort him. He again looked at Rhys who rode stiffly, back straight, as Loralyn teased him, and didn't think he would mind.

"As Rhys told you, he had been his prisoner as well, a short time ago..." He paused at Tarian's strangled sound, muffled against the horse.

"Hush," he murmured, rubbing Tarian's back through the rich burgundy robe he still wore despite his protest. But Luka was warm enough in his old cloak, and the child needed to be reminded of his worth, that what Aethan had done had not diminished him.

"Aethan uses people. And will hurt them, if he can," he continued, and laid his hand flat on Tarian's back, speaking to him earnestly, "But I see you, and the beautiful light inside you is not lessened."

Tarian made no reply, but in a moment he sat up and scrubbed at his eyes with the back of his hand. Luka sighed, heart sore, knowing Tarian would never fully heal from his abuse at the hands of a monster. But perhaps he could still find joy in life. Rhys's laugh floated back to him and he looked reluctantly ahead, saw Rhys push the fae from his lap once again, and wondered if he witnessed his own happiness slipping from his grasp.

If so, then that was how it would be. He couldn't afford to dwell on it longer. They were out of time.

"Loralyn, we must go," he said. He had no need to raise his voice. The fae glanced at him, nodded, and the horses sprang forward on her whispered word. Time twisted as they ran, Luka losing track of the moments flitting by, hours or days or even years. To the Fae, time worked differently than that of human born. A hundred years could pass for a mortal, seeming a mere heartbeat in their glittering, enchanting company. He could only hope Loralyn steered them true, bringing them where they needed to be at the necessary juncture.

His lips twitched with a faintly desperate smile. He needn't worry. Loralyn knew what she was about. The forest flowed past, and he put an arm around Tarian as his head bobbed and he dozed, unaware of the leagues sliding away beneath them. Luka longed for the forgetfulness of sleep, to put his burden down for a single moment. But he had pulled the Well of Hope from the earth. It was his responsibility to return it.

At long last, the stallion slowed into a walk, muscles shaking beneath Luka's thighs. The evening was far advanced, darkness gathering under the trees. Loralyn drew the white mare to a stop and Luka halted beside them, gaze intent on Rhys's hunched back. Rhys glanced at him, blinking sleepily. He must have gotten a little rest. Rhys smiled at him and yawned, captivating him, and Luka's heart quickened. He had the sudden urge to kiss him, but Tarian woke at that moment, forestalling him.

He swung from the stallion's back and helped Tarian down, curious about the faint blush in his pale cheeks, but then Loralyn came up to him, snatching his attention. She was beautiful, a bright flame against the gray sky and lightly falling snow. A few flakes clung to her brilliant hair, and he smiled fondly. Despite the pain she had cost him, she had loved him in her own way.

"This is as far as I will go, sweet witch," Loralyn told him, her pretty lips twitching, laughter in her eyes as she used Rhys's endearment for him.

"Thank you." Luka noted they had reached the edge of the forest. He picked up Loralyn's slim hands and placed a kiss on them. "Did my mother have any other message for me?"

Loralyn nodded and cupped Luka's face. "She said to go with care and her love." She paused, cocked her bright head, and there was concern in her brilliant eyes.

"I know the strength in you, Luka, but I echo her words. Aethan would tear this world asunder to gain what he desires from you, with little thought to the cost. This makes him dangerous, his atrocities beyond nightmare. At the end, do not hesitate, my love, for he will not." Her lovely face clouded, a dark note entering her musical voice, "There will be death."

Luka sucked in a breath, his heart chilled. The fae's words filled him with a terror he dare not give in to, and he swallowed the wish hovering on his tongue. Loralyn rose on her toes and kissed his eyelids, his lips, and then she walked into the forest and was gone without a sound except for Tarian's gasp behind him.

"What did she mean?"

Tarian's frightened words brought Luka's attention back to him. The young man's face was white, his blue eyes wide with lingering horror and growing fear. Luka sighed. Aethan had much to answer for.

"Aethan is nigh upon us," he began and watched Tarian pale further. "But you need not be part of what is to come. Please, take one of the horses and go. Aethan comes from the south. Travel east for one day, until you reach Silver River, then follow it downstream. It will lead you to the Black Oak Valley and then home."

Unexpected dismay touched Tarian's face and hurt clouded his bright eyes. "I wish to stay with you, lord."

Luka frowned, puzzled by his words. "But it will be dangerous for you here. Can you not see that? Aethan—"

"Has already hurt him," Rhys put in as he joined them, setting his heavy pack at his feet then assisting Luka to remove his own. Luka's face heated. He'd forgotten all about it and it was a relief to be without the extra weight.

"That is why he should go," Luka pressed, confused by their hesitancy.

Tarian moved closer to Rhys, turning his back on Luka. "I wish to keep him safe. Why does he not see this?" Tarian's tone turned stubborn. "He requires my help."

Rhys nodded. "He needs both of us. But he is a truly humble man and doesn't see his own worth. Doesn't understand our compulsion to protect him." Rhys met Luka's astonished gaze and winked, drawing a gasp from him. "We will stand at his side despite his protest."

Luka gaped, then closed his mouth, emotion tightening his chest. Finding no words, he stepped back and swept them a low bow. On raising his head, he found them staring at him, and the love brightening Rhys's gaze and the blush staining Tarian's face brought tears to his eyes. All this for him?

He swallowed the lump forming in his throat. "Well... We'll sleep here tonight—"

"Aethan—" Tarian shot in, then bit his lip, flushing red as he dropped his gaze.

"Will not approach us tonight," Luka said firmly. "Ash Swale lies beyond the next ridge. He waits for us there."

Fear returned to Tarian's light eyes and Luka gave Rhys a helpless look. How would he be able to protect the boy? Rhys gave a thoughtful nod as if puzzling the question, then dropped a hand on Tarian's shoulder. "Come, lad. Let's fetch wood for the fire while Luka sets the wards."

Luka watched them a moment as they gathered fallen limbs and twigs, Rhys using a small axe from his pack on the larger pieces. He glanced skyward, blinking at the flakes of snow striking his face.

"Mother, am I doing right?" he asked, anxious and scared, but not expecting an answer in return. This was all his doing. By making his wish, he'd pulled hope from the world. All he could do now was return it before Aethan wrested it from him.

"Keep them safe," he whispered, not sure she could hear him, or if the spirits of the earth cared about the prayers of a frightened, foolish witch. Sighing, he drew the small granite stone from his pocket. He used it to focus his intention, then walked the perimeter of their camp while Rhys started a fire in its center. Luka set the ward with determination, in case Aethan sent a surprise. They would have one last good sleep before the morrow came with its terrors.

When finished, he joined the others at the crackling fire. Tarian removed a pot of water and oats from the flames that had been set to heat for the horses. Rhys handed out the last of their dried fruit and the remainder of the bread. Tarian dug in hungrily, his strength returning.

"We'll need to forage tomorrow," Rhys observed, sliding a dried berry between his lips. Luka's mouth went dry as he watched. Every sense he had was heightened, nerves stretched taught for the coming ordeal. He could imagine those lips on him, warm, moist, the rough flick of a tongue...

Rhys's eyes widened and Luka glanced hastily aside, begging his errant cock to subside. His gaze fell on Tarian, bent over his meal. It had been a long, strange day for him. Perhaps he'd sleep soundly. Rhys touched his knee and Luka raised his head and caught his breath at Rhys's crooked smile and the promise in his eyes.

Luka felt his face heat, embarrassed and aroused, and Rhys rose to his feet. "I'll care for the horses," he said, picking up the cooling pot of oats. "Tarian, will you see to the fire?"

"Of course, my lord," Tarian climbed to his feet to lay more wood on the dwindling flames. Luka watched the fire dance across the logs as his tired mind wandered. Thoughts of Aethan and the coming confrontation tugged at him, but he firmly put that aside, preferring to dwell on Rhys's smile and the mischief in his blue eyes.

Chapter Twenty-Three

"My lord, may I ask you something?"

Tarian's troubled voice broke through Luka's musing, and Luka blinked him into focus where he sat across the fire, the smoke rising between them swirling into the growing darkness. A few stars twinkled between the snow clouds.

"Yes?" he asked kindly. The delicate skin under Tarian's eyes appeared bruised, his face lined with exhaustion.

Tarian viciously chewed his lips, then drew a breath and squared his shoulders, bravely meeting Luka's gaze. "Why did you come for me? If my father is now indebted to you, please, let me fulfill his contract in his stead. I would not see him suffer further."

Luka's heart smote him. "What do you mean?" he asked cautiously, not sure he wanted to hear the answer.

"Mother died two years ago, thrown from a horse that bolted during a thunderstorm. Father...wasn't himself for a long time afterwards. He must have been beside himself when I was taken, ready to swear to anything for my return."

Tarian rose and knelt beside Luka, and to his dismay lowered his face to the ground. "Please, Luka. You are a great witch. Have mercy on my father. Let me bear the burden of his debt."

Luka gazed at him in shock and more than a little shame for his violent thoughts against his father. He put a hand on Tarian's shoulder, urging him up. Tarian sat cross-legged, hands clenched in his lap, his look pleading as he waited for Luka's answer.

Luka shook his head, sorrow spilling into his voice when he spoke, "My dear boy. Tarian, you have it wrong. There is no debt between us. We would have saved anyone from Aethan's cruel imprisonment."

"But how did you come to meet my father?"

Luka hated this part. Hadn't Tarian suffered enough? A grim look stole over Tarian's face when Luka hesitated.

"Tell me," he demanded, sounding older than his years.

Luka nodded. "Aethan has many eyes in the world, to watch and report back to him. I am to blame, Tarian. Aethan searched for me. For Rhys, knowing his connection to me. He needed someone near Sweetbrier and used you to...persuade your father to help him."

Tarian hissed in pain as if Luka had struck him. "Father has been aiding Aethan? After what he—" He broke off, looking with horror at his tortured hand with its missing fingers, then covered his face, chest heaving as he fought for control.

Without thought, Luka leaned forward and pulled Tarian into his embrace. He stroked his red hair, a splash of color in the gathering dark.

"He did what he must, for a son he loves more than life," Luka fiercely assured him. Tarian shook in his arms, perhaps weeping for more than a father's betrayal. Luka didn't have to imagine what he'd suffered at Aethan's hands. He saw it every day in Rhys's eyes. He firmed his lips. No more. Aethan couldn't be allowed to continue.

In a moment, Tarian pulled away and Luka reluctantly released him.

"I'm sorry." Tarian rubbed at his eyes, clearly embarrassed.

"You need never apologize to me." Luka softened his voice. "You're tired, Tarian. Sleep now. Tomorrow will bring its own concerns."

Tarian drew a ragged breath, and then a fleeting confusion took hold. "I still have your cloak," he said, plucking helplessly at the thick garment. He went to remove it, but Luka put a hand over his.

"Keep it, Tarian. I have no need of it," he assured him with a smile. Color mounted in Tarian's cheeks, but he nodded gratefully. He moved a few paces away and lay on the ground, hunching into the burgundy cloak for warmth.

Luka sighed and watched the fire. Life could be a trial, he knew that well enough, but it was hard to see Tarian's struggle. Looking up, his glance found Rhys with the horses, and his growing anxiety eased. Tomorrow would take care of itself. He pulled his pack close and dug inside, his fingers brushing the packet he sought.

"Thank you, Ravan," he said with love as he pulled out the smudge of woven sage and sweetgrass and cedar. Putting aside his pack, he then added more wood to the fire and sat cross-legged beside it.

He stilled his mind and watched the flames dance on the wood, smoke curling into the cold night, a sharp scent, warm when it brushed his face. The snow had stopped, melting in a circle around their fire, showing the short grass beneath. He thanked the fire for its warmth, the earth for their refuge. Focusing his thoughts, he lit the smudge then blew lightly on the end, and a tendril of smoke wound from the twisted bundle.

Drawing a deep breath of the fragrant smolder, his mind cleared, calmed. He knelt up and wafted the smoke with his free hand toward Tarian where he lay, sending thoughts of sleep and peace and healing. Soon, the tension eased from Tarian's youthful body and he slept. Luka allowed the sweet smoke to surround the young man, then settled back on his heels, laying the smoldering grass on a rock near the fire.

He sat cross-legged again, a fond smile lifting his lips as Rhys approached him. Rhys stopped across the fire, his answering smile warm.

"The horses are set for the night, Luka." His gaze fell on Tarian, sleeping soundly, and returned to Luka, his eyes now bright with mischief and hunger. "Is there anything I can do for you, sweet witch?"

Heat swept Luka at the desire underlying his words. He shook his head, helpless with longing, and flushed hotly when Rhys laughed at him, saying even while he licked his full lips, "I see that there is."

Luka's heart pounded as Rhys came around and sat behind him, legs on either side of his body.

"Rhys—"

"Hush," Rhys whispered, breath warm against Luka's ear as a shiver ran through him. Rhys kissed his neck and pulled the string from his hair, undoing Luka's braid with deft hands. His fingers felt incredible over his scalp as Rhys loosened the locks, letting them fall in long strands around his shoulders.

Rhys placed kisses along his jaw then eased Luka back against his chest.

"Relax," he teased, and Luka drew a quivering breath, inhaling the smoke from the burning smudge, allowing it to swirl in his mind. It made him dizzy, giddy, as Rhys undid the buttons on his coat and teased his nipples through his tunic. Luka stretched his legs out, leaning boneless against Rhys, turning his head for Rhys's kiss. Long, languorous kisses that drugged his senses. He realized he should reciprocate Rhys's attention, but Rhys stilled his hands.

"Be at peace, sweetheart. Rest here in my arms," Rhys enchanted him. "Let me pleasure you."

"But Tarian—"

"Sleeps. But if it eases your mind..." Rhys pushed him forward, undid his cloak, and threw it over them both. "Better?"

"Yes," Luka managed, then gasped when Rhys pinched one of his nipples. He gave himself over then, leaning back, his world narrowing to Rhys's strong body around him and Rhys's skilled fingers lifting his tunic. They teased over his abdomen, sending shivers of anticipation through him. He tipped his head for another kiss, Rhys's sweet lips pressing to his, and gasped into his mouth when Rhys's hand slipped inside his pants.

A finger stroked along his cock and Rhys swallowed his deep moans as he became lost in overwhelming sensation. Rhys's kisses were hungry, demanding, starting an ache deep inside. He silently pleaded for Rhys to grab his cock, bring the delicious torture to its climax. In answer, Rhys chuckled and nipped his earlobe, sucked it and fondled Luka's balls while his free hand continued to pluck his nipples.

Luka whimpered, losing control, rocking his hips in the hopes of gaining friction. Rhys dropped his hand from his nipples to a hip, holding him down. Then finally, at long last, he took Luka's dick in his right hand and stroked him. Slowly. Maddeningly.

Luka threw his head back. "Please!" he gasped, shivering, desperate, body aching with the need to thrust into the tight fist grasping him.

Rhys moaned against his throat. "You are beautiful like this, my sweet witch." He pumped him in earnest, quick, practiced strokes. Luka shuddered with the pleasure washing through him. Too much. Too sweet. With Rhys holding him as if he were cherished, loved. Rhys fondled his balls while he continued to work his cock. Then slid a finger downward, touched his hole.

Luka arched his back, mouth opening in a soundless shout as he came in hard, hot pulses in Rhys's hand. He floated in pleasure, inhaled when he realized he needed to breathe. Rhys's pleased chuckle rumbled through him. He sighed, satiated, tranquil, and gradually became aware of the earth beneath him and Rhys's strong arms. He felt the hard lump of Rhys's erection against his back and stirred, but Rhys held him firmly in place.

"Peace, darling," Rhys said, and kissed his neck. "Sleep now. I'll keep you safe."

Luka wanted to argue, to give Rhys the bliss he drowned in, but found he couldn't move without great effort. His eyelids grew heavy, refused to remain open, and he slipped into dreams without realizing it.

Only to awaken in what felt like a heartbeat, stretched on the ground, Rhys's cloak covering him. Something had disturbed his warding. He turned on his back and blinked at the blue sky overhead. The storm had passed, the rising sun filtering through the trees heating the chill air. He felt a warm presence curled against him and tilted his head to brush a kiss against Rhys's cheek, unwilling to wake him unless necessary.

Turning the other way, he found the fire burned down to ash and a few coals. The horses stood nearby, undisturbed by whatever pushed against his ward. He sat up cautiously, his glance falling on Tarian where he lay across from them, who gazed back with wide, troubled eyes. Luka motioned for him to stay still and climbed to his feet. His heart jumped. A figure leaned against a tree outside his ward, wrapped in a deep red cloak.

"Ravan," he murmured in relief, and beckoned her over, lowering his warding until she had passed through. He stirred up the coals and added wood to the struggling flames while Tarian sat up and slid fingers through his red hair in an attempt to tame the wild curls.

"Hello," Ravan greeted them, a smile on her face as she came up. She looked at Tarian curiously and Luka introduced them, Tarian sketching an awkward bow from where he sat.

"A pleasure," Ravan told him, and ignored the blush that stained his cheeks, saying to Luka, voice turning grave, "Everything is in place, Papa." She hesitated, pressing her lips together. "It's not too late to turn from this path," she urged, and would have said more if Luka hadn't raised a hand to stop her.

"Peace. I set this in motion long ago with a foolish wish. It's time to return the Well to where it belongs."

Ravan drew a breath as if to argue, then sighed and unslung a brightly colored sack from her shoulder.

"If we are going to do this, we should at least have a decent meal to start. I fear it will prove to be a long day." She sat by the crackling fire and removed tightly wrapped packets from her bag. Sunlight glinted in her red hair. "Tarian, will you put water on to heat? I've brought tea."

Luka smiled at her fondly, his love for her a warm spot in his heart. Glancing across the forest, he chewed his lips as thoughts of the coming trial intruded. Wispy fog moved between the trees as the sunlight melted the thin layer of snow on the ground. It would burn off soon enough, and they would be on their way. Dread filled him for what they would find in the swale.

Loralyn's warning returned to him. *There will be death.* What had the Fae foreseen that she wouldn't tell him? He glanced at Tarian's innocent face, at Rhys behind him, and a cold shiver traveled down his spine.

Chapter Twenty-Four

Rhys frowned, coming reluctantly awake as voices broke through his pleasant dream of Luka's hearth and eager arms. Where was Luka? He'd slept pressed against the warmth of his body. He grinned smugly, remembering how Luka had moaned and trembled in his arms and came so beautifully. He'd wanted to give him a little pleasure before they faced the danger awaiting them this day.

Opening an eye, he sighed on spotting Luka with Tarian and Ravan by the fire. He was unsurprised to find Ravan there, though he'd hoped they'd have a little time before the trials of the day started.

"Good morning," he murmured, sitting up and running a hand through his mussed hair, and his heart rushed when Luka sent him a heated glance, a secret smile on his lips. What he wouldn't give to steal away with Luka at that moment. Travel across country, the sea. Leave the Well of Hope behind, forgotten. Chances were, Aethan would never find it in Ash Swale.

But if he did…

Rhys hung his head. They couldn't take that risk.

"There's tea, lord," Tarian offered, pulling him from his dark thoughts.

"Thank you." Rhys joined them, taking the cup Tarian offered him with a grateful dip of his head. The lad looked more rested today, though fear lingered in his blue eyes, as well it should.

"Luka, is it true the horses will not go into Ash Swale?" he asked out of hand, an idea forming.

Luka gave him a considering look. "Nothing living would go without duress into the swale. It's a dangerous, loathsome place."

"A good location to hide the Well, then." He blew on his tea, purposefully not looking at Tarian. "Do we need someone to stay at camp with them, then? Keep a fire going in case one of us is injured? Our packs ready in case we need to leave in a hurry?"

"Those are good points." Luka nibbled on a dried cranberry.

Rhys risked a glance at Tarian, hoping he would volunteer. It would be a way for him to avoid the swale and yet be of help.

Tarian glared back, lips pressed together. "You won't keep me from his side," he vowed in an unconscious challenge.

Luka looked between them, clearly confused, and Rhys's heart warmed with fondness. Luka had his long hair unbound, framing his handsome face and dark, compassionate eyes. He appeared young and unsure in the soft morning light. Small wonder Tarian had lost his heart. Rhys had given his to Luka long ago.

"My horses will be fine on their own. They would never stray," Ravan put in dryly. "We need Tarian with us."

"As you wish," Luka said. He still seemed puzzled by the exchange and blushed at their attention. Self-conscious, he deftly braided his hair. Rhys cast about and came up with the bit of leather Luka used for his hair and tossed it to him. He couldn't help a sly wink and laughed softly when Luka reddened further.

He caught Tarian's eye and they shared a grin, Rhys relieved to see he didn't begrudge him Luka's affection. He was turning out to be a strong, reliable young man. He must be a great comfort to his father and a son to be proud of. Rhys looked forward to the day they could return him safely home.

They finished their meal then Luka rose to his feet, stretching his lean, taut body.

"It's time to be going," he said gravely. "Tarian, you will be with Ravan. Do her bidding without question or hesitation."

"Yes, lord," Tarian answered, climbing to his feet.

"Rhys." Luka hesitated, reluctant when he needed to be resolute.

"I am yours to command," Rhys assured him. Luka had to know he would die for him if necessary. Sadness touched Luka's eyes, and he covered Rhys's hands with his own. Ravan and Tarian moved away, calling to the horses.

"We will end this today, dear heart," Luka vowed, and Rhys gave him a firm nod.

"That we will," he answered, and leaned forward to kiss Luka's lips to seal the promise. Luka gathered the packs while Rhys dowsed the fire, then they joined the others near the edge of their camp. Rhys felt the wards fall as they mounted the horses, Tarian on a rust colored roan with Ravan, Luka taking the stallion.

Rhys swung onto the white mare and they moved out; Rhys unsurprised when Luka took the lead as they trotted the last few leagues to the edge of the forest. He wrinkled his nose at an unpleasant odor on the air. "Sulfur?" he guessed.

"Yes, and limestone pools." Luka slid off his mount, and the others followed him, lining up on the slopes into Ash Swale. "Watch the mud pits. Many are bottomless."

Rhys stared at the terrain below them in disbelief. He'd heard rumors of this land, where the entrails of the earth had ruptured, spilling to the surface. The sloping sides of the swale were as gray as volcanic ash, the swale itself spreading to the horizon north and south and a league across. Steam rose from noxious pools splashed across the desolate landscape, the pools and ledges stained icy blues to mustard yellows, pinks, and deepest rusts.

The air was heavy, unpleasantly warm, stinking of vile fumes and rotting earth. Sickly grasses struggled to grow in the marshy earth between the bubbling springs.

Rhys pinched his nose. "You hid the Well in there, Luka?" A rumble halted his words, steam hissing from a funnel directly below them, water surging upward in a geyser of heat and the stench of sulfur. Rhys shuddered. "I'd rather not go down there, unless necessary."

Ravan snorted inelegantly while Luka simply ignored him, as well he should. Tarian said nothing, hunched in Luka's cloak, though his expression was troubled and more than a little frightened.

While Ravan spoke to her horses, whispering unintelligible words in their ears, Rhys surveyed the gray slope with his eyes, searching for a safe way down. The horses trotted away, probably to hide themselves in the woods until needed.

"There seems to be a path over there." Rhys pointed out the barely discernable track to Luka, though he couldn't image what animal would use the trail down into the horror below.

Luka nodded. "Follow me. Stay close," he murmured, but Ravan put a hand on his arm, halting him.

"We go to battle, Luka," she said gravely. "This is a time to put off your humility, for Aethan will use it against you. Wear the cloak I gave you and face him from a position of strength." Luka shook his head but Ravan went on, "You must. I know it means nothing to you, but Aethan will view it, and you, as the challenge of an equal. Someone he should be wary of. It will shake his confidence, and we need all the advantage that will bring."

Luka sent Rhys a pleading look, but Rhys shrugged. "I must agree with Ravan, my witch. You've been Aethan's captive, even for a short time. To him you appear weak and he may attack instantly. But if you meet him as a lord, with strength gathered around you, he may hesitate, and lives might be saved."

Grave brown eyes studied him a moment, then Luka inclined his head, though his dusky cheeks reddened. "If this is your wish," he murmured and undid his coat. Rhys watched him, his heart reaching out to his shy lover and the role he was forced to assume. But he could see no alternative.

Tarian hastily removed the thick cloak from his shoulders, red-faced, clearly self-conscious of his mutilated hand as he exchanged garments with Luka and pulled on Luka's coat almost reverently. Luka swung the rich burgundy cloak around himself and Rhys stepped forward, settling it on his shoulders, fastening the silver clasp. He tilted his head to take in the effect while Luka blushed and bit his lips under his gaze.

"Here." Rhys reached over his shoulders and undid his hair, loosening the silky strands so it fell in a dark wave around his face. Rhys put a finger under his chin, lifting it. "Handsome and proud, sweet witch," he murmured, and gave Luka a swift kiss despite their audience.

Luka laughed slightly, running his hands over the lush fabric. "Ravan, this is gorgeous, and I thank you for it. But I still feel a fool and pretender."

"Don't fuss, Luka. When this is over you can wear what you please." Ravan reached for something in her pack, and Luka's lips parted on a sharp inhalation, his eyes growing wide.

Rhys stood taller, the solemnity of the moment settling over him as Ravan laid a thin crown of woven oak on Luka's head. "Luka, you are the son of the forest, the child of nature, with the earth's power in your fingertips. No more hiding, or Aethan will steal all hope from the world and leave us in despair."

Silence hung in the air, Rhys's chest tightening with love and pride. He felt as if he were seeing Luka for the first time. Not as his lover and savior, but as a man of magic and energy and force. Beautiful and virile. His blood surged. He would have gone to his knees, would have let Luka fuck him into the ground then and there.

Instead, he took a step back and made Luka his most elegant bow. "My lord."

Tarian was quick to do the same, eyes shining. But Luka looked uncomfortable and turned away, making for the narrow path Rhys had pointed out. Ravan laughed fondly and followed him.

"He is a great lord, is he not?" Tarian asked, awe in his voice as he watched them, their cloaks a splash of color in the bleak landscape, burgundy and blood red. Rhys glanced down at his own brilliant blue cloak then at Tarian wearing Luka's rust brown coat.

"Just a moment," he murmured and dug in the pack at his feet, retrieving the moss green cloak Ravan had packed for him for everyday use. He shook it out. Not as ostentatious as theirs, but it would suffice. He lifted a brow at Tarian, implying he remove Luka's coat, but Tarian's lips settled into a stubborn line.

"Very well. Now, you're one of us," he added and settled the cloak around Tarian's shoulders. He took a moment to arrange his lovely red hair around his blushing face and smiled. Clearly the lad wasn't used to such attention.

Picking up his pack, he motioned for Tarian to lead the way and caught his shy smile as Tarian passed him. He'd seen the tears in his blue eyes and cursed Aethan that the small act of kindness could so move him. He sighed. He'd been around Tarian's age when Aethan had taken him the first time. It had required Luka's infinite patience and kindness to make him feel...human, and worthy of love. He would strive to do the same for Tarian.

They came to the head of the trail and peered down. Luka and Ravan were already midway from the bottom, disturbed gray ash swirling around the hem of their cloaks.

"When we reach the bottom of the path, stay close. The swale can be more than dangerous," Rhys cautioned Tarian and planted his feet carefully as they descended the path, slippery with ash. Tarian proved sure-footed and quickly caught the others up. Rhys was several steps behind when they reached the bottom, and the earth erupted.

Chapter Twenty-Five

The ground rumbled like thunder and Rhys shouted a warning, horrified as steam spewed from a small cone less than twenty steps from Luka. Water surged skyward from the opening, scalding hot, if what Rhys had heard was true. Instantly, Luka and Ravan dodged to the left, skirting a stinking pool of boiling mud to escape the steaming spray.

It lasted too many long moments, the water cutting off with a hiss and gurgle as if a valve had been closed. Heedless of the slippery, mineral encrusted ground, Rhys and Tarian hurried to join the others, Rhys's concerned gaze traveling from Luka's face to his exposed hands, looking for blisters or burns.

"We're well," Ravan assured them, shaking water droplets from her cloak.

"What was that?" Tarian asked, eyes wide with an understandable alarm as his gaze darted between the myriad of pools and craters surrounding them. They stood on a swath of the sickly yellow, short grass that grew between the steaming, reeking caldrons and mud flats and poked through the ash.

"We must be careful," Luka warned. "The pools will emit gasses harmful to breathe, the bubbling mud will burn, while even the smallest cones will spill out steam or scalding water without warning."

The bleak, nightmarish landscape spread out around them and a low moan escaped Tarian. "Why have we come here?" he asked, sounding lost, panicked.

Rhys dropped a hand on his shoulder and Tarian looked up, his eyes wild.

"We are here because Luka needs us at his side," he said in calm, resolute tones. "He needs us to be strong." Tarian stared at him a moment, and then drew himself up, squaring his slender shoulders. He firmed his lips and nodded, visibly clutching at his courage.

Luka looked heartbroken. "I am so sorry, Tarian. Please forgive me. You were not supposed to be here." He ran a shaking hand over his face. "This is not what I planned. By all rights, you should be home safe with your father. If I could change things…"

"He may yet have a role to play, Luka," Ravan said soothingly. "We do not know why the fates have brought him here, with us."

"Fates," Luka repeated. For the first time since Rhys had met him there was a bitter note in his voice. "The fates aren't involved here, just my own foolishness that has endangered all of you."

"That is where you are wrong, my sweet witch," Rhys put in hastily, knowing Luka's just heart was hurting. "We are here because we choose to be. Because we love you."

Luka's dark eyes shimmered as he looked at them one by one, and he drew a deep breath. "I have spent most of my life alone," he told them quietly, and a sad smile lifted the corner of his mouth. "I don't know what I have done to deserve your love, but I will try to be worthy of it."

Ravan promptly touched his arm. "We give our love freely, Papa. All you need to do is allow yourself to accept it."

Luka's lips parted, then he shook his head helplessly, clearly overcome. He turned abruptly, taking several steps away from them. His shoulders shook as if he wept and Rhys's heart twisted. Tarian moved under Rhys's hand as if to follow him and Rhys gave his shoulder a soft squeeze.

"I don't want him to suffer," Tarian confessed brokenly. Rhys searched his face, so young, troubled, wet with tears.

"He's strong, Tarian. Stronger than we know, I think. But he is also deeply compassionate and gentle and ridiculously shy. At the moment, he is embarrassed and humbled, but I suspect joy underlies his tears. He'll be well."

Tarian nodded, sniffed, and wiped at his tears with his sleeve. Ravan shifted her pack on a shoulder, her own eyes bright, and they crossed the stubby grass to stand beside Luka. The ground turned a chalky white at their feet surrounding a pool of brilliant green water, seeming bottomless, with a strange yellow scum floating on its edges. The farther side, some ten paces across, was lower, a thin layer of water spreading across the ground with a froth of rust and sulfur and other minerals Rhys couldn't name clouding its surface.

Tarian strayed to a pool on their right, perhaps drawn by its vibrant colors. Brilliant orange and yellow stained the earth under a thin layer of water dipping to glowing green, which then plunged to a pool of deepest blue, again without a visible bottom.

Rhys touched Tarian's hand in warning, pointing to a hissing cauldron of mud close to their boots. "Stay with us," he urged. "I have no desire to see you harmed by anything here."

"Yes, lord," Tarian said, white lipped, clearly disturbed and frightened by the bleak, astonishing landscape. Rhys found it unsettling as well, needing to fight off a growing despair, the foul, oppressive air fraying his spirits.

Luka skirted the pool and headed toward the center of the swale, Ravan and Tarian behind, Rhys in the rear. He kept a hand on the knife at his belt, though he knew this battle would not be fought with common weapons. Mud pools continued to bubble and belch on either side of them, the rumble and hot spray of a geyser halting them at intervals, too close to be comfortable.

The gray sides of Ash Swale drew in, growing taller, forcing them onto narrower paths between the painted pools. The bright yellow of sulfur appeared through the grass until it surrounded them, spanning out into the distance. Rhys made a sour face at the strong, unpleasant odor. The mineral encrusted grass crunched under their boots and he winced, knowing they would be heard by any enemy lying in wait for them. Had Aethan brought an army with him? Men in armor and steel who would throw his broken body, along with those of his companions. into the deep pools to be dissolved in the acidic baths?

Or did he come with only Lorin as his companion? Rhys thought of his half brother then, and sadness welled inside him.

"Did you have any chance at all?" he whispered in the sulfur laden air. He'd been his father's captive on two occasions—terrible months of brutality and degradation and despair that ate at his soul. What had it been like for Lorin, living in the same household with the monster? How young had he been when Aethan had gone to his bed—

Rhys's mind shied away from the horror of that. The years upon years of beatings and unwanted touches and rape in the darkest nights. Worthless and unloved. Small wonder Lorin hated him, the one who'd escaped. Had become like his father and tormenter. Perhaps, when this was done, Rhys could find a way to reach him, through the pain and horror, to the man he could have been.

A small cone hissed beside the path, startling him back to awareness. There was a slight dip in the swale ahead of them and Luka brought them to a stop on the edge of what appeared to be a mud flat, twenty paces across and equally as wide, bubbling gently. Rock poked here and there through the slime, the mud seeming only a hand span deep. Sunlight shimmered off a thin layer of water on its surface.

"They've come," Luka said, and the grief in his voice shook Rhys. A silence settled around them and he peered across the mud. Gradually the shapes of three men became discernable in the distance, advancing through the bewildering landscape. They stopped on the opposite shore, and a chill ran through him. Lorin glared at them, hate on his face. But Aethan stood loosely, confident, holding the end of a rope looped around a man's hands tied at his back.

Tarian gasped and took an impulsive step forward, but Luka grabbed his arm to hold him back. Anger and panic swept Tarian's face, but he waited, body visibly shaking.

"What do you do here, Aethan?" Luka called across the distance. "The Well is not yours to take. Go home before you lose all you have."

Aethan's laugh was cut off by a rumble in the earth, then on their right a geyser spewed into the air, towering above their heads. Hot mist landed on their upturned faces and Rhys threw an arm up to protect his skin. It lasted only moments, but as the water settled into the earth, he found that Aethan and Lorin had started across the mud flat toward them, pushing Calan out in front.

The man stumbled on the slick ground but regained his feet. He looked up, his frantic gaze going at once to Tarian. Relief washed over his comely features, and he straightened to his full height as if the sight of his son renewed his strength. Aethan noticed and muttered a curse, kicking the back of his knee, sending him sprawling into the mud. Lorin's scornful laugh hung on the thick air.

Tarian made a frustrated sound, rocking on his heels. Rhys put a calming hand on his shoulder. "Let Luka deal with them," he urged, though his heart burned as well.

Calan regained his feet and Luka instantly put up a hand. "Far enough," he warned as they took another step closer.

Aethan's look of disdain was easy to read. "You don't frighten me, Luka. I know your heart. You can't, won't, hurt me. Your principles won't allow it. They make you weak. It's why I'll always win."

He motioned to Lorin, and they took another step forward, reaching the middle of the mud flat. At that moment, unexpectedly, Ravan shouted and dropped to a knee, slamming her hands on the edge of the mud. Instantly, the mud lost its firmness and the three men sank to their knees, their waists. Aethan shouted in anger while Lorin flailed as they sank deeper.

"Don't fight it," Ravan warned calmly. "You'll only sink farther."

Fear whitened Calan's face, but he didn't struggle, his gaze locked on Tarian as if urging him to be calm, brave. Tarian nodded, shaking under Rhys's hand, and Rhys's heart hurt at the love apparent between them. What would it have been like to have a father to nurture and guide him? Not be the cause of his nightmares nor put his life in peril now.

Ravan's trap had been well planned. It must have been what she'd gone ahead of them to prepare. A rueful smile touched Rhys's lips. He'd been acquainted with Ravan most of his life, Luka for years, but he wondered if he really knew them at all. Their power was more than he had ever imagined, more than they'd hinted at.

"Aethan, please," Luka entreated. "Listen to me. You will never have the Well. Go back. I don't want to fight you."

"You shall surely lose, witch," Aethan hissed. To Rhys's horror, he drew a long slim knife from his belt and placed it against Calan's back. "Release us."

"If you kill him, there will be *no* talking," Luka warned, his voice deadly cold.

Aethan's smile grew cruel. "I don't need to kill him. There are many ways to inflict pain, to torture a man until he begs for release."

Tarian growled in his throat and Rhys fisted his cloak, holding him in place. He stiffened and flashed Rhys a look, fury and terror sparking in his eyes. Rhys shook his head, mouthing, "Not yet," though he found it difficult to hold his place when Aethan moved the knife and drew a line across Calan's cheek.

"If we walk away now, Aethan, you will surely die. There is no escaping the pit." Luka looked at the liquid oozing to the top of the mud. "I doubt the water here is drinkable."

"And if I gouge his eyes out, spill his entrails in the mud, the carrion birds will gather that much sooner." Aethan made an impatient sound. "Enough. We all know, Witch, you won't see this man harmed. That pure, good conscience of yours won't allow it. Let us out, and we'll talk,"

Rhys's heart sank. Luka couldn't have foreseen the complication of Aethan having a hostage. What was to be done?

Luka let out a frustrated breath and tilted his head to Ravan. She scowled but made a sharp motion with her hand. The mud shivered, air bubbles bursting across its slick surface with the stench of rot and decay. The mire hardened, and with a shout of panic, Lorin struggled to gain his feet, hauling himself from the mud. Aethan merely looked annoyed, pulling Calan upright with him until they stood on firm ground.

Despite the circumstances, a spiteful smile tugged Rhys's lips. From the waist down, the three men were covered in stinking mud, with slime on Lorin's forearms and lower face from his struggles. Lorin caught his gaze and temper flared in his blue eyes. He strode toward him, boots sticking in the mud. Rhys couldn't help but laugh out loud, waiting for Lorin's angry words. It caught him off guard when Lorin stopped in front of him and clamped a hand on his neck, squeezing hard.

"You find this funny, *brother*? I'll flay you alive." Spittle struck Rhys in the face as he struggled to breathe, pulling on Lorin's arm. Lorin leaned close to his ear, his hot breath brushing against his skin. "Then I'll do the same to your witch, listen to his screams as I peel him open, fucking him as he dies."

"Lorin," Rhys gasped out, a plea, staring into his brother's eyes, searching... The blue eyes, so like his own, widened slightly, the grip on his neck easing. For a moment Lorin looked bewildered, uncertain, but then a hardness settled on his features and he clutched Rhys's throat again, making his head spin from lack of air.

"Enough, Lorin," Aethan drawled, sounding bored. "Let him be. I wouldn't want you to...damage him." The lewd tone underlying his words sent a shudder through Rhys.

Lorin grunted, loosened his hold, and shoved Rhys from him, stepping back to Aethan's side, who'd come up to the edge of the mud. Rhys rubbed his throat, gulping in air. He slanted a glance at the others, embarrassed to have been caught so easily, but Luka and Ravan's attention was on Aethan while Tarian inched closer to his father.

Luka stirred. "What now, Aethan? You cannot force me to reveal the Well of Hope to you."

Aethan looked them over, one by one, his gaze lighting on Rhys. "No more of this. Rhys, kill Luka, now."

What? Rhys's gaze darted between Luka and Aethan. Was he in jest? A cruel smile curled Aethan's lips, his eyes cold.

"It's easy, love. Kill the witch, or I will slice this man open ear to ear, then do the same to the boy." Aethan kicked the back of Calan's leg, knocking him to his knees in the mud.

Tarian gave an angry shout and dashed forward, boots squelching in the stinking water covering the mud, but Lorin intercepted him, trapping him against his body with a strong arm around his neck. Rhys looked at them helplessly then jerked his gaze to Luka and Ravan. Why weren't they reacting? Ravan ignored him, eyes on Aethan. Luka wouldn't meet his gaze. But there was something...

Luka held himself still, silent, his handsome face growing pallid as if under strain. Rhys's heart clenched, and he made a move to touch him, but Ravan sent him a sharp glance from under her brows, giving a slight shake of her head.

Rhys hurriedly looked away to find Aethan's speculative gaze on him. "What will it be, Rhys? Your lover or the people he's promised to protect? What would Luka wish you to do?"

"Luka wouldn't wish—"

"But he has wished, hasn't he? Isn't this how the Well came into his possession?" Aethan scowled. "Come. Decide. I'm growing impatient."

Rhys drew his sharp knife from his belt. Sunlight glittered off the long blade, shining in his eyes. How could he stall? Surely, Luka had a plan. The mud bubbled with soft plops, small cones hissed. The earth complained, and he heard a geyser go off behind them. Lorin and Tarian both looked over his shoulder, eyes wide, but Rhys and Aethan locked gazes.

Rhys's heart pounded. He'd never seen himself in his father's face. Both he and Lorin took after their mother's family. Nevertheless, he'd always feared there was a part of himself, buried deep, that reflected Aethan's cruelty. At that moment he could easily have plunged his blade into his father's chest. There was a glint in those dark as night eyes. A twist to his lips that betrayed his pleasure in wanton brutality. In inflicting pain. He would kill Calan without a thought beyond the joy of drinking in their grief and horror.

Aethan's eyes narrowed as if sensing Rhys's thoughts. "You refuse? So be it," he snarled, and pressed the edge of his knife to Calan's throat.

"No!" Rhys shouted, springing forward, and Tarian's scream of anguish rang in his ears.

Chapter Twenty-Six

Luka vibrated with the energy he drew in from the earth, nerves sparking as he anticipated Aethan's move to violence. Rhys spoke with the sorcerer, though Luka couldn't hear their words as his pulse rushed in his ears. He kept his focus on Aethan's hand, the wicked knife he held. All of a sudden, the sorcerer's wrist twitched.

Luka exhaled, energy bursting from him in a wave that engulfed both Calan and Aethan, capturing them in that instant before Aethan's blade sliced through Calan's jugular. Calan's breath left him in a strangled sound, his eyes going wide. Aethan blinked, his only gesture of surprise, then he dropped his arm, the knife falling from his fingers as if his hand had gone numb.

"Well, well," Aethan murmured. "This is interesting." He rounded Calan and a few steps brought him up to Luka. He reached in a quick movement for Rhys beside them, and a startled look flashed across his face when he couldn't touch him, as if there were a barrier between them. He tilted his head, taking in the others, who seemed frozen in place, and thrust out his hands.

Luka felt the push against the pocket of time he'd created as a thrum of pain throughout his body, but he swallowed his moan. He could do this. He had to and cursed the trickle of sweat alongside his eye that gave away his effort.

Aethan turned his attention back to Luka, standing with hands on hips. "This is something I've never encountered before. Are you drawing from the Well, Luka? Is that wise? Do you want to leave the world without hope?" His lip curled with derision when Luka didn't respond, and ran a caressing finger along his cheek, played with the clasp of his robe. "You won't answer? Could this"—he waved, encompassing the group—"be too much of a strain for you?"

Luka remained quiet, hoping to goad him to anger. Aethan was most dangerous when he was silent and focused. They stared at each other a moment, then Luka allowed a mocking smile on his face, to be rewarded with a flash of temper in Aethan's dark eyes.

"Go home," he urged, knowing it wouldn't be that simple. He braced, willing the circle tighter, and it flowed over Calan and snapped around the two of them, leaving an ache he felt to his bones.

Aethan glanced over his shoulder at Calan, still kneeling, but looking at them with awe on his face, frozen with the others. He was slow to turn back to Luka, unable the hide the fear betrayed in the white about his lips, the tremble in the hands he folded behind his back. "What do we do now?" he asked hoarsely and coughed to clear his throat.

"Go home. Promise to leave us in peace, and I will let you go."

"And if I stay and fight you?"

"You will lose." Luka clamped his teeth together, hearing the tremor in his voice.

Too late. Aethan noticed it as well and triumph flashed in his eyes. He clasped Luka's shoulders and leaned into him, bodies touching. "Well now, lovely. Let's see what happens when I *push.*"

The energy around them vibrated as Aethan's will clashed with his own. Pain sliced through Luka's skull. A soft cry escaped him as wave after wave of agony struck him, Aethan shoving back against the ward. His concentration slipped, and he drew it in with great effort. Aethan's body shook against him, his face whitening, sweat glistening on his pallid features. The sorcerer threw his head back and screamed, cracking the wall.

Luka moaned as his strength gave out. He could only hope Ravan was ready.

"Now!" he shouted and dropped the ward. Several things happened simultaneously. Rhys jumped into motion, shoving Aethan away from Luka, back into the mud.

"Run!" Ravan shouted at Calan. Without hesitation, Calan leaped at Lorin, who seemed dazed, and slammed a fist against his head and grabbed Tarian's hand. They sprinted from the mire just as Ravan dropped to her knees and smacked her hands against the earth, calling forth the mud pit once again.

Luka watched, shivering, spent, unable to gather his thoughts, as Lorin and Aethan sank, though not as deep as before. Ravan's strength must be failing. Rhys wrapped an arm around Luka's waist and pulled him after the others racing back the way they'd come over the sulfur flat. But Luka quickly tired and soon had to pause, chest heaving. He motioned Ravan to continue with Calan and Tarian while he took a moment to catch his breath. Rhys looked over his shoulder and cursed and Luka turned to see what had caught his attention.

His heart turned cold with dread. Lorin had worked his way over to Aethan's side and stood with his hand on his shoulder, head bent. Aethan had his hands cupped in front of him. He obviously took energy from Lorin, a flame growing in his palms, brightening. Their gaze clashed across the flame and the hate smoldering in those dark eyes made Luka flinch. He'd never wanted this to happen. How had they become such bitter enemies, when all Luka wanted was to live a quiet life in his cottage? Have time for the animals, raise a few herbs. Make love with Rhys.

With a sudden flick of his hands, Aethan threw the fire from him, and Luka watched in horror as it splashed across the yellow layer of sulfur. The mineral instantly bubbled, melting into a deep blue liquid that spread at a rapid pace, flames rising from the surface.

"Go! The air is poisonous," he urged Rhys, pushing him back. He heard Rhys's retreating footsteps, but stayed a moment, captivated by the unearthly, glittering blue liquid flowing toward him, strangely beautiful. Fire danced across its surface and he was caught in a moment of wonder.

Rhys's shouted warning woke him. He saw Aethan and Lorin crawling out from the far side of the mud flat. Aethan rose to his feet on solid ground and swirled toward him, flinging out his arms. Wind swept across the bubbling mud, lifting the slick water on the surface. It rained down on the burning sulfur and fumes rose in the air, noxious, deadly.

Luka turned and sprinted up the narrow path, knowing it was already too late. The wind struck his back, engulfing him in heat and the stench of sulfur. The thick air choked his throat, searing its way to his lungs. He shut his burning eyes, flinging up an arm to protect his face from the sting of acid rain.

He stumbled a few more steps, but the hiss of a geyser warned him he'd left the path and he stopped, uncertain what to do, the fumes he'd breathed disorienting him. It seemed an age before the crunch of boots pounded up to him and a hand gripped his arm.

"Don't open your eyes. Come with me." Not Rhys. Tarian sounded panicked, afraid for him, and Luka went with him without protest as Tarian led him by the arm, Tarian sure-footed on the wet grass. In a moment another, joined them, and Rhys's arm once again slid around his waist. Rhys's breathing sounded labored and Luka prayed the killing air had dissipated before reaching him. Merciful earth, what had he done?

The nightmare terrain muttered and rumbled around them, the hiss and steam from its various caldrons and pools a soft caress against his wounded face. His foot caught on the rough ground and Rhys murmured in sympathy, his arm tightening.

"A little further, darling," Rhys urged, and Luka set his lips against the pain wracking his body, his chest on fire. A broken cry left his raw throat when they finally stopped, and Rhys eased him to the ground.

There was a flurry of movement around them, then Ravan's practical tones took over, though there was no mistaking the love and concern underlying her words. "Keep your eyes closed, Papa," she said as she knelt beside him, touching his shoulder. "The exposed skin on your face and hands is burned. We will have to wait to see the extent of the internal damage."

Her voice broke and Luka reached for her hand as she drew a shuddering breath. He was still unable to speak, his throat in agony as if he'd swallowed broken glass. The taste of blood filled his mouth, though that could be from the sores on his lips. But he gave her hand a reassuring squeeze, awaiting her instructions. He felt strangely detached, thoughts muddled, unable to focus. Panicked, though he fought that down.

He became aware of someone sobbing quietly beside him and reached out, catching Tarian's sleeve, and made what he hoped was a reassuring sound.

"Tarian saved your life," Ravan told him, then choked on a caught breath, well knowing she might be wrong.

"I'll go for the horses," Rhys offered, clearly distressed.

"They won't come into the swale," Ravan cautioned, near tears.

A gruff voice broke in, impatient, determined, "Then I will carry him. Tarian, get up. Gather the packs." Calan's sturdy presence hovered over him, an arm going around his back, another under his legs. "Permit me," he muttered, and without waiting for Luka's answer, lifted him with a grunt of effort.

The stink of sour mud filled Luka's senses as he stifled a moan against Calan's rough coat. Pain hit him with each step they took, and he swooned, welcoming the gray fog of semi-consciousness. Time spiraled out in hazy moments, the gurgle of a nearby pool, the hurt of being shifted in Calan's arms.

He couldn't suppress the small cries that escaped him as they started up the steep slope of the swale. Calan's boots slipped several times on the ash, jolting his already aching body. Tears streamed from his burning eyes, inflaming the delicate lids. A terrible thought came to him, making his sluggish heart thump. Was he too damaged to heal? Would he leave Rhys unprotected, vulnerable to Aethan's dark whims?

Hurting in mind as well as body, he was only vaguely aware when they reached the top of the swale and Calan's steps hurt him less. They stopped and he was lowered into Rhys waiting arms, pulled against his chest. He clutched feebly at him while Rhys murmured loving words in his ear, rocking gently. Luka's heart swelled with longing, wanting more time with him. He'd only just found him again!

He didn't know how much time passed while he breathed in his lover's scent, pushing off the black hole waiting on the edge of his mind to drag him away from all he loved. It felt like decades or an indrawn breath, then Rhys shifted and laid him on the ground. He whimpered in distress, reaching blindly for him. Sweet lips touched his, calming his panic.

The sting of water and a soft cloth on his face roused him from a crowding darkness.

"Keep your eyes closed, love," a voice of music and magic whispered in his ear. His thoughts scattered. *Who?*

"It's me."

The tinkle of laughter made him smile. "Loralyn," he croaked, and winced at the agony tormenting his throat.

"Don't speak, sweet witch. Rest now."

Fingers, light as butterfly wings, fluttered against his face, chest, hands, while a song of pure joy and sunshine wound through his head. He floated while his body healed, grounded by Rhys's hand on his shoulder. He hoped with all his heart to kiss him again. He wished... No. He'd done enough damage with a wish. He would *will* himself better.

An eternity passed while he dreamed of summer days, a child holding his Mother's hand while they walked sunlit paths through the forest. The splash of sunlight in a dark pool of a rippling creek. Squirrels chittering overhead. The scent of pine and leaves underfoot.

A meadow at dawn, mist on the grass, and a brief, stolen moment as a stag in dazzling sunlight, stared at them from the edge of the towering trees across the meadow. Luka's heart leaped and thrilled as Mother squeezed his hand, and he knew without words that his father's spirit was with them, and that Luka was loved.

Luka sucked in a breath, the pain wrapping his chest easing with each heartbeat. He became aware of hands cupping his face as he came back to consciousness. Soft lips brushed his, not Rhys's, and he frowned, and felt his skin pull tight.

A bright laugh teased a smile from him. "Open your eyes, sweet one."

Luka slowly parted his eyelids, blinking at the sudden light. Tears formed, but no longer burned, and he looked at the lovely face bending over him. "Loralyn," he whispered, and swallowed, throat dry. Concern touched him at the exhaustion in her face. What had she done? He struggled to sit up, and an arm went around his waist, supporting him.

"Luka," Rhys murmured, voice choked with tears. Luka tilted his head and Rhys's concerned face filled his sight. Rhys gave him a tremulous smile, eyes glittering. "Here." He held a water flask to Luka's lips, allowing him a sip before pulling it away. "A little at a time, sweet witch," he warned, and trickled more into his parched mouth.

The cold water eased his throat. Rhys pulled Luka back onto his shoulder, and Luka heard the pounding of his heart as he nestled against him. His gaze fell on his own hands, red and raw, with open sores scabbing over. He imagined his face looked the same and ducked his chin. Tired, shaky, it took effort not to fall into sleep.

"Loralyn, are you well?" he asked when he caught the fae's trembling breath. He blinked her into focus and her full lips lifted in a wan smile. She pushed her brilliant hair off her face with a shaky hand. Luka struggled up in sudden fear, remembering her warning of death earlier, and gripped Rhys's hand against a wave of dizziness.

"What have you done?" he demanded when the black spots cleared from his eyes.

Loralyn lifted her slim shoulders in a shrug, but there was a frailty about her that hadn't been there before. Luka sent a panicked glance at the others sitting around them. Calan and Tarian tended the fire while Ravan hurriedly joined them, kneeling at the fae's side. She picked up Loralyn's hand. "You're cold," she said worriedly and removed her cloak, draping it around her shoulders.

Luka shivered, filled with foreboding. For a fae to be cold was unnatural. Something was desperately wrong with her. He took her hands in his. They were icy to the touch. He exchanged a troubled glance with Ravan, who took Loralyn into her arms while Luka kissed her palms.

"What can we do?" he begged, staring at her in disbelief. The fae was already fading, her brightness dimming as he watched. "Anything."

Loralyn's smile squeezed his heart. "Everything has been done, sweet witch. You are to get well and finish your task."

"And you? Loralyn, why would you do this?" His sudden tears fell on their clasped hands. Nothing made sense.

"Because we once loved, my heart. Luka, do not be sad. Do not blame yourself. I chose this, giving my life energy so you can be healed. A small payment for the terrible hurt I once caused you."

Luka snorted despite himself. "Don't pretend you regret leaving me, Loralyn. But I would not have chosen this for you. Why, when it was my own foolishness that put me in harm's way?" He never should have let the sulfur fire startle him into hesitation.

Familiar mischief sprang on her sweet face. "You know me too well, my witch. But I did love you, once upon a time. A moth to your flame. I stayed as long as I could. But the forest called..." She sighed. "I promised to watch over you. I would not fail in my task." She dropped her gaze, ashamed. "Not like I did with Calan. I thought him safe, and I left and gave him no further thought. Aethan must have come afterwards."

"Yet Mother would never have wanted you to give your life for mine," Luka chided gently, heartbroken. "I would never ask it."

Loralyn tried to lift a hand, but dropped it, strength failing. "This was my choice, Luka. Do not grieve! It is but this shell that passes. My spirit will live on, in my beloved woods. Walk under the trees this spring and you will hear me in the flutter of leaves in a sweet breeze."

She tilted her head to meet Ravan's gaze. "I'm sorry, daughter. I should have come to you sooner." A small shrug and laugh. "Time does not pass for fae as it does for others. It seems a mere blink of the eye since I cradled you as an infant. But know I've always held you in my heart." A shiver ran down her slim frame, and she gave a soft gasp and sank into Ravan's waiting arms.

Luka felt her spirit flit away as a tug on his heart. A sob broke from Ravan and he scrambled up, wrapping his arms around both her and Loralyn, grief making it hard to breathe. He welcomed the pain of his aching body, matching the agony of his broken heart.

Long moments passed before Rhys put a hand on his shoulder. Luka sighed and sat back on his heels, blinking his stinging eyes, Rhys a solid presence behind him. "I wonder if it had been her own death she'd foreseen, yet come anyway." His voice trailed off, then he gathered his thoughts. "We shouldn't stay here with Aethan so close."

Rhys made a sound of regret and sorrow. "I know, my heart. What would you have us do?"

Luka held Ravan's gaze, and she inclined her head, deferring to him. He tongued the sores on his lips, deep in thought. "She would like to be buried in the forest, I think," he said at last. "A shallow grave, to become one with her beloved trees." Weariness fell on him. He removed his cloak, laying it over his lost love. It was hard to believe her fierce heart had left them for whatever awaited her beyond this life.

He made an effort to stand and Rhys helped him up, keeping an arm patiently around him until the world stopped spinning. Luka drew in a breath, his chest still painful, but he would heal in time. He sighed and bent to pick up Loralyn, but then Calan was at his side. "Permit me."

In pain, heartsore, Luka didn't argue. "Thank you," he murmured when Calan lifted her up in his strong arms.

"She weighs nothing," Calan said in awe, looking at the still lovely woman whose head rested on his shoulder. Tears welled in Luka's eyes.

"Come, Luka, show us where," Rhys said gently.

Luka hesitated while Ravan wiped her eyes on her sleeve. She gave him a pleading look. "I would like to stay here with Tarian, Papa. In my mind, I still see Loralyn singing while she danced in the sunlight. I wouldn't want to see her put in the ground."

"Nor would I," Luka confessed. Tarian came up to Ravan, sadness on his face, but he nodded at Luka's questioning look, a promise to care for her while they were gone. "We will be back shortly." He slipped his arm through Rhys's, and with a nod to Calan, headed into the trees, his chest tightening with grief as the forest with its heady scent of pine and rich earth closed in around them.

Chapter Twenty-Seven

Rhys set the last rock in place and rose to his feet with a heavy heart. It had been a terrible, frightening day, though it was still early afternoon. He ached for Luka. He'd helped them scrape out a shallow trough between Aspen trees in a small meadow, which would fill with wildflowers come spring. But for now, the grass was shorn and dry, covered with the golden leaves of autumn and patches of snow.

Luka had knelt by Loralyn, kissed her lips, then wandered to the edge of the trees while Rhys and Calan covered her with the dark, fertile soil. Luka now stood beneath a towering oak, a forlorn figure in his tattered tunic, braid tangled. His hand rested on the trunk of the tree, skin brown as the bark, though red sores dotted his face and hands. Rhys sighed, knowing how much Luka's gentle heart was hurting.

Calan cleared his throat, his gaze on Luka as well. A stray snowflake landed on his face and he glanced at the gray sky. "We should go soon, before the snow in those clouds begins to fall in earnest," he said gruffly. His breath plumed in the cold air and he hunched into his coat.

Rhys nodded in agreement, then put out his hand. "Thank you for this, and for carrying Luka to safety as well. I am in your debt."

Calan clasped his hand in a firm grip. "You saved my son. We will not speak of debts between us, only abiding friendship."

Rhys studied his grave, appealing face, and inclined his head, grateful to have the strong man on their side.

"Return to camp. I'll bring Luka shortly," he requested, and waited until Calan was hidden by the trees before going to Luka. His lover stiffened slightly at his approach, and kept his face averted, though Rhys could see the tears wetting his raw skin.

"Luka?"

Luka glanced at him, sorrow swimming in his eyes, but he averted his face at once. Rhys's heart jumped when he realized Luka was self-conscious with him, as if Rhys would give a damn about his appearance, as long as the dear man still lived. Going to him, he put his arms carefully around him and pulled him back against his chest.

"Are you well, sweet witch?" he murmured in Luka's ear, placing soft kisses on his turned cheek.

"No. My heart is broken, Rhys. But it will mend, like the rest of me, at its own pace. Is it time to go?"

"Yes. Calan thinks it will snow soon, and we should be on our way."

"Very well." Luka straightened, squared his shoulders, and Rhys was relieved to see the spark return to his dark eyes when he turned toward him. Luka smiled, tentative, and put a hand on Rhys's arm. "I am more thankful than I can say that you are with me. It would prove too hard, otherwise."

"I'll always be with you," Rhys promised, and placed a chaste kiss on his abused lips. They made their way to the others, Rhys catching the aroma of a stew on the air before they came up to the fire, and his mouth watered. Luka's stomach grumbled, and they exchanged a small grin.

"Something smells delicious," Luka said, his glance moving between Tarian and Ravan, Calan standing over them.

Tarian blushed with pleasure while Ravan explained, "Tarian worried you'd be hungry and gathered herbs, mushrooms, and tubers from the forest while I melted snow and kept the fire going. There are nuts drying in the coals as well."

Luka looked touched and smiled sweetly at Tarian. "Thank you, lad. This is kind of you."

Tarian mumbled something, clearly embarrassed, and Rhys came to his rescue. "Bowls and spoons are in my pack, if you'll help me hand them out?" he asked and Tarian nodded, happy for something to take the attention off him. They dished out the stew and ate crouched around the fire, Rhys grateful for its warmth and for the savory burst on his tongue. The company finished quickly, in silence, then Tarian took the dishes to clean in the snow while the others packed.

When all was ready, they gathered to stand at the fire, a tired, forlorn group as the first flakes of snow fell. Rhys wished he could think of something heartening to say. Luka was especially discouraged, wrapped in a wool coat dug from Ravan's pack, his lip bloody where he chewed on it.

Luka sighed, lifting his hands in a helpless gesture. "I'm sorry, my friends. This is not how I pictured the day going."

"You could not have foreseen Aethan taking a hostage," Rhys cut in. He wasn't about to let Luka spiral. "He won this match. So, what is next, my witch?"

Luka opened his mouth, closed it again, peered at them one by one. "Calan, please take Tarian home." He held up his hand when Tarian scowled. "Aethan will only find a way to use you against me again." He moved closer and put a hand on Tarian's shoulder. "I need to know you're safe, before I do what I must."

Tarian nodded, setting his lips, in that moment looking older than his fifteen years. "If that is your wish, lord," he said stiffly, and bowed, high color in his face. Luka turned to Ravan. "Will you see they arrive home safely?"

"Of course. You will call to me if needed?"

"Have no doubt." A tired smile tugged Luka's mouth, squeezing Rhys's heart. "I will meet you at the cabin afterwards, my dear."

Ravan nodded, seemed about to say more, then simply embraced Luka and glanced at the others. "Will you come with me?"

"Of course, my lady," Calan said, while Tarian bowed to her, his youthful face working. He hesitated beside Luka, but stomped after his father without speaking, not ready for open rebellion, though Rhys could feel his anger and frustration.

Luka watched him, confusion on his face, and Rhys smiled to himself. Luka would never realize how much the tragic hero he appeared to the young man. And once he'd saved Calan's life, he'd earned Tarian's love and loyalty, probably for life. They hadn't seen the last of him, whatever Luka might wish. Though hopefully he stayed away until Aethan was dealt with.

Ravan whistled, and in a moment her horses trotted out of the trees, neighing when they saw her. She laughed and held out her arms, caressing each as they came up.

"Calan, will you and Tarian take the roan?" she asked, then looked back at Rhys and Luka. "Paddy is yours, Father, as long as you need him." The stallion passed her and came over to nudge against Luka's shoulder. Luka rubbed his nose.

"Thank you. Take care, Ravan," he replied, and waved when she mounted her white mare and the three of them disappeared into the trees.

Rhys scattered the ashes of the fire, packing snow over a few glowing coals. Luka watched him, troubled, unsure, and Rhys gave him time to think. Their next move would be crucial, of that he was sure. It wasn't until he gathered the packs and put a hand on the stallion to mount that Luka stopped him with a touch on the arm.

He didn't quite meet Rhys's searching gaze. "You could travel with Ravan," he said quietly, and moistened his cracked, abused lips.

Rhys's heart thumped, but he put a finger under Luka's chin, tilting his face so their eyes met. "Is that what you want?" he asked, keeping his voice even, though his pulse ran riot. "You know I will follow you wherever you go."

"Even if I take the horse?"

"Then I will be tired when I catch up."

Temper flared in Luka's eyes, but then his shoulders slumped, his face crumbling. "I made a grave error today, Rhys, that proved fatal. I can't keep you safe."

Rhys gently pulled Luka to him. He resisted, but Rhys merely smiled, tugging him closer. Their thighs touched, chests, and hunger crossed Luka's face. He knew Luka wanted to kiss him and Rhys would have been happy to oblige. Instead, Luka dropped his head on Rhys's shoulder with a deep sigh. Rhys would have none of that.

He nudged Luka's face up again and placed a tender kiss on his lips. Luka's blood didn't worry him, though he mourned Luka's pain, both physical and the anguish of losing Loralyn.

He didn't deepen the kiss, pulling back sooner than he would have liked, and studied Lukas face. "You seem to be healing," he said with some surprise, the ugly red of his burns fading, the open sores closing.

Luka nodded. "Loralyn is strong—" His voice caught, tears shimmering in his beautiful eyes.

"She was amazing," Rhys agreed. He held him a moment longer, then, "Shall we go, my sweet witch?"

"Yes. At least a short distance. I want to be away from here."

Rhys swung his pack on a shoulder while Luka did the same, and they mounted the stallion, Luka in front of him. Rhys nudged the horse, and they headed into the woods the way they'd come. In a short time, Luka was nodding, and Rhys eased him back against his chest, cradling him between his thighs when Luka fell asleep with a murmured word of love.

Snow fell lightly as they traveled, filtering through the evergreen branches overhead, but steadily giving way to watery sunshine. Rhys opened his cloak and wrapped Luka snug against him, welcoming his warmth. A shuddering breath at last escaped him, and he felt he couldn't fill his lungs as he allowed the terror of nearly losing Luka to overwhelm him. Damn Aethan to the void. If he'd lost him...

Rhys scrubbed the tears from his face with a shaky hand, trying to calm the mad beat of his heart, and huffed a laugh, knowing Luka would chide him for his anger and close despair. But then Luka would kiss him and tease away his dark mood with soft caresses that turned sure, his gaze heated and hungry...

Rhys's arms convulsed around Luka and a desperate sound escaped him as his pulse surged, lust pounding through him. He groaned as his prick swelled. It was crazy! But his fear turned to an overwhelming *need* for Luka, who was sprawled against him. Luka's thighs were warm under his hands, lean and strong. He knew the taste of the nut-brown skin; lighter colored and softer between his thighs, heating as it neared his balls and that beautiful, thick cock...

He moaned and hid his eyes against the top of Luka's head. What was he doing? Luka was injured and in mourning. It didn't seem to matter. He felt out of control, reckless, the horror and grief of earlier culminating to this moment in time and this man in his arms. The horse moved beneath them, knowing where to go, and Rhys shifted closer to Luka so that his dick rubbed against him with the powerful motion of the stallion.

A soft gasp escaped Luka, and he tilted his head back, blinking sleepy eyes. Naked, open, Rhys stared down at him, unable to hide the lust pulsing through him. Luka's eyes widened, and flashed, and he shifted about to slide a hand up Rhys's tunic, cup the back of his neck, and pull him down into a kiss.

Rhys groaned into his mouth, drowning in the sweet heat that welcomed him with delight and an answering need. He tried to pull back when his tongue slid over a rough patch on his lips, but Luka murmured and held him in place, tangling their tongues further. Frantic now, Rhys worked the buttons on Luka's pants, shoving his hand inside when they loosened.

Luka growled low in his throat, urging him on, and he wrapped his fingers around the hot, thick member waiting for him. A groan broke from Luka, and he laid his head on Rhys's shoulder, his face flushed, lips parting on desperate pants. Rhys ran his tongue up the column of his neck, tasting sweat and salt and warm skin. He craved Luka's cock in his mouth to suck and lick until they were both shaking with the pleasure of it. But Luka collapsed against him, hips bucking as he thrust frantically into Rhys's fist.

Rhys nipped the tender skin under his ear and Luka arched his back, coming close to unseating them as he came with a strangled cry. Rhys held him as he shook, then released him straight away and pulled the horse to a stop. He slid from the stallion's back, taking an unresisting Luka with him. Luka staggered and Rhys went with him, pushing him up against the trunk of a nearby tree, thrusting a knee between his thighs as he captured his delicious mouth again.

He drew back, heart thumping madly. "I'm sorry. I—"

"No." Luka fisted his cloak with both hands, a wild, feverish look on his face. "I'm cold and achy inside. I need you to love me, Rhys. Fuck me hard. Please. Help me... Remind me I'm alive."

Rhys groaned; his cock painfully hard, unable to stop himself from turning Luka to face the tree. After stripping off Luka's pack and his own, he planted a hand on either side of Luka's head, then took a moment to calm his breathing, cool the madness racing through him. He wouldn't hurt him, not this sweet man, anguished and lost. He tugged down Luka's pants, nudged his legs apart, then knelt behind him. Luka sighed in surrender, crossing his arms on the oak tree and resting his forehead against them.

Hands shaking, Rhys cupped Luka's ass and opened him, breath catching, his own white skin a stark contrast to Luka's beautiful rich brown flesh. He pressed his face close, inhaling Luka's musk, and ran the tip of his tongue along the lighter crease, over his opening. Luka shuddered, a soft moan escaping him, and Rhys's chest swelled, love and desire swirling in his head.

He moved lower to take his tender sack in his mouth, sucked gently until Luka trembled in his hands, moaning raggedly. Unable to maintain control any longer, Rhys stood, planting kisses on Luka's neck as he undid his own pants. Spitting on his hand, he stroked himself a couple of times, then opened Luka again and eased into him, massaging Luka's balls until he could slip deep inside.

They groaned together, an erotic sound in the stillness, and Rhys paused, Luka hot and tight around him, hard again in his hand. A single, exquisite moment in time, poised on the edge of bliss. And then Luka shoved back against him, startling him into motion. Their lovemaking was usually a slow build to completion, pleasure mounting with each touch and taste and stroke. But Luka had a wildness to him this time, pushing to meet Rhys's thrusts, shoving into Rhys's hand.

Then Luka raised his arms to twine their fingers together against the tree. Rhys gasped, jolted as Luka's pleasure in their coupling rolled through him, confusing and fierce, intense, his own pleasure building feverishly, hurdling him toward orgasm. Luka convulsed, arching back into Rhys as he came with Rhys's name on his lips. Overwhelmed, experiencing Luka's ecstasy on top of his own, Rhys shouted as he came hard, buried inside his lover.

He floated for a moment, then remembered to breathe, and became aware of shaky legs and Luka trembling against him. He eased out gradually, already missing Luka's glorious heat around him. He tucked himself away while Luka did the same, then pulled him back in his arms, turning him to see his face.

Luka gave him a tentative smile, dark brown eyes shining. Recalling Luka's delight in him, Rhys's chest tightened, and he dipped his head, tenderly kissing him. "I love you, my sweet witch," he whispered, and deepened their kiss, pouring all his affection into it. Luka murmured approval, but he still trembled, betraying his exhaustion.

Rhys pulled reluctantly away and picked up their packs. "Shall we find a safe place to sleep tonight?" he asked and hated that their moment had passed and sadness returned to Luka's eyes. The stallion stood grazing a short distance away and came when Rhys called.

Chapter Twenty-Eight

Dusk was falling before Luka drew the stallion to a walk, head lifted. Rhys scanned the area with sharp eyes, the trees close, boulders tumbled at the base of a rocky hillside.

"What is it?" he whispered against Luka's ear, feeling the tenseness of his body.

"I'm not sure..." Luka dismounted, and Rhys was quick to follow, stifling his swift anger, knowing it was caused by fear. Luka was never as careful as Rhys could wish. He ran a hand down the horse's neck, which stood, ears pricked, head turned to the closest group of rocks. Luka headed in that direction and Rhys walked behind him, to his left, senses alert for any hint of danger in the air.

They drew near to the boulders and Luka stopped abruptly, making a sound of distress. Rhys stared into the shadows between the rocks, and frowned at a deeper shadow, a man, obviously asleep on the ground beneath them. The light would soon be gone, but it was easy to discern the brilliant splash of his red hair. Tarian.

Luka's sigh sounded loud in the quiet, animals and insects dropping silent at their intrusion. "Why would he do this? I wanted him safe."

Rhys made no reply. It was not his place to betray the young man's heart. Instead, he went to the rocks and knelt, reaching into the small space to place a hand on Tarian's shoulder. Instantly, Tarian flinched and scrambled back, a long knife gleaming in his hand before he was completely awake.

"Peace," Rhys urged. "It is only us."

Tarian sucked a breath, gave a sharp nod, and climbed out of his haven, slipping the knife away. They stared at each other, then Tarian bit his lip and turned his glance aside. "I had hoped you wouldn't find me."

"But what are you doing?" Luka asked, clearly confused.

Tarian reddened, drew another deep breath and swiveled to face them. "You saved my life, my lord. Saved my father's life. I will not abandon you while Aethan is free."

"But..." Luka sent Rhys a distressed look.

"What does your father say?" Rhys put in, going carefully. Tarian's pride was at stake.

"He understands my reasons."

"And is he here as well?" Luka cast about helplessly.

"No. He has gone on to see to the farm. He didn't want me to come but knew he could only stop me by tying me to a chair." Tarian's calm broke, and he held out his hands, pleading, "Let me help you, lord. It would shame me not to offer what little aide I can give."

"It would be good to have another set of eyes and a strong arm," Rhys observed. Tarian was young, but there was strength in him and courage in his face.

Luka's glance held a question and Rhys nodded in answer, and Luka placed a hand on Tarian's arm. "Your help will be welcome. Thank you."

Rhys frowned at the small space between the boulders Tarian had hidden in, and Tarian offered, "There's more room behind here, enough for us and the horse."

He picked up his pack and led them to a trail between the tall rocks, barely discernable in the growing shadows, opening into a grassy area with snow piled against the boulders. The stallion crossed to the far rocks and nibbled the green blades, seeming content. Rhys stared at Luka, hunched in his coat. It would be unwise to start a fire to warm him. He undid his cloak, but Luka knelt, cupping his hands in front of him.

A soft gasp escaped Tarian, and Rhys met his wide-eyed gaze, biting his lip on a smile. It was one thing to know Luka was a witch, another to see him use his magic in this way. He was grace and power, face kindled, earnest, achingly beautiful as he conversed with the earth he loved. After a long moment, Luka placed his hands flat on the ground, and warmth spread out from him, drying the melted snow, heating the air around them.

Rhys drew Tarian aside. "Luka will ward the area for us. Try to sleep now. I'll wake you later to take a watch."

Tarian nodded, though his gaze traveled back to Luka, who'd risen to his feet. Luka was still, face raised, a small granite stone in his hand. Rhys knew he gathered energy, to push out in a circle around them few, if any, would have the strength to break. Pride swelled in Rhys's chest, understanding Tarian's awe completely.

Tarian settled on the warm ground, head on his pack. Rhys went to Luka and embraced him. "You should sleep, sweet witch. I'll guard for a while."

"In a moment." Luka sounded distracted, and tugged Rhys's sleeve, drawing him across the small space, away from Tarian. He sat, pulling Rhys down with him. He didn't speak, his gaze trained on Tarian's slight form, a darker shadow in the gloom.

"What's wrong? Luka, talk to me." Rhys cursed the growing darkness that kept him from seeing Luka's expression.

Luka drew a troubled breath. Another. "He's been in Aethan's hands," he said in little more than a whisper.

Rhys's heart clenched, but he pushed away the spurt of panic. "I was in Aethan's hand as well. Twice."

Luka took up Rhys's hand, twined their fingers. "You frightened me at first. So young, beautiful, full of pain. You tugged at my heart where no one had reached in many long years. I nursed you to health, falling more in love with your courage and sweetness every day, until I was lost in you. We'd made a connection the moment I found you. If you had proven my downfall, I would still have cherished every moment we had together.

"I am proud of Tarian, of his goodness and bravery in the face of Aethan's abuse. But...we didn't make the same connection." Luka rested his head on Rhys's shoulder, played with his fingers. "I don't crave him like I do you."

Rhys snorted. "I should hope not. I would take offense at that. What are you afraid of, my love?"

"That he might betray us to Aethan. Never on purpose," he answered Rhys's startled breath. "But because Aethan has been intimate with him, he may be able to find us through him."

"Aethan has had me, Luka," Rhys reminded him grimly. "He and Lorin both."

"And since you and I are lovers, darling, I can sense when his magic touches you and block him. I do not have that with Tarian."

"No, you do not." Rhys paused. He'd never thought to take another lover. Luka was all he desired. But what did Luka want? They had never discussed it. He glanced across at Tarian, wrapped in his cloak. The young man slept, thankfully. He picked up Luka's hand, kissed his palm.

"He would not be opposed to it, I think," he murmured against Luka's skin, and felt his startled jolt. Luka looked at him, his eyes a mere gleam in the darkness.

"I have no wish to bed the lad," Luka told him firmly, sounding somewhat shocked. "I love you."

"One does not always need love to—"

Luka pressed urgent fingers to his lips, stopping his words. "I could not, Rhys. When we...fuck, it is an extension...an expression, of my love for you. I could not... Not with anyone else."

Rhys heard the slight distress in his voice, and it dawned on him that Luka didn't know how *he* felt. That he worried Rhys wasn't content with him. He wished he could see his face more clearly. Luka had just lost his wife for the second time, old wounds opening. She'd left him without a word of explanation. How that must have torn his tender, lonely heart. Hurt that profound could burrow deep, leave an uncertainty behind Luka should never feel.

"Come here," he said gently, sliding his arms around Luka. Luka trembled, drew a quivering breath and rested his head on Rhys's shoulder.

"I love you with all that I am," he murmured against Luka's ear. "Your touch sets me on fire. In my darkest, loneliest nights, you were my dream. My lover and friend. I could not want another—"

Luka kissed him hungrily, passionately, and Rhys gloried in it. That this beautiful, powerful man could want him still amazed him, humbled him, filled him with wonder. He kissed him back with all the love in his heart, but soon Luka's exhaustion registered, and Rhys eased away with a final nibble of his tender lips, once again bleeding.

Luka gave a soft, self-conscious laugh and wiped at his eyes with his sleeve. "I must be more tired than I thought."

"Then sleep, sweet witch. I'll keep guard."

Luka glanced around the small clearing. "No need. The wards are sound."

"Excellent." Rhys lay down, pulling Luka into his embrace. Luka shifted, getting comfortable against his side, and it wasn't long before his breathing evened into sleep. Rhys closed his eyes, mind drifting.

And opened them again in what seemed moments, though morning light had found them between the tall stones. Luka still slept, a warm presence against him, and he tilted his head to look at him. His face had completely healed besides a few red scabs marring the rich brown skin. His braid had loosened, and wisps of dark hair brushed his cheeks. He appeared young, defenseless, in the soft sunlight, despite the strands of gray threading his hair.

Fondness filled Rhys's heart, and he wished, not for the first time, that they were in Luka's cottage, free of Aethan's threat, where they could live in peace and joy. He firmed his lips, resolving to bring it about. Luka deserved it. They both did.

The scent of wood smoke drifted to him and he eased away from Luka and rolled to his side. Tarian sat by a small fire cooking something on a spit. Luka's ward would keep the smoke from traveling, but what... Rhys widened his eyes in alarm even as his stomach growled. He hadn't eaten meat since they'd escaped Aethan's stronghold. He rose to his feet, careful not to wake Luka, and hurried across the short space.

Tarian glanced up as he approached. "It's cooked, if you'd like to share?" he said, and Rhys winced at the note of pride in his young voice.

Rhys crouched across the fire from him. "This is very kind of you," he began cautiously, and sighed as a troubled look touched Tarian's face. "Luka doesn't eat meat. The loss of any life wounds him. Don't be upset," he hastened to add at his dismay, "You are very skilled to have snared a rabbit in winter. But it would be polite not to eat him in Luka's presence."

"I'm sorry, my lord. I didn't know. I'll get rid of it at once." Tarian's hands shook as he pulled the rabbit from the fire, coming close to dropping it in his haste.

"Tarian, it's all right. Simply eat him in the rocks where Luka won't see. This is my fault. I will instruct you on the things you will need to know while you serve our lord."

"Thank you, lord—"

"First thing. I am not a lord. You are to call me Rhys, and ask me any question concerning Luka's wellbeing. He is all that matters."

Tarian ducked his head. "Thank you, my... Rhys," he said, and gave a short bow, then hurried with the rabbit through a gap in the stones.

Rhys watched him go, worry gnawing at him. What did the young man want from them? Better question, what were they to do with him? Did he hope to become Luka's apprentice? Work beside them? His depth of feeling for Luka would ensure his loyalty, but would discovering Luka didn't return the sentiment change that?

Luka stirred and sat up, and Rhys ran a hand over his face. Questions for another day. Luka approached and Rhys smiled at him as he sat across the fire. Luka looked disheveled, weary, and utterly adorable when he blushed at Rhys's scrutiny.

"Where's Tarian?" Luka wrinkled his nose but made no comment about the strong odor of cooked meat. At that moment Tarian returned, red-faced, but cupping something in his hands. Berries and a few wild onions.

"It's all I could find in the area," he apologized.

Luka hastily rose and accepted the offering. "Thank you, Tarian. This is lovely."

They sat by the fire, and Luka held his hands out to Tarian for first choice, who picked out a few berries. Rhys took half of the remainder. "This is wonderful, Tarian. You have my gratitude," he said and Tarian blushed and smiled at the praise. Then he looked down at the berries balanced in his mutilated palm and a troubled expression crossed his face.

Luka touched his hand, startling Tarian into glancing up, and Rhys's heart squeezed at the distress in his sky-blue eyes.

"I am more sorry than I can say about your hand," Luka told him, and wouldn't let go when Tarian tried to pull it back. "Aethan was beyond cruel and left a tragic reminder that will be with you all of your life. But this is not who you are, and you have no reason for shame. You are brave and intelligent and generous, and I am honored to call you my friend."

Tarian's lips parted, eyes widening at Luka's words. He blinked, and tears glittered in his eyes. Rhys studied Luka's face, looked at his dark palm holding Tarian's mangled hand. There was no magic being used here, only Luka's certainty and the moment of Tarian's acceptance, when joy swept his face and he ducked his head to hide his tears.

They ate in easy silence after that, then Tarian doused the fire with snow while Rhys gathered the packs. Luka crossed the small area and caressed the stallion, speaking quietly in his ear until they came up to him.

"I'll walk for a while. I would enjoy stretching my legs," Rhys decided, ignoring Tarian's protest. He slipped out between the boulders, the others following, and Tarian mounted, Luka swinging up behind him on the stallion. Once settled, they started along the game trail in the rough direction of home.

The forest closed in around them as they traveled, Rhys setting a steady pace, eating up the miles. They paused occasionally for him to rest and for Tarian to melt snow for water. Tarian walked at midday, followed by Luka. But Rhys balked at that, and took over before his time, overcoming Luka's objections by pointing out he walked too slowly. An absurdity, since Luka easily held the pace, but Tarian took Rhys's side and bustled Luka onto the horse despite his protests.

The sun broke from the clouds to their left in late afternoon, unaccountably lightening Rhys's mood. He glanced over his shoulder at the others and smiled. They dozed, the stallion seeming content to follow Rhys wherever he led. He calculated they'd reach Oak Knoll an hour after sunfall. It would be wonderful to sleep in a bed, Luka tucked against his side. Tarian on a pallet by the fire, stomach full of Ravan's delicious stew.

He walked on, humming a stray tune he heard on the edge of consciousness, and stumbled, realizing he'd come close to falling asleep on his feet. He glanced again over his shoulder. The stallion had fallen back a bit and Rhys saw with concern he had his head up, ears pricked, as if sensing danger. He swiveled forward at a thud on the path ahead, heart pounding, and found Lorin blocking the way.

"Hello, brother." Lorin smirked, and punched him in the face, knocking him to his knees. Rhys surged up, head ringing as the song he heard grew louder, deafening, and Lorin easily stepped out of his path and struck the side of his head, dropping him to a knee again. The chains of the spell woven in song weighted him down and he could have wept with relief when Luka shouted behind him and the clomp of hooves rushed up.

Lorin snarled in fury, and perilously close to too late Rhys spotted the knife in his hand glittering in an arc toward him. He threw himself to the side and cried out as the blade sank into his back, behind his left shoulder, searing like fire. Darkness gathered in his vision. Lorin dodged into the forest just as the stallion reached him, then the song hit its crescendo in his mind and he screamed at the pain and dropped into unconsciousness.

Chapter Twenty-Nine

Luka crouched low over Rhys on the stallion as they raced from the forest, the powerful animal barely slowing on the downward trail into Oak Knoll. It was fully dark, though firelight spilled onto the streets from the clustered houses. Fury rose in Luka along with self-reproach. He'd let go of vigilance for one moment, fallen asleep, and Rhys had been wounded. The stallion had snorted and reared, rousing him enough to drive Lorin back into the forest. But too late to stop him from plunging a knife into Rhys's back.

The stallion thundered to a stop in front of the cottage Ravan kept in Oak Knoll. The house of Luka's childhood. It stood dark, cold. He sent a plea out on the wind, searching for Ravan. He slid off the horse, easing Rhys into his arms.

"Go for Tarian," he urged, and the stallion leaped into the night, a dark streak back the way they'd come.

Luka climbed the steps of the cottage, shifted Rhys in his arms to fumble for the latch, and pushed inside. No one had been there since they'd left. Who would be foolish enough to enter a witch's hut? He crossed to the couch by the cold hearth, lighting candles with a thought, and sank carefully to his knees, arms shaking as he lowered Rhys down on his side, his back to Luka. Blood soaked his cloak, the handle of the knife protruding from the muscle above his left shoulder blade.

Panic momentarily seized him, but then Luka set his lips, scrubbed the tears from his face. What did they need? A warm room. And salt and boiling water to clean the wound. He got up and went to the hearth. Gray ash lay in a pile in the center of the fireplace from their last morning there. Normally, he'd scrape out the dead coals, but there was no time. He went to a knee and quickly layered kindling and short logs on the ashes.

Closing his eyes, he centered his thoughts to one purpose, and pulled power from the earth and air until his body thrummed and ached with it. He peered through his lashes and thrust out his hands, and fire ignited the wood in a roar and whooshed up the chimney. Luka gave a shaky laugh. He may have overdone it.

The flames settled, and he rose. There was still water at the sink, and he filled a clean cooking pot, setting it on the hook to swing over the fire. A glass jar of salt rested on the mantle and he put it down on the hearth, in easy reach to add to the water when it boiled. Clean cloths rested on a shelf and he took the lot, returning to Rhys.

Luka bit his lip, hard, to steady his nerves. Rhys took shallow, gasping breaths, sweat slicking his face lined with pain. Fresh blood spread a bright stain across his shoulder, soaking his cloak. Luka set the towels on the back of the couch, keeping two in his left hand. He bent over Rhys and curled his right hand around the thick knife handle. *Damn them!* The blade slipped cleanly from muscle when he pulled, and he instantly jammed the cloth against the open wound. Luka dropped the knife and used both hands, pressing as hard as he dared against Rhys's shoulder.

In a moment, he had to switch the sodden rags for new ones, wishing with all his heart for the wound to clot. In this instance, he would have wished for anything to save Rhys. Rhys had lost enough blood. It took longer this time before he had to change the cloth, and he became lightheaded as relief swept him. Rhys breathed easier and his dark lashes fluttered, a moan escaping him.

"Peace, Rhys. I have you. Go back to sleep," Luka murmured, wishing slumber to take him, at least until Luka had him bandaged. Rhys licked dry lips, murmured, but couldn't stay conscious, slipping away once again.

Luka shook as exhaustion and fear took its toll while slow moments passed. He wondered if the stallion had reached Tarian yet. He'd hated to leave him behind with Aethan so close, but there had been no choice, and Tarian insisted he wouldn't know how to treat a wound like this. Nor have the skill to ready the house for Aethan's coming assault.

"Stick to the path, but will you hide yourself if necessary until Paddy comes for you?" he'd urged, worry knotting inside him, not wanting Tarian to be reckless. He'd almost ordered him on the horse as well but could already feel the life slipping from Rhys's body as the blood poured from his wound. He had to travel swiftly. He'd been so scared...

"I will, lord. Go," Tarian bade him, and ducked into the trees.

The cottage door opened, but Luka didn't look around as someone came inside in a swirl of cold air. The door closed and latched, and footsteps approached. He caught Ravan's concerned presence from the corner of his eye, and she placed a competent hand on his shoulder.

"I'll see to the salt and water," she told him.

The tension eased from his shoulders. Ravan shored up his courage. He could do this. They'd save Rhys. Tarian would come soon, unharmed. Then he would deal with Aethan. By all that was good, he hoped he had the strength for it all. And the wisdom.

The water hissed in the quiet cabin and Luka's heart thudded as Ravan set the pot and a large empty bowl on the floor beside him, placed a bright lamp on a table by the couch. Luka winced in the sudden illumination, the smell of the saltwater and blood making him queasy. Elements of a sickness and death. He bit his lip to steady his nerves. Ravan leaned to get a better look at Rhys's face, pressed a hand to his sweat drenched forehead. "Are you ready?" she asked without taking her gaze off Rhys.

"Yes," Luka lied.

Ravan took it in stride, undoing the clasp on Rhys's cloak and unlacing his tunic.

She flicked a glance at Luka, assessing. He nodded sharply and lifted his hands. Ravan tossed back the sodden cloak, then eased his tunic down, baring Rhys's muscular shoulder. Luka winced at the raw, gaping wound, two knuckles long and one wide, the edges bloody.

"It looks clean," Ravan said, matter of fact, calming Luka's racing heart. She picked up the pot of water, checked the temperature, then drew a ladle full. "Hold him," she warned, and waited while Luka shifted to grip Rhys's arm and hip to keep him from jolting.

Ravan poured the saltwater on Rhys's shoulder immediately above the wound, allowing it to flow in and over it and collect in the bowl positioned on the floor. A hard shudder ran through Rhys and he cried out, coming awake. Luka kept a firm grasp on him, hating it. "Easy, honey. We're nearly done."

Rhys panted under his hold, bitten off groans escaping him as Ravan poured water again and again over the wound, rinsing away blood and any dirt that may have entered with the knife blade. At last, she finished, Rhys trembling under Luka's hands. Luka helped him to sit up sideways on the couch, back and shoulder presented to Ravan, while she fetched a jar from the kitchen and her sewing kit.

"I'm going to cut away your shirt," Luka told him, rather than wrestle with the wet, stained material.

"You'll owe me..." Rhys teased through white lips. Luka looked at him helplessly, and Rhys's lips lifted as he tried to smile. "I'm well, Luka. Hurts. I'm tired. But I'll be fine."

Luka nodded, throat tight. Ravan handed him a pair of sharp snips, and he set to work, cutting Rhys's shirt from the hem upward. His face was close to Rhys, who brushed his lips against his cheek. Luka swallowed a lump of emotion, knowing he was being ridiculous. He'd suffered his share of wounds and knew Rhys had been lucky with this one.

Ravan dried Rhys's shoulder with a soft cloth then tilted her head, surveying the wound. "I won't stitch it yet, merely bind it. If there's still no infection by morning, I'll close it up."

Rhys nodded, pain evident around his white lips, and Luka resolved to fetch more water for a restorative tea when they were done.

The door rattled and Luka rose to his feet as it opened, releasing a held breath when Tarian walked in on a wave of cold air and rich earth and the scent of horse, dropping the packs Luka had left with him by the door.

"I'm very happy to see you," he said with feeling, leaving Ravan packing the wound with moss a moment to cross the floor and embrace him. Tarian sighed in his arms, relief, and Luka searched his face, white and weary, but no shadows in his blue eyes. "Are you well?"

"I am, lord," Tarian said as he removed his cloak. "And Rhys?"

"Come and see." Luka waited while Tarian hung his damp cloak by the door, then they crossed to the couch. Rhys glanced up at them and gave Tarian a warm smile.

"I'm glad to see you safe," Rhys told him, and winced as Ravan bound his shoulder with strips of cloth.

"And I, you," Tarian replied fervently.

Luka put a hand on his shoulder. "Paddy found you easily?"

"Yes, lord. Thank you for sending him back. I stayed on the trail, as you suggested, ready to hide if I heard anything. But I saw no sign of Aethan and Lorin, and the stallion returned sooner than expected."

"Finished," Ravan told Rhys, who yelped when she tied the last knot on his binding.

Luka looked at him and couldn't help but relish the sight of his bare, leanly muscled chest, slick with sweat. Rhys caught his gaze and winked, making his heart thump. But Tarian had glanced away, color in his cheeks.

"Here." Luka plucked a brightly colored blanket from the back of the couch and set it gently around Rhys's shoulders. He pulled it closed in front, then glanced up. Rhys's face was inches from his, eyes bruised with pain, sleepy. A small smile played on his full lips and Luka cupped his cheek, caressed it with a thumb. "Don't scare me like that," he whispered, unable to hide the terrible fear that had struck him.

Rhys shushed him, a warm breath on Luka's face. "I'll be fine. Just tired," he promised, and gave Luka a kiss, barely there, a brush of lips that sent his heart pounding. Tarian retrieved a pillow from one of the bedrooms for Rhys's head, and Luka eased him down onto his right shoulder again and set another blanket over him. Ravan put out the lamp by the couch, leaving them in the soft light of candles and the glowing fireplace.

They adjourned to the hearth, Tarian carrying the pot and used bowl to the sink and fetching water from the outside well while Luka built up the fire. Ravan warded the room then retrieved fruit and cheese from the cellar. Luka felt the weight of her gaze on him while they ate, the warmth of the room making him drowsy, but put her off as long as he could.

"Well?" she asked at last, exasperated with him. "I can try to heal him, though I don't have near the strength as you."

Luka stared into the cup of tea Tarian handed him, hesitant, uncertain and heart sore. At last he raised his eyes, taking in Ravan's compassionate gaze and Tarian's anxiety. "Do I have the right, Ravan? Aethan is dangerously strong. If I weaken myself..."

"I don't think you can," Tarian said breathlessly, then flushed red when Luka and Ravan both looked at him. Luka searched his young, open face, his translucent skin and vibrant red hair. Tarian bravely met his gaze, inviting him to search deeper. His sky-blue eyes widened, and Luka peered inside, straight to his pure, wounded soul. Aethan had been brutal, cruel, to an innocent. Yet he couldn't destroy Tarian's bright and sensitive heart, nor extinguish the touch of magic running through his core.

"Your mother was one of the Fae?" Luka asked gently.

"No. But there is Fae blood in her family." He glanced between him and Ravan. "She taught me to recognize the magic in others."

"Curious. How do you see me?" Ravan asked, brow quirked.

"Your magic glows around you, vivid and warm."

"And Luka?"

Luka squirmed, uncomfortable, as they turned to him, and flushed hotly when Tarian answered in an awed whisper, "He burns."

Silence hung in the air, then Luka climbed to his feet and went over to Rhys, conscious of their gaze on him. He knelt by Rhys's shoulder. His blond hair was tangled and clung to the sheen of sweat on his skin, face white with pain. Luka tenderly brushed it back and placed a kiss on his warm forehead. "Be well, my heart," he whispered in his ear, and kissed along his jaw.

Rhys's hands were clenched against his chest, and Luka touched them, feeling the tension running through him. There was a soft gasp at the end of Rhys's indrawn breath. His still slept, which was a blessing. Luka blinked, realizing Rhys clenched something in his hands as if his life depended on it. Peering closer, his pulse jumped and surged, overflowing with emotion. Tears filled his eyes, blurring the pink quartz stone pressed against Rhys's heart. He must have carried it in his pocket this whole time.

"Rhys, my love, my heart." Luka choked on the painful lump in his throat. He placed both his hands on the blankets over the wound in Rhys's shoulder, hiding his wet eyes against them. "You are my life," he whispered, chest tight as his love filled him. "I give you my life in return."

He breathed in, filling his lungs. A held breath. Exhale, the life-giving blood moving through his body. With his inhalation he took in light, peace, joy. Allowed it to spread through him, centering his thoughts on one ideal. He let out tension and worry and doubt with his breath. Inhale, filling with the energy of the earth, letting it flow through him to his hands. Life.

With a silent prayer, he spilled the energy into Rhys, a faucet, fully opened. He would give all he was to Rhys, if necessary, forgetting Aethan, forgetting everything but the man who owned his heart. But Rhys's sharp inhale reminded him of the fragility of the human body, however precious. He reined in his power, let it flow smoothly, steady and sure.

Rhys moaned, eyelids fluttering.

"Darling?" Luka trembled. He'd never healed anyone in this manner before. But flesh had knitted under his touch, he was sure of it, the fever leaving Rhys's body with his exhales.

"Wake up," he murmured, pressing his lips to the tender skin of Rhys's throat, overcome, fearing to want something so intensely. A weakness Aethan wouldn't hesitate to exploit. *Damn him, then.* Rhys was worth any risk.

Rhys sighed, waking, even as Ravan stood abruptly, hands raised toward the door. "They come," she warned.

Luka's pulse leaped, and he rose, hurrying to Ravan's side, Tarian on her left. Ravan's ward vibrated, setting his teeth on edge.

Chapter Thirty

Rhys woke by degrees. Had he been dreaming? He hoped not. For a moment he'd felt Luka in his heart and mind. *Joined* with him. It had been...amazing. The power...

It thrummed through him still, fire and energy and joy, overwhelming. But there was something else, a tension in the room. He rolled to his back, peering at the ceiling as he tried desperately to clear his mind of a lingering fog.

He'd been wounded, he remembered now, stabbed in the shoulder by his brother. He struggled to sit up, the blankets falling to his waist, and swung his legs over the side of the couch. Luka stood in the center of the room with Ravan and Tarian, and a cold dread crept over him. This was it. Aethan and Lorin were coming, with Rhys weakened when Luka needed him the most.

Clenching his teeth, he pushed up from the couch, and swallowed a moan as pain radiated from his shoulder. He swayed, and closed his eyes against the swell of dizziness, hoping it passed swiftly. Sweat broke out on his forehead. He gulped air, pushed the pain aside, and stumbled forward a few steps, but had to grip the edge of the table to keep from falling.

He sensed Ravan's ward then, thrumming in the air as Aethan attacked it. Rhys had felt the bite of Aethan's power often enough to recognize the dark malignancy that ate at light and hope. The air grew taut, a pulled bowstring, then snapped, the ward was failing. Ravan made a strangled sound of pain but recovered, the three of them spreading out to face the door. Rhys rounded the table, desperate to join them, when something smashed into the door, the crack of wood resounding in the small room. Silence settled, fraying Rhys's nerves.

The fire snapped, making him jump. Another crash at the door and it splintered, falling away in chunks of heavy wood. Aethan stepped over the pile, arrogant, assured, though Lorin took a moment to shove the boards aside before joining him. Rhys sucked in a breath. Lorin's face was battered, hardly recognizable, dark bruises circling both eyes and his jaw, scratches scoring his neck. The attack had been vicious, brutal, done in a fit of uncontrollable rage. Punishment.

Lorin stood to Aethan's left and slightly behind him, a position of servility, his place with his father. Unexpectedly, Rhys's heart contracted, hurting for a half brother he had despised and feared, and now pitied. He willed Lorin to look at him and was surprised when he raised his head and met Rhys's gaze, his eyes stormy with misery and shame.

"Lorin," he whispered hoarsely and held out his hand.

Lorin shuddered and took an involuntary step toward him, but stopped, confusion sweeping his face. Rhys wanted to go to him, but Aethan's cruel laughter froze him in place.

"You will hold your ground, Lorin." Aethan gave him a scathing look. "You had your chance and failed, miserably. It's my fault. You always disappoint me. Why had I expected anything different on this occasion?"

A dark flush stained Lorin's face, and he dropped his gaze to the floor, though Rhys caught the flash of anger in his eyes. His brother clenched a hand around the knife hilt at his belt and Rhys had the sudden thought Aethan was treading on perilous ground without being aware of it.

"You should go, Aethan. You have no business here," Luka put in and Aethan's attention snapped to him. Luka had sounded calm, though energy surged under the surface of his words in a twisting coil, waiting to spring forth. How did Aethan not feel it? Or perhaps he did, but his hunger for power had gone beyond reason. There was that terrible light in his eyes...

Aethan curled his lips into a cold smile. "Give me the Well, witch. I will not ask you twice."

"Don't be a fool, Aethan. You cannot wrest it from me without great damage to yourself."

A cock of the head. "Truth, Luka. But what of the child?" Aethan flicked a hand, and instantly Tarian made a strangled sound and clutched at his throat, eyes widening in terror as if he couldn't draw breath. He dropped heavily to his knees, grasping for Ravan's tunic. Ravan reached for him, but Lorin was the swifter, a knife flashing in his hand as he lunged forward and slammed the hilt against the side of her head. She crumpled to the ground and didn't move.

"Kill her," Aethan commanded dispassionately.

Lorin hesitated, indecision sweeping his face.

Aethan turned on him with a snarl, vibrating with instant rage, "I said kill her! Fool! Useless offal. You insist on defying me, first with Rhys and now this whore. Get from my sight." He darted a look at Rhys, eyes wild. "Perhaps I will take your brother instead. The better son. Prettier, who doesn't go limp at my touch." He ran a contemptuous glance over Lorin. "You are less than nothing. Go."

Lorin paled, bewildered, in pain, lost without the bindings of Aethan's power. "Father..." He met Rhys's compassionate gaze. "What do I..."

"Come to me—"

"Ha!" Aethan's scornful laugh cut off Rhys's words. Lorin flinched, knuckles whitening around his knife hilt as Aethan's hateful words dripped poison into the tense silence. "You think anyone could want you after the things you beg me to do to you, your own father? The way you moan and writhe at my touch? Depravity. You've fucked your brother—" He snapped a command. "On your knees, cur. The only place you belong."

Lorin made a strangled sound, a mixture of fury and anguish, and swung the knife at Aethan. Power crackled instantly in the air, and several things happened at once, as they often did with magic in play. Aethan flung up his hands to ward off the knife just as Luka moved, a wave of energy surging from him toward Aethan. Aethan was the quicker, power slamming into Lorin, sending him flying back against the wall with a terrible crunch of bone. He swung to Luka, hands outstretched. Their power collided, Luka stumbling back as Aethan stepped forward.

Rhys caught Luka in his arms. Already weakened from the torturous day, Luka swooned under the crushing attack, and Rhys could do nothing but watch in helpless horror as Aethan reached for him, his gaze frantically searching for any weapon at hand.

Chapter Thirty-One

Luka listened while waves of energy beat against him. A heart thumped, strong, steady. *What?* Not his. His was a trapped dove, wild with fear. This other beat true, with purpose, and quickened, aware of Luka's notice. Luka tilted his head back onto Rhys's shoulder and met the flame in his eyes. Luka's lips parted on a breath of wonder. Rhys's gaze was filled with love and desperation, his mind open, barriers down. His love poured into Luka, pleading with him to take what he needed from him.

"Stay with me, sweet witch," Rhys's thoughts urged.

"Always, my white knight." Happiness flooded Luka, mirroring Rhys's pleasure at his absurd endearment, a memory of happier times. He grew strangely calm; it was time. "We will put an end to this monster's cruelty in the world. Will you yield to me?"

"In all things," Rhys murmured in his ear, breath warm on Luka's neck.

Luka straightened and Aethan pulled his hands off him with a cry as if burned, widening his eyes in alarm.

Luka drew breath, Rhys's arms tight around him, and called humbly on the energies of the earth. "If it is your will, lend me strength."

Rhys's arms convulsed around him and Rhys screamed in terror and ecstasy, the Well of Hope opening inside him where Luka had hidden it one winter's night while he slept, knowing this day would come. Aethan took a step back, horror on his face, but Luka couldn't stop what was to come. Power surged from Rhys, Luka's senses igniting as it filled him, every cell afire, alive.

It swept from him into the room, knocking books and papers from the shelves. Aethan convulsed as it struck him, a scream of pain and terror bursting from his throat, and he fell to the floor, unmoving, as the wave passed him to crash against the walls with a deafening boom that smashed open the shuttered windows and broken door.

Luka blinked in the silence that followed the surge of energy, watched the last fluttering papers land on the floor in the firelight. Aethan lay crumpled in a heap at his feet. Compassion swept Luka. Had they taken his life? *Please, no.*

Rhys took a shuddering breath behind him, dropping his arms to his sides. Luka turned and made a soft sound of concern. Rhys's head hung, body drooping, sweat slick on his skin, utterly spent. Luka took his arm and guided him to a nearby chair, going to his knees beside him.

"Are you well, my heart?"

"Aye," Rhys said, voice heavy with exhaustion. "What happened, Luka? I felt...outside myself, blind, and yet powerful beyond measure."

Luka's heart ached, and he picked up Rhys's limp hand, kissed the hot skin of his palm. He placed Rhys's hand against his own face, needing the closeness as well as Rhys's understanding. But first...

"I will explain everything, Rhys. I promise. But I must check on the others. And Aethan hasn't moved. Will you be patient a moment?"

Rhys nodded, then leaned his tired head against the back of the chair. Sweat trickled down the side of his face though cool air swept into the room from the burst windows and broken door. The extra heat in his body would leave Rhys soon enough.

Luka turned his gaze to the room and sighed. Moonlight found its way through the clouds and flooded the space with light. But more snow massed in the coming storm. He'd have to shore up the windows and door before too long.

He pressed a kiss to Rhys's forehead, gathered himself, and rose painfully to his feet, bones aching from the power that had raged through him. A tender smile touched his lips. His mother had warned him of the danger in opening the Well.

"I had no choice," he told her image in his mind, and felt the comfort of her love warm in his chest. Ravan was already rousing, and he helped her sit up. An ugly welt marred the right side of her forehead. "Are you badly injured?" he asked in concern. "I would have stopped him, if I'd known—"

Ravan's inelegant snort stopped his apology. "You can't see the future, Papa. Don't take the blame for everything." She groaned and settled cross-legged on the floor, hand to her head. "This hurts."

"Let me check on the others, then I'll see what I can do," Luka promised, giving her shoulder a squeeze before he turned to Tarian. The young man sprawled on the oak floor, his breathing once again even, though healthy color was slow to return to a face that had tinged blue. Luka straightened Tarian's arms and legs, making him more comfortable. He remained unconscious but was slowly waking.

Luka stood and rounded Aethan's crumpled form, wanting to see to Lorin who lay at an awkward angle against the wall. His heart thumped, sorrow filling him as he approached Rhys's half brother. Lorin had set out to deceive him from the beginning, but still, he didn't deserve this tragic death at the hand of his own father. To see his handsome face, so like Rhys's, with blood on his lips, eyes wide and unseeing, broke his heart.

"No," Rhys murmured at his elbow and sank to his knees, gathering Lorin's broken body into his arms. "You never had a chance, did you?" he whispered against Lorin's pale cheek, his voice choked.

"He never did," Luka agreed sadly. "Aethan bound him as a child to his dark machinations. Yet he showed courage at the end, refusing to kill Ravan. For that, I owe him a debt I would gladly repay." He brushed the shiny hair from Lorin's face, bent to place a kiss on his forehead. "Be at peace, Lorin," he murmured, and sighed for one whose life had been endless days of torment and despair.

He left the brothers alone and approached Aethan with care, not sure what to expect. It startled him when Aethan moved with a shuddering intake of air and sat up, knees against his chest. Luka knelt beside him, placing a hesitant hand on his hunched shoulder. "Aethan?"

The man who had been his enemy for years raised a face streaked with tears, the lost look in his eyes going straight to Luka's heart. "Where am I?" he asked, lips trembling. "What's going on?"

The last word caught on a sob and Luka sat cross-legged beside him, keeping a hand on his knee. "What do you remember?"

Aethan drew an unsteady breath, bewilderment and fear in his expression. "I was in the forest...searching...for something. I don't remember..."

Murmuring words of comfort, though uncertain what he'd find, Luka touched Aethan's sweat slicked forehead with careful fingers, and pity filled him. The Well's energy had scorched through Aethan, hollowing him out, stealing his memories as well as the power he'd held since childhood. He blinked at Luka, an empty vessel longing for reassurance.

Luka wasn't sure he had any comfort to offer, but perhaps he could guide him on a true path in life. They would have to remain vigilant. Would a man's nature change without the burden of memory? Luka had no way of knowing. Only time would reveal the answer.

He cupped Aethan's face to gather his wandering attention, hurrying to assure him at his frightened gasp, "You're safe here. I'm a friend. No one will hurt you. But you must rest now. Come with me." Taking Aethan's hand, he led him to the couch, where he murmured words that sent him to sleep.

There was still much to be done, and Luka's strength was quickly ebbing, the day catching up to him. Ravan was with Tarian, helping him sit up. Rhys had laid Lorin on the floor and sat beside him, his bare back pale in the moonlight. He stirred when Luka drew near, turning his head to look at him with such pain in his eyes, Luka trembled. He went to his knees and gathered Rhys in his arms, careful of his injured shoulder.

"Are you well, my heart?" he asked, face pressed to Rhys's neck, lips against his strong pulse. Rhys's embrace tightened and Luka thrilled at the strength in his arms, feeling safe. He breathed in the scent of drying sweat and Rhys's skin.

Rhys's lips brushed against his hair, then he tilted Luka's chin up, making him meet his gaze. "I'm fine, though more tired than I've ever been. Heartsore." He sighed and asked the question Luka had been dreading, "Tell me, Witch, how is it I have the Well of Hope inside me? How long?"

Luka withdrew with reluctance from Rhys's arms, troubled. But he'd known the risk, known this day would come. He sat back on his heels, but kept a hand on Rhys's knee, unable to keep from touching him.

"It was soon after I rescued you from Aethan the first time and brought you to my cottage," he confessed, gaze intent on his hand curling into a fist on Rhys's knee. He willed his panic to subside. The story needed telling, whatever the outcome. But merciful earth, he didn't want to be without Rhys again.

He took a steadying breath. "I knew without a doubt Aethan would come back for you. A selfish man never lets go of what he considers his. I needed to keep you safe, at least from mortal danger, and this was all I could think of to do. Yes, Aethan could hurt you, as he did, but if he threatened your very life, the Well would rise up and stop him. It was the only reason I sent you from me later. I could not have let you go without its protection."

"Surely, there are safer places to keep so powerful a weapon?" Rhys asked. His eyes were dark with bewilderment and Luka prayed silently for his understanding.

"The Well of Hope is not a weapon. It is an idea, powerful and life-giving. Aethan meant to deny hope to the world, dole it out in small measure to those who curried favor with him. I needed to hide the Well where he would never think to look."

He dropped his gaze again. "And the Well would keep you safe from him. Even if he tried to wrest it from you, the power would rise up against him. As it did today."

Rhys covered Luka's hand on his knee with his own, a firm touch. "So, you hid the Well inside me, without my consent or knowledge, and sent me from you, heartbroken, thinking you had no use for me."

Uttering a soft cry of pain, Luka lifted Rhys's hand, pressing his lips to it. "Forgive me," he whispered, throat tight and aching. "I needed you safe. And if Aethan found you in my home, and suspected what I had done... Also, if I had told you, and he read your thoughts—" Luka broke off and groaned into his hands, covering his face. "I tried—"

Rhys grabbed his shoulders, stopping his desperate rush of words. "Come here," he urged, pulling Luka up into his lap.

"I'm so sorry," Luka said again, voice quavering as he struggled with overwhelming emotion. He couldn't regret what he'd done, but knowing he'd caused Rhys to doubt him was unbearable.

Rhys's arms tightened around him. "I understand. But Luka, you must trust me." He made Luka look at him and Luka's heart bounded at the fondness in his gaze. "What happens to the Well of Hope now?"

Luka put a hand over Rhys's heart, feeling its strong beat, and put his worries aside. "It remains with you, if you will. At least for the moment." Heat touched his face. "I like knowing you're safe from harm."

Luka snaked an arm around Rhys's neck, pulling him down for a kiss, glorying in the life and strength in his limbs, the passion in his hungry embrace. The power of the Well whirled between them, then gathered in Rhys's heart, sealing closed until needed. Luka pulled away from him, the knowledge of the depth of Rhys's love both wonderful and humbling.

He wanted to be home, all this behind them, and take Rhys to bed, prove his devotion. But he felt the utter exhaustion in his lover, the dull ache of bone and muscle in a vessel unused to expending such energy. He stood and held out his hand. "It's bed for you, my heart, and a rest you sorely need. Don't worry. I'll be here in the morning when you wake."

Rhys nodded, leaned to give his brother one last kiss good-bye, and allowed Luka to help him to his feet. His face was wane and tired in the flickering candlelight, grief covering his features when he looked down at Lorin's porcelain face.

"I wish I could have saved him. I think, at the end, he wanted me to."

Luka nodded, taking his hand. "I am sure of it. Come, my heart. You must sleep." He led Rhys across the cottage to the room they had shared once before. Ravan had stirred up the fire in the main room and added wood, its bright light driving back the shadows. Tarian shivered on a chair drawn up to the hearth while Aethan slept on the couch. Luka passed a trembling hand over his face. There was much to be done before he could join Rhys under the covers. And a decision to make in the morning. But that was a worry for later.

Their room was dark when they entered, and Luka lit a candle with a thought and preoccupied word of gratitude, then pulled back the blankets on the bed, tucking them around Rhys once he'd removed his trousers and climbed in, being gentle with his shoulder.

Rhys took his hand when he straightened. "Stay with me, my witch."

"Always, my heart. But right now, I need to board up the windows and door or we'll have snow in the cottage by morning."

Rhys nodded, though his eyes begged him to hurry. Luka bent and kissed him, Rhys's lips warm and soft. His sweet tongue teased at Luka's lips, kindling a fierce need in him, though he merely gave a low chuckle and withdrew from Rhys's arms twining about his neck.

"Sleep, my love. I'll return soon."

Covering Rhys's eyes with his hand, he sent his lover's thoughts into pleasant dreams. After a last stolen kiss, he crossed to the cold hearth and ignited the old coals with a thought, his power still near the surface. He added several small logs, then returned to the main room, leaving the door open behind him to let in the fire's warmth until the room heated.

"How are we doing?" he asked as he approached the crackling hearth, its warmth scarcely keeping the cold from outside at bay.

Ravan smiled faintly from where she was binding the broken shutter closed in the kitchen. "My headache has eased, but you might see to Tarian," she suggested, and nodded meaningfully to the lad huddled at the fire.

Tarian looked up from the mug of tea in his hands. "I am well. Thank you," he protested, though he sounded tired, voice strained. Luka went to him, ignoring how his eyes widened with uncertainty.

"Permit me," he murmured, and placed a hand on Tarian's red curls when he nodded. The lingering horror of his near strangulation jumped out at Luka, a black swirling mass weighting Tarian's spirit. Luka gathered it while Tarian shuddered and gasped under his hand. When he had it all, he placed a kiss on his forehead.

"Peace," he murmured, and sent the horror into nothingness. He drew back but Tarian startled him by clasping his hand, kissing his palm.

"Thank you, lord," Tarian said fervently, and forced down his tears. "I've been lost for so long, trapped by the dark weaving of Aethan's magic, even after you rescued me from that cabin. It was hard to fight against him." Wonder touched his comely face. "But I am free now." He moved, going to his knees at Luka's feet. "I would bind myself to you, lord, if you would have my service."

Luka looked into his passionate face and embarrassment flushed through him. "Please, stand," he begged, helping Tarian to his feet. "You answer to no one but yourself. But if you will," he amended, "I may have a task for you in the morning."

"Anything, lord," Tarian promised recklessly, eyes shining.

Luka shook his head, an embarrassed smile tugging his lips. "Finish your tea now, then sleep. We'll speak more in the morning."

"I could help—"

"Sleep, Tarian. You need to heal, in both body and mind."

"Yes, lord." Tarian gave a small bow and resumed his chair. Luka looked at his bowed head and sighed. He would need to tread carefully, not allow Tarian to exchange him with Aethan as his master. Tarian needed a friend, someone to guide him toward finding his own confidence and strength. Rhys could help him with that.

Ravan had finished with the window and Luka took up wire, hammer, and nails to help with the others. He crossed the cottage to the shattered window in the west wall while she took the east. Moonlight flooded the forest and Luka gazed out in awe, captivated by the glittering winter scene. Breathtaking. But even as he watched, clouds scurried in and covered the moon and the first, cold snowflake kissed his upraised face. A wolf howled in the distance; an owl swooped from the trees. Hope stirred in the world and in Luka's heart at that moment. Hope slept in his bed. If he could hold on to it... But that was not the way of things, and morning would come with its own troubles.

With a last deeply drawn breath of the bracing air, he sent a silent prayer of peace into the night, then worked on closing the crooked shutters.

Chapter Thirty-Two

Luka woke, and smiled at the warmth of Rhys's body spooned against him, the huff of his soft snores tickling his neck. Luka rolled carefully to his back, easing Rhys onto his chest, where Rhys snuffled and buried his face in Luka's shoulder and continued to sleep. Luka's heart swelled, not large enough to hold the love he felt for this man in his arms.

He ached to be home, where he could make love leisurely, kiss and lick every inch of Rhys's skin. Worship his delicious cock with mouth and tongue. Bury himself deep in his warm, pliant body.

He laughed a little, self-conscious, and willed his instant erection to subside. This was not the time nor place. A line of worry formed between his brows. Would the time ever come again? Grief struck him then, hard, and he clung to Rhys while helpless tears spilled down his face. If the plan he'd worked out last night succeeded, he may not return, or worse, Rhys might not love him afterward.

Rhys's hand rested over Luka's heart, rose and fell with his labored breathing. Not wanting to wake him, Luka slid carefully out from under him, and shivered in the cool morning air as he dressed. With a last, lingering, hungry glance at his lover, Luka crossed the bedroom floor and slipped into the main room, easing the door closed behind him.

Sunlight made its way through cracks in the battered shutters and poured through the broken planks in the door across from him. Sadness stirred in his heart. Last night, Ravan and he had built a cairn for Lorin and burned him, scattering his ashes in the forest with a prayer of peace from Luka. They'd shored up the door afterwards as best they could with wood from the barn.

The cottage had grown chill during the night, and Luka went to the fireplace. Tarian lay on a pallet by the hearth, a soft blanket over him, face sweet and peaceful in sleep. Luka had an errand for him and Ravan that day, but hoped to return him to his father soon, if that was Tarian's wish. Or he would stay with them in Luka's cabin, learning how to care for the earth and all its myriad creatures. Luka may have doubted him, once upon a time, but no more.

All that was a matter for the future. For the moment, Luka contented himself by making up the fire and putting water on for tea. He rummaged Ravan's kitchen and put together porridge sweetened with honey and dried raspberries, setting the pot over the fire to cook. With nothing else he could think of to do, he turned with some reluctance to the couch and the problems it held for him.

Aethan slept curled into a tight ball, his face creased in troubled lines. What had the Well done to him? The power that had struck him had been great indeed. Had it shattered his mind? Luka went to him and knelt by his head. Aethan breathed rapidly as if his dreams distressed him. Pity stirred in Luka and he placed a hand on Aethan's forehead, finding it hot to the touch.

Aethan's eyes fluttered open, catching Luka in their glittering gaze. His lips moved as if he struggled to speak and Luka bent an ear close to hear him. "You have killed me," Aethan hissed. Luka felt the sudden surge of power, the last of Aethan's energy. Tarian bolted from his chair with a bewildered shout. Ravan stumbled from her room, still dressed as if she hadn't yet been to bed, hair in wild disarray.

Luka focused his attention on Aethan, feeling the sorcerer's power center on his own struggling heart, halting its frantic beating.

"No!" Luka bent his will, pushing against Aethan's desperate hold, but in this instance, when Aethan attacked his own body, Aethan's power proved the stronger. His proud heart faltered and stumbled to a stop.

"Please." Luka called on all the strength he had. It couldn't end like this. They had already lost Lorin in this terrible struggle between them. Would they lose another life to it? It was unthinkable. He pushed against Aethan's will until he was shaking, but time was running out, and Aethan's heart refused to beat again.

"I'm here."

Luka's pulse leaped. Rhys was in his head, power flooding to Luka in a wave of love and joy, the Well opening between them. Energy sparked in Luka's fingertips, and he sent it into Aethan's body, jolting him into life. Aethan's heart leaped, pounding strongly. Aethan gasped in a lungful of air, then another, and he pushed Luka away and sat up, bewilderment in his once keen gaze.

"Why did you save me?" he cried out in anguish and scrubbed at the tears on his face. "I don't know why I am here."

Luka searched his eyes and saw the rising panic.

"You are safe, Aethan. All is well," he began, but Aethan shook his head violently and scrambled to his feet.

"No! What is happening? I don't recall who I am… Why…" Aethan gave a strangled cry and dodged past Luka, grabbing a long knife from the counter. "Stay away from me," he snarled, holding the knife toward Ravan, who stood closest, paranoia and fear apparent in his hunched stance.

"What have I done?" Luka whispered, pain flooding through him. All his choices were proving wrong, time after time. He reached a hand toward Aethan. "Let me help—"

"Stay back." Aethan's frantic gaze darted between them, and he edged along the counter. With a sudden feint of the knife at Ravan, he bolted around her and sprinted for the door.

Luka made to follow, but Ravan's sharp call stopped him. "Leave him be, Papa," she cautioned, going up to him. "I see his mind. He would not hesitate to kill you."

Aethan pushed aside the boards bracing the door and shoved it open with his shoulder. He hesitated at the sight of the pristine snow glittering in the sunlight beyond the threshold but then stomped through the thick layer, quickly disappearing into the opposite trees. Luka quivered with the need to go after him, Ravan's hand on his arm tightening.

Tarian had watched the scene with wide eyes, but now he searched Luka's face with a keen gaze. He nodded once, bowed, and trotted after Aethan, snatching up a cloak on the way out. Luka wondered helplessly what he had read in his expression, when he'd tried so hard to mask his panic and fear.

Ravan sighed after them. "Come and sit, witch," she told him with a tug on his sleeve. "You are not responsible for all the harm in the world."

Luka took the chair Tarian had used and propped his chin on his hand, not caring when cold air swirled into the cottage from the broken doorway while Ravan stirred the porridge.

"I am at fault, in this case," he said after a moment, despair licking at his senses. "It was I who pulled the Well of Hope from the earth and set all this in motion." He buried his face in his hands. "I don't know what to do."

Ravan made an impatient sound, but before she could comment, the bedroom door opened, and Rhys's familiar tread crossed the room. He knelt by Luka's chair and Luka allowed himself to be pulled against his shoulder, finding comfort in the strong arms holding him.

Rhys ran fingers over his hair, soothing Luka's troubled heart. "We have discussed this before, my witch."

"I know. I would save him though, if I could." In a moment, Luka sighed and sat up, brushing at a stray tear. "I would not have hurt him like this—"

"Do you regret saving our lives, Luka?" Ravan snapped, clearly out of patience with him.

Stung, Luka thinned his lips, refusing to reply. Rhys patted his knee, then drew up a stool beside him, putting his hands out to the fire.

"Tarian went after him?" Rhys asked in the tense silence.

"Yes," Ravan answered, handing him a mug filled with tea. She passed one to Luka as well. "Perhaps when they return, we can sort out what to do with Aethan. He's clearly not the same man."

"I wouldn't think so," Rhys stated, and sipped his tea.

Luka drank his as well, and thanked Ravan when she handed him a bowl of porridge, not meeting her eyes. He wouldn't look at Rhys either, though his lover tried to catch his gaze. The time was coming to implement his plan, Aethan's panic only reinforcing his resolve, though his heart froze with fear. Yet he could think of no other solution to all that had gone wrong since that fateful, terrible day he'd called the Well to him. They would never agree to it, though, these two whom he loved the best.

The door creaked on its broken hinges and Luka put aside his bowl and stood when Tarian entered the cottage, trailing snow behind him as he came up to the fire. His face was pale, eyes wide and haunted, and Luka's heart clenched, but he bit his lip against his questions, allowing Tarian to gather himself.

Tarian held his hands to the fire, the scars from the missing fingers on his left hand white with cold. His voice choked with emotion when he spoke. "I followed Aethan half a league to the north, to a crevasse plunging to the river far below. I called to him and he paused, but then stepped over... He made no sound as he fell..." Tarian swallowed convulsively. "I climbed down to him, but he had broken on the boulders at the water's edge. Dead when I finally reached him..."

Tarian's voice trailed off in remembered horror, and Ravan put an arm around him, pulling him against her when he broke down, and he sobbed quietly on her shoulder. Luka exchanged a look of compassion with Rhys, grieving hard for the tragic loss of yet another life. He sighed, then drew a deep breath, resolving to bring matters to an end the only way he knew how.

Chapter Thirty-Three

"I want to go with you," Tarian fumed and settled his lips into a stubborn line, temper and jealousy in the glance he shot Rhys waiting with the horses. His fierce loyalty touched Luka's heart. There was so much strength in the young man. Tarian had chosen to return to his father to help during the planting and harvesting seasons. The rest of the year he'd be with Ravan, learning herb lore. And once a week, he'd climb the hill to learn from Luka as well.

Tarian wanted to live with him, he'd made that clear. But no... Luka looked at Rhys and his blood heated. He wanted, needed, to be with Rhys alone for long days and nights before he'd let anyone intrude. The thought made him blush warmly. Rhys caught his gaze at that moment and his eyes flashed in answer, hot, demanding, making Luka hastily swallow a groan.

"One more task," he promised his aching heart. Impatient to have it done, he put a hand on Tarian's arm, startling him into silence. "I ask you to stay and help Ravan repair the damage to her cottage, in payment for her kindness to us. Will you do this for me? I will return when I can to help with it."

Tarian's fair skin reddened, and he sketched a quick bow. "Of course, lord… I mean Luka," he amended, and his flush darkened when he spoke Luka's name.

Luka patted his arm and caught Ravan's wry glance. His own face heated as he turned to her. Tarian would lose his infatuation soon enough, once he learned there was no glamour in selling herbs at market. Luka would return to his quiet life, mix his potions and care for the small creatures he shared his house with. The peculiar witch in his isolated cabin.

Ravan embraced him and searched his eyes with her keep gaze. "What are you doing, Papa?" she asked in concern. Luka hadn't told her his plans, merely that he had an errand to run and would be back by nightfall.

Luka found he couldn't let her go, his precious child. She had been conceived in love, Loralyn carrying their child for nine months with joy, and stayed as long as her wild spirit permitted after her birth. Ravan had been his reason to wake each morning after Loralyn had left him, his ally and champion in his lonely life. He'd miss her.

He eased back but Ravan gripped his shoulders, searching his eyes. "What are you doing? Papa, I'm frightened."

Tears formed in Luka's eyes though he tried not to let them fall. "So am I. But it must be done." He embraced her again, brushed the hair from her face and saw Loralyn in her lovely features. He placed a tender kiss on her forehead. "I love you," he whispered, throat constricted, and let her go.

"I love you too," Ravan said to his departing back.

Luka didn't turn. He joined Rhys, not meeting his eyes as he grabbed a handful of the stallion's mane and swung onto his back. Rhys mounted the white mare and Luka led the way through the snow to the road leading deeper into the village. Rhys came up beside him on the wider path, though he didn't speak, and they walked the horses, Luka in no hurry to reach the end.

Sunlight flooded the world around them, bright and clear, its beauty creating an ache in his heart on the point of being too exquisite to bear. Crisp air kissed his cheeks. He could keep going. Take Rhys home. He had enough wood for the rest of the winter and food in storage until Tarian brought supplies from the village on his first visit. He could hole up with Rhys, relearning the plains and contours of his sleek body. What touch made him moan in that breathless way that drove Luka wild for more. Watch him come, beautiful in ecstasy.

Luka turned toward the center of town instead, the villagers watching them pass in silence and suspicion, and the oak grove rose above their heads as they climbed the steep road. Rhys made a soft, wounded sound as if guessing Luka's purpose, and Luka winced at the violent longing and sorrow that filled him for the life he desperately wanted and might never have.

"Why have we come here?" Rhys asked as they drew rein outside the grove, his tone more of a plea than a question.

Luka didn't answer immediately. Instead, he slipped off the horse. Rhys did likewise, and Luka went to him and pulled him into his arms, clinging frantically as fear rolled through him, leaving him helpless and yearning, tears blurring his eyes.

Rhys stroked his hair as if comforting a child. "What can I do?" he whispered, choked with emotion.

Luka drew a hard breath, gathering his courage. "Do you still have the heartstone I gave you?"

Rhys pulled the pink quartz from a pocket, and Luka took it in his hands, pressed it against his chest over his heart. He felt a spark of his life in it, and closed his eyes, pouring his love once again into the crystal, charging it with his life's energy. "Keep him safe," he entreated, and brought the stone to his lips.

"I love you always," he said simply, and returned the stone to Rhys.

Rhys clenched it in his hand, his expression anguished. "You're saying good-bye."

"Walk with me," Luka said gently and held out his hand. Rhys tucked the stone away, and they strolled under the gnarled branches of the oaks, the horses finding a patch of grass, though they watched as they moved away.

It was peaceful in the grove with the natural rustle of small animals under the thick layer of old leaves, the occasional chirp of a bird carried on the soft air. Rhys's hand was warm in his against the coolness under the trees, the sunlight bright in a blue sky far above the twined limbs, and Luka sighed. The world was beautiful. It would be hard to leave it.

As they drew near the center of the trees, Rhys pulled him to a stop, turning Luka to face him, and claimed his lips in a fiery, hungry kiss, flooding Luka's senses with his love and longing. Luka responded, kissing Rhys over and over, murmuring endearments while his pulse ran riot and his cock ached.

He whimpered a protest when Rhys broke off their kiss, turning it to a gasp of surprise instead as Rhys slid down his body to kneel at his feet. Rhys ignored him, deft fingers at Luka's pants, and, in an instant, his cock was free. Rhys licked the glistening tip, making him jump, before sucking it whole into his warm mouth. A cry of pleasure burst from him, echoing through the grove, and Rhys's chuckle vibrated against his cock.

Rhys released him and Luka swayed, dizzy with lust, going willingly when Rhys pushed him back against the rough trunk of a nearby tree. They were both out of control, desperate with need. Rhys fumbled with his own pants, then took both their cocks in a firm grip, sealing his lips over Luka's moans as he stroked them both. Luka reached blindly between them and closed his hand over Rhys's. The feel of Rhys's cock grinding and thrusting with his into their fists an intense pleasure bordering ecstasy.

They kissed frantically, faces wet with tears as joy and pain crashed together, building toward intense release. Luka came first, a shattering surge of bliss and grief. Rhys shouted as he came in a warm burst over Luka's fingers and gave a broken moan as he collapsed into his arms.

Luka pressed his lips against Rhys's damp forehead, throat tight, but Rhys pushed back from him, passion and sorrow on his face. He gripped Luka's hand and brought it up, holding Luka's gaze as he purposefully licked their spunk off their twined fingers. Luka shuddered, gloriously aroused by the blatant act, cock twitching to life, and he laughed a trifle desperately as Rhys kissed him and he tasted their mingled flavor.

"We have to do this," he whispered urgently against Rhys's lips.

"I know, my witch," Rhys hissed back. "But know this, I will not let you go."

You may not have a choice.

Luka kept the thought to himself. They righted their clothing, then Luka took Rhys's hand again, and they crossed the threshold into the center of the grove, green with moss, treeless except for the ancient, powerful oak standing at its heart.

Utter silence filled the grove, broken by Rhys's shuddering breaths, his only sign of fear as they approached the venerable tree. Power rode the cool air, brushing against their skin. They halted at the base of the oak's gnarled roots twisted in moss. Luka glanced skyward through the thick, heavy limbs over their heads to catch a glimpse of sunlight and blue sky, freedom. He drew in a lungful of air, felt the solid earth beneath his feet vibrating with energy.

He took Rhys's hands and squeezed his eyes shut against the sight of his beloved face.

"Mother?" he whispered, fearful, courage faltering. How could he leave this man he loved beyond his own life? Leave an existence grown precious to him? "I'm afraid," he confessed in the darkness behind his closed lids. What if he couldn't do this?

A presence formed at his back, warmth and love, and Luka's breath left him in a sob.

"I'm here," his mother murmured and wrapped him in a blanket of peace and strength. He felt like a child again, safe in her arms.

"What if I fail?" he asked her, anguished, hurting, part of him rebelling at his sacrifice.

"You won't," she assured him. "Look."

Luka's eyes snapped open, and he sucked in a breath. A door had opened in the magnificent breadth of the oak's trunk, spilling light around them, Rhys at his side exquisitely lovely in its scintillating brilliance, his lips parted in awe. Luka wrenched his gaze from him, and terror struck him as a form took shape on the wide threshold.

The terror fled as the image resolved into a proud stag, antlers branching, head lifted. It captured Luka's gaze, and Luka gasped, chest swelling, overwhelmed as understanding dawned. Tears burst from his eyes. His father's love was with him, filling his heart, pulsing in his life's blood. His mother's hand warmed his shoulder, reassuring, full of pride and joy in him.

"It's time," she whispered in his ear, and leaned to kiss his cheek.

Luka nodded and gathered Rhys in his arms, heart to heart. "Will you yield to me?"

"In all things," came Rhys's immediate, breathless reply.

Luka closed his eyes, drinking in Rhys's scent. He rested his forehead on Rhys's, enjoying the length of his body against him. "I love you," he said, in case it was the last chance he had, and opened himself to the Well of Hope. Power surged from Rhys to him, an open valve, flooding his senses. Too much! And still it came, an agony as his heart neared bursting, his thoughts spiraling into a chaos of pain and joy.

He couldn't do this! But his mother stood behind him, stalwart, lending strength and boundless love. His father's love surrounded him, held him up. With a soundless cry of agony and bliss, Luka fell to his knees and slammed his hands down on the ground, a conduit, the power bursting from him back to the earth. It lasted a lifetime, his blood molten, his brain on fire as energy drained from him, emptying him out.

He felt his life going and sank to the ground, buried his face in the moss, and wept. But even as life left him, Rhys gripped his shoulders, shaking him roughly.

"Hold on, damn you," Rhys demanded savagely, voice rough, shocking a surprised laugh from him, holding his fleeing spirit to the earth.

Luka sucked in air that sliced into his lungs, his body aching, feeling battered and broken. In time, he rolled to his back, Rhys's sobs penetrating the ringing in his ears. He groped blindly and sighed when Rhys clasped his hand in both of his.

"Rest, sweet witch. Take your time," Rhys pleaded, voice choked. His pain bruised Luka's heart, and he forced his weighted lids open. Rhys's dear face blurred, and Luka blinked at his tears.

"I'm well," he croaked, and his heart clenched at the helpless relief in Rhys's expression. He seemed overcome, and picked up Luka's hands, kissing his palms repeatedly while he fought for control.

It was too much and Luka pushed to a sitting position, unable to stop the groan that rose up in him, his every movement painful. Rhys quickly settled beside him and eased Luka against his shoulder. "Slowly, Witch. For a moment there, I thought I had lost you."

"Not so easily done after all, my heart," Luka whispered, throat raw. He longed for water, and Rhys pulled a flask from his belt, holding it to his lips. Momentary panic swept Luka. Had he wished? No. Rhys was a practical man. Of course he had brought water with him.

Luka sipped at the cool liquid, murmuring his gratitude to both Rhys and his beloved earth. He was exhausted, in pain, but restlessness seized him. The clearing was silent, energy a dull thrum beneath him, his father and mother's love nestled in his heart. It was time to go.

"Allow me?" Rhys asked as Luka struggled to stand, and Rhys put a hand under Luka's arm to help him to his feet. Luka swayed in momentary dizziness, but it passed, and he allowed Rhys to lead him to the tree line.

He sighed as they passed across the threshold into the grove of ancient oak. He felt woken from a dream, the warmth of the afternoon sun making its way to them. Rhys would have continued on, but Luka tugged him to a stop.

They looked at each other, the air fragrant and rustling with the sounds of life. Luka tilted his head, listening, reaching for the power under his feet. Relief swept him. Hope had been returned to the earth. He smiled, content, and touched Rhys's face with gentle fingers. "Thank you for standing with me. I might have slipped away altogether without you as my anchor."

Rhys turned his head, kissed his fingers. Then his eyes twinkled, and he sucked one into his mouth, his teasing smile capturing Luka's heart forever. They lingered over several sweet kisses, then Luka slipped an arm around Rhys's waist and started for the horses.

"Let's go home," he murmured, heart full.

"With pleasure, my sweet witch," Rhys replied, with a flash and promise in his eyes that sent Luka's spirit soaring.

About Dianne Hartsock

Dianne is the author of m/m romance, paranormal suspense, fantasy adventure, the occasional thriller, and anything else that comes to mind. She lives in the beautiful Willamette Valley of Oregon with her incredibly patient husband, who puts up with the endless hours she spends hunched over the keyboard letting her characters play. She says Oregon's raindrops are the perfect setting in which to write. There's something about being cooped up in the house with a fire crackling on the hearth and a cup of hot coffee warming her hands that kindles her imagination.

Currently, Dianne works as a floral designer in a locally-owned gift shop, which is the perfect job for her. When not writing, she can express herself through the rich colors and textures of flowers and foliage.

Facebook

www.facebook.com/diannehartsock

Twitter

@diannehartsock

Website

www.diannehartsock.wordpress.com

Other NineStar books by this author

Callum's Fate
Sweet William
The Mirror Maze
Little Match Girl

Also from NineStar Press

Kelpie Blue by Mell Eight

When a beautiful blue horse asks Rin to go for a swim, Rin doesn't realize how much his life is about to change. Blue is unlike anyone else Rin has ever met, and the magic of the fae, and of this particular kelpie, is wondrous, but deadly. Rin learns too late he might be in for a swim he won't survive.

Cassadaga Nights by Jana Denardo

Santino Bellomi and his coworker, Cam, are sent to Cassadaga, Florida by the Aspida Pneuma, a group of psychics and mages. Their job is to rescue a nixie from a polluted lake and to check out the town, which is known for its psychics. New recruits to the Aspida are always welcome and where better than a spiritualist camp to hunt for them? What Santino wants most, however, is to finish the assignment quickly. He isn't a fan of heat and humidity, and he'd looking forward to a well-earned vacation once the mission is over.

Ryan Doyle grew up in Cassadaga, where being psychic runs in the family. Ryan has never roamed far from home, though it's hard being a geeky gay, wannabe urban fantasy author living in a small town. His job as one of the town psychics is fairly routine until he meets someone new. Ryan has never encountered anyone with a psychic shield so strong until Santino sits down for a reading. Intrigued, he asks Santino out even though Santino is as secretive as he is fun.

Santino hopes to win Ryan over both for himself and for the Aspida. And he's hoping his skills in the kitchen will swing the balance in his favor. Ryan has almost given up on finding love, living in rural Florida. Can a seductive tourist be the answer to his dreams?

Things never run smoothly for those in the Aspida. What should have been a simple rescue mission is plagued by mosquitoes, enraged ghosts, and someone or something draining residents of their life force. Ryan's first foray into adventure may be his last.

Awakening by Connal Braginsky and Sean Ian O'Meidhir

Nathen was recently diagnosed with autism, and he's a newly created vampire. His maker, a multinational corporation with its finger on the pulse of the technology industry, has recruited him to stop a terrorist plot. In the process, he meets Cameron, a telepath and psychologist, who has a troubled past he keeps locked up in the shadows of his psyche.

Nathen is confused by social cues and Cameron can barely block out the thoughts of others.

Together, they find common ground, and with the help of their friend Syn, they work out the secrets of the terrorist

group and learn that the plot is far greater than they could
have imagined.

Connect with NineStar Press

www.ninestarpress.com

www.facebook.com/ninestarpress

www.facebook.com/groups/NineStarNiche

www.twitter.com/ninestarpress

www.instagram.com/ninestarpress

www.ingramcontent.com/pod-product-compliance
Lightning Source LLC
Chambersburg PA
CBHW051606100726
47898CB00001B/244